BIRDEYE

PRAISE FOR *SNEGUROCHKA*

'A captivating story about foreigners in Ukraine in the 1990s. In *Snegurochka* grand historical and political narratives – of Ukraine's newfound independence, of the Second World War – interweave with the very personal stories of the book's female protagonists – Rachel, Zoya, and Elena.'

—EMILY COUCH, *The Moscow Times*

'It's a very interesting and clever read. With no narrative trickiness it shows us the author's knowledge of that time and place, and more importantly a wonderful character, one who struggles with her new-found family and her new-found sense of displacement. Rich and readable, this is well worth turning to.'

—JOHN LLOYD, NB *Magazine*

'An unnerving and enthralling novel set in newly independent Ukraine, *Snegurochka* is a captivating story of motherhood, betrayal, belonging and control.'

—*Hampshire Life*

'It is a joy to read a novel in which the elements fuse so harmoniously: taut but lyrical prose, an exceptionally vivid sense of place, politics and culture but also of a pivotal time which is neither recent nor of the distant past. I regularly say that a good novel makes me feel I've seen the film; this one made me feel I was there, confronted with the vertigo-inducing view from that balcony.'

—ISABEL COSTELLO, *The Literary Sofa*

JUDITH HENEGHAN is a writer and lecturer. She spent several years in Ukraine and Russia with her young family in the 1990s and now teaches creative writing at the University of Winchester. She has four adult children.

JUDITH HENEGHAN

BIRDEYE

SHEFFIELD

PUBLISHED BY SALT PUBLISHING 2024

2 4 6 8 10 9 7 5 3

First published in Great Britain in 2024 by
Salt Publishing Ltd
18 Churchill Road, Sheffield, S10 1FG United Kingdom

www.saltpublishing.com

Salt Publishing Limited Reg. No. 5293401

A CIP catalogue record for this book is available from the British Library

ISBN 978 1 78463 326 4 (Paperback edition)
ISBN 978 1 78463 327 1 (Electronic edition)

Typeset in Neacademia by Salt Publishing

Printed and bound in Great Britain by Clays Ltd, Elcograf S.p.A

In memory of my parents, Michael and Gill Heneghan

Rose looks, but the noisy dog is gone.

No yapping mouth. No pushing nose.

The noisy dog is gone, and the quiet dog is watching
with its ears.

PEACE AND LOVE PEOPLE

H E WAS PROBABLY just a hiker.

Liv Ferrars hadn't noticed him as she walked through the trees, but when she turned away from the river, his bright blue jacket caught her eye. He was standing on the bridge a couple of hundred yards downstream, between the struts, near the public information sign. Young, she guessed, by the way he raised his arm. He wasn't waving at her; he was taking a selfie.

Liv didn't wait to see if he would cross over to her side, or head back into the town. Instead, she continued up the slope towards the dead end of Dutchman's Road, where a track climbed between still-bare beeches to the old house, her home, snug and safe from rising floodwater. Run-off could still cause problems though, after heavy rain, or during the spring thaw. Sonny had asked her to check the drain beneath the road, so when Liv reached the outlet pipe, she peered in. Immediately she put a hand over her nose. The matted fur of a dead racoon showed through a mesh of twigs and other debris. They'd need the gaff pole to clear it.

She winced as she straightened up, out here where Sonny couldn't see her. Her limbs were sinewy after decades of hiking, but arthritis was taking its toll. Numb fingers fumbled with the blister pack of Advil in her pocket. Gunther, her German Shepherd, regarded her from a few yards away with pale, reproachful eyes.

'I know,' she said, raising her voice over the rush of the river below them. 'Do you lay down and die, or wait for breakfast?'

The dog lifted his tail, once, then picked his way across the fallen leaves towards her. The leaves had been compressed by almost five months of snow, and now, where Gunther's paws had disturbed them, they sloughed up like flakes of dry skin. Liv tugged gently on one of his ears and looked around. The trunks that rose about her seemed like a veil, mournful, as befitted the back end of winter. The light between the mountains was subdued and still, washing everything in a palette of fawn and slate and rust. High up on Sheridan and North Dome the snow lingered among the conifers, while down the valley a few vestiges clung on in clefts and the corners of backyards. The only thing that moved was the river, gushing and spilling towards Apollonia and the reservoir beyond. At this time of year its waters were muddied by silt and its wide, winding course was littered with brush and fallen branches. No pokes of skunk cabbage yet, no hint of spring green, if you didn't count the dark sludge of the spruce firs, or that hiker – she could see him more clearly now – making his way along the narrow road towards her. His khaki backpack, too cumbersome for a day tripper, made him stoop a little.

Another one, then. This was how they came, hopping off the Trailways bus or hitching up from Poughkeepsie.

She tipped her head back and swallowed her pill.

'Hello!' The young man took a step towards the edge of the asphalt and stared down at Liv. 'I'm looking for Birdeye – the Birdeye Colony?'

His accent was from the city. Gunther raised his head and sniffed.

'Poor old Gunth,' said Liv, pushing up her glasses with the back of her hand. She took in the stranger's formal-looking chinos and heavy, unyielding boots, and wondered what they said about his intentions. 'He hopes that someday his real owner will step out of the trees and take him home to a bowlful of meat.'

'Oh.' The young man looked at the dog.

'Been with me for ten years, and still resents our veggie ways. You like dogs?'

'Yeah, but I don't have one. I think it's cruel in the city. Yours has all the space he wants up here.'

Liv smiled, warming to him. 'Well, this is Birdeye. Did you call ahead? We're not expecting anybody.'

The young man shifted his feet and nudged a couple of small stones off the asphalt. His black hair lay flat against his scalp, and his clean-shaven skin was so white it was almost blue.

'No, I didn't call – I hope that's okay. I mean, I couldn't find a website. I read *The Attentive Heart* – you're Olivia Ferrars, right? I'm Conor. Conor Gleeson.'

'Hello, Conor. Call me Liv, please.'

He bent down to shake the hand she offered, and his grip was soft, as if he didn't know what to do. He looked tired, too; his eyelids were grey and puffy. Maybe he hadn't slept in a while.

'We don't see many visitors this early in the season,' she went on, 'but if you're hungry we can find you some breakfast. First, though, I'm going to need some help.'

Conor's gaze faltered. As always it was a question of trust, and trust cut both ways. She raised her arm again, ignoring the pinch in her shoulder.

'Haul me up there, will you?'

'Sure!' He sounded relieved, and pulled firmly, without yanking.

Liv led the way across the road, then walked alongside him as they started up the track that led to the house. Conor kept glancing over his shoulder to where Gunther had stopped beside a paper birch.

'Your dog seems kind of sad,' he said.

Liv nodded. 'He's pining.'

'What for?'

'Well, his pal Pinto died of a stroke a couple of days back. The whole night, Gunther lay beside her.' She paused, once again assailed by loss: Pinto's brindled coat, the brush of white down her nose, her cloudy, cataracted eyes that never dimmed her yapping. The little dog had appeared on the porch during the dark days of Liv's mastectomies a decade before. 'People drive up from the city, their

3

dogs go crazy after squirrels and that's it. They're gone. Owners should tag them, or microchip. I've had dogs for thirty years, and each one came off the mountain, dehydrated, half starved.'

'So it's not just people you fix, huh?'

Conor's tone wasn't flippant, but Liv had dealt with this before – a cynicism, often unconscious, usually to hide the longing. Visitors came to Birdeye for all sorts of reasons, bringing their problems, their pain and loneliness, hoping to be mended, made whole. Some still expected a loved-up summer camp with herself as an earth-mother messiah. In recent years, several visitors had wondered openly why they'd bothered to make the trip to such a hokey Catskills backwater. Go pick some peas in Mishti's garden, Liv would tell them. Take a hike up the mountain or sit with Rose in the yard. Then they started to unfold.

'We don't *fix* anything,' she said, letting Conor down gently. 'There's no cure here. Just listening and accepting.'

'That's what I read,' he said. 'In your book.'

They had reached the bend in the track, and Conor raised his head. Liv looked too, as she sometimes did – a sort of dry-eyed reckoning of the old place with its peeling purple clapboards above the deep, old-fashioned porch that wrapped itself around two walls and shored up the drooping south-east corner. The circular attic window that had given the house its name was set high in the steep-angled front gable; someone had spray-painted a sooty outline, like smudged kohl, a good twenty years back, then picked out the surrounding shingles in rainbow colours. The wide stretch of back-yard was hidden, mainly, to the rear, but to the left, an eight-foot-high scrap metal sculpture of the goddess Artemis giving birth to twins squatted in front of Mishti's winter-wasted veggie garden. To the right of the house hunkered the donkey barn, where visitors used to sleep in bunk beds and hammocks, sun-kissed limbs akimbo. Nowadays the metal legs of the swing-set stuck out like shin bones through the unglazed window, and a string of Tibetan prayer flags hung limply from the chimney.

4

'Awesome.' Conor's face twisted momentarily, as if he were wistful, or disappointed. Before Liv could ask, he walked on, then stopped beside the tan pickup parked near the steps with his head tilted to one side. 'Who's that?'

A figure hovered on the porch above them, behind the stack of shelves that Mishti used for seedlings in the spring. The see-through plastic covering was blotched with mildew, but Liv could still make out an angular nose that mirrored her own, fading copper hair cut short, and a long, flapping hand.

'Hey, Birdie,' she said, using an old nickname. 'Were you waiting for us? This is Conor. Conor, this is my daughter, Rose.'

Conor seemed to hesitate as Rose moved into view. Rose would be forty-nine soon, and she was tall, like Liv. Her sweatpants and cardigan only partially disguised her thin frame; she put her arms behind her back and clasped her fingers in a way that pushed her shoulders forward and made her chin jut out. Like a heron, Liv often thought – her Argus-eyed child.

'Great to meet you!' said Conor, recovering. He shrugged off his backpack and leaned it against the steps before holding out his hand.

Rose did not reciprocate. Instead, she made a sound that might have come from some large-winged bird, wheeling and keening. Arms flailed. A white neck; wide damson eyes.

'What did I do?' Conor pulled his arm back as she veered around the porch corner.

'She's fine,' said Liv, keeping her voice quiet and firm. 'Everything is fine. Please go inside. Say hi to Sonny. I just need a minute.'

Rose, meanwhile, had stumbled down the side steps and disappeared towards the rear of the house. She never went far; the house was her lodestone, and in the ten or so seconds it took for Liv to skirt the goddess sculpture and the veggie garden, she was already circling the backyard, weaving between the boulders at the edge of the treeline where the ground rose sharply. She had stopped crying out, but her shoulders were pulled up to the base of her skull and her knees had locked, causing her to move stiffly, painfully. Liv knew

5

what was coming. As she tried to take her daughter's elbow Rose lunged at her, grasping her hair in both her hands and yanking Liv's head down with some force. Liv held her then, one side of her face pressed against Rose's abdomen, her arms around Rose's waist, not resisting, and in the minute or so while she waited for the sharp tugs to subside, she, too, felt a kind of release, at once unsettling and familiar.

How much had Conor seen, she wondered, as she reached up to uncurl her daughter's fingers. She and Sonny and Mishti had agreed that, moving forwards, they wouldn't take in anyone new without each other's explicit agreement, but the winter had been long, and the old hope was stirring within her.

He could stay one night, she decided. One Sharing.

⁂

By the time Liv had coaxed her daughter indoors, Conor was sitting in the kitchen at the back of the house, eating a plate of Sonny's crispy paprika potatoes. Liv could see Conor's legs stretched out across the floorboards as she walked along the gloomy passageway. Sonny stood at the sink beyond him, a familiar silhouette against the window, framed by the spider plants and aloe vera shoots that dangled in macramé holders around his head. He was wearing faded cargo pants with a woven belt and his Janis Joplin t-shirt, which made him look like a college professor. The wispy remnants of his hair were gathered in a ponytail, and the burnished dome of his head shone in the electric light that accentuated his stooping shoulders.

'Hey,' said Conor, drawing in his stockinged feet.

'You two have met, then.' Liv pulled out a chair and sat down. 'Conor found me checking under the road. There's a dead racoon in there.'

'Yep,' said Sonny. 'I'll deal with it.' He was scooping up potato peelings and didn't turn round.

Conor nodded his head towards Rose who wavered in the

passageway. 'Is she okay?' He pushed another piece of potato into his mouth.

'Rose,' said Liv, glancing up towards her daughter. 'Conor is asking if you're okay. He's here to visit.'

Conor stopped chewing, as if he'd worked something out. 'If that's cool with you, I mean,' he said to Rose.

Sonny flicked on both faucets suddenly, splashing water across the counter. 'Have you checked with Mishti?'

'Mishti won't mind.' Liv leaned back in her chair, trying to catch Sonny's eye. He knew perfectly well that she couldn't have checked with Mishti, because he'd just dropped Mishti at the high school where she worked and there was no cell service along the valley. But what Liv really wanted him to know was that she couldn't turn Conor away. This was never how they'd lived the communal life. Birdeye welcomed all comers.

Conor was staring around at the scuffed orange walls and shelves crammed with dusty tins and jars. 'I'm not a freeloader,' he said. 'I'm good with tools. I work at Home Depot.'

'Home Depot, huh?' Sonny turned off the water. 'Gas grills and wallpaper.'

'I could fix this table.' Conor nudged it with his knee so that it creaked. It was actually three small tables screwed together, made level with back issues of the *Catskill News* and covered with a bedspread that one visitor had liberated from the Zen Mountain Monastery. Like most of the house it smelled of dog and several decades of sandalwood incense, as well as Sonny's cooking spices. 'Eau de Sixty-Nine,' they called it. Eric, Liv's ex-husband, was always joking that they should bottle it for the second-homers down in Saugerties.

'There's nothing wrong with the table,' said Sonny. 'We have outside jobs to do.'

Rose, who had ventured in and was standing straight-backed beside Conor, lunged towards his fried potatoes. She grabbed a handful and immediately dropped them near her feet. Gunther padded under the table and began to eat.

'You're very welcome.' Conor looked around again. 'Who else lives here? I thought there'd be more of you.'

'Used to be.' Liv smiled at his growing confidence. She took a brown egg from a bowl on the table and broke it straight onto the floorboards, next to the dropped potatoes. 'Twenty or twenty-five, most summers, back in the eighties, early nineties. The four of us have been here from the start – that's Rose, Sonny, Mishti and I – but others come and go, travelling, off to college, off to the city. Even Mishti goes out to work, these days.'

'And Mishti is Sonny's sister.' Conor tipped his head to observe Gunther as he lapped the glistening egg.

'Right. You'll meet her later. Eric, Rose's dad, lives in Tukesville now, but he still calls by to take care of the plumbing and electrics. Karin walks up a couple of times a week. She helps out with beds and cleaning.' Liv watched Sonny's shoulders move up and down as he swabbed the wet counter. Sonny still thought they should live by their hands – growing things, teaching yoga, reiki, running the stall at the flea market in Woodstock. It wasn't practical anymore though; they'd stopped all that after Liv's surgeries. 'We're a bunch of old hippies,' she added, as much for Sonny's benefit as Conor's. 'Always will be. Visitors come and go. Some like you seek us out, while others show up because they can't find a room in town. But anyone who stays must be open and humble in our Sharing. If you've read anything about us, you'll know that we have very few rules, but the rules we do keep are how we survive. "Listen first. An attentive heart—"'

'"Responds with love."' Conor stressed each word and tapped his fingers on the table in time with their beat.

Liv studied him over the top of her glasses. 'It's what keeps us alive.'

'Oh, sure!' said Conor, swiftly. 'You've done a ton of stuff here. Seen it too.' He nodded towards the piece of blackboard that hung from a nail next to the refrigerator. 'What does that mean?'

A long time ago, Mishti had painted 'Peace and love thoughts' in

8

gold nail polish across the top of the blackboard's frame, and visitors had scrawled their slogans and exhortations: 'Human Be-in!' and 'An Army of Lovers Cannot Lose' and 'If not you, then who?' Lately it had been used for little more than lists of shopping or gardening tasks, but Liv could still make out the letters that someone had once scrawled in greasy pink Crayola across the bottom.

'"Communi"-something, exclamation mark,' Conor read out. '"Communition!" Is that an actual word, even?'

Liv smiled again – warmly, she hoped – and got up from her chair. 'People have expressed themselves on that board in all kinds of ways, over the years – not all of it in English, not all of it making sense. I'll show you where you're sleeping. Then, if you feel up to it, Sonny could use some help in the yard.'

Conor rose, too, but seemed in no hurry. He was wearing a white button-down shirt half-tucked into his chinos: a little formal, to Liv's mind, as if he'd come for an interview. He reached for the backpack he had propped against the wall. 'Where's Rose's twin?' he asked as he shouldered its weight. 'I thought she'd be here.'

Rose, still hovering, made a soft sound like a hum, with her lips open.

'Mary visits,' said Liv, gently. 'She lives in England, doesn't she, Rose?'

'Where you're from,' said Conor. 'I guess she didn't subscribe to the Birdeye manifesto.'

At last Sonny turned around. He gripped the dishcloth in his hand. 'We're not a cult.'

Liv waggled her fingers at him, willing him to let it go, but Sonny's frown deepened.

'Oh, come *on*,' he said, as if it were Liv who had suggested something outrageous. 'You know what we've put up with. I'm tired of the insinuations. He'd better not be a reporter, or I'll—'

'Whoaa!' Conor put up his hands.

'Let's rewind a little,' Liv said hastily, troubled more by Sonny's hostility than Conor's choice of words. 'We don't get much interest from anyone, these days, although even if you were a reporter, Conor, we wouldn't turn you away. Because everyone is searching. That's why you're here, isn't it? Sonny's just concerned—'

'I'll speak for myself if you don't mind,' muttered Sonny, throwing the cloth into the sink. He stomped past Conor and exited the kitchen, heading for the study, his moccasined feet sticking slightly along the painted wooden floor.

'Peace and love, man!' said Conor, once he'd gone. Two pink spots had appeared below his cheekbones, and Liv felt her colour rising too. She wished Sonny could have shown his tender side: the Sonny who drove fifty miles out of his way to fetch a visitor, or who knelt in the wet grass to remove Rose's slippers on summer mornings so that she could sweep her toes through the dew.

Instead, her old friend was being an asshole. Sure, they knew nothing about Conor. Wasn't that the whole point?

AREA OF DETAIL #1

C ONOR HUNG BACK in the kitchen when Liv followed Rose along the passage to the big room next to the front door. 'The parlour', as Liv had called it, was opposite 'the snug', which was full of craft stuff. Mishti's space, he guessed. Another door, between the snug and the kitchen, was firmly shut. Sonny was in there. It didn't matter. He had plenty of time.

He breathed in deeply through his nose, then extracted his cell phone from his back pocket. After swiping to find voice memos, he tapped the red circle and brought the device up to his mouth.

'Communition,' he said, speaking slowly and deliberately.

He looked at the screen again, scrolled down to a previous file and tapped the play arrow.

'*Flooding hazards.*' The voice didn't seem like his, but it was. Earlier that morning he had recorded himself reading the information about river restoration and flood defences on the board for tourists down by the bridge. '*Before restoration. After restoration. After the flood.*' The phrases sounded biblical with the rushing river in the background, and while he wasn't religious, he knew that if he wanted to, he could give them another meaning.

He refreshed the screen and tapped the play arrow one more time.

'*Area of detail.*'

These words had appeared several times on the information board, next to a yellow magnifying glass that zoomed in on a specific feature such as a strand of river weed or a bald eagle. He repeated them under his breath, noting their out-of-context blandness, but also their precision. Such thoughts helped him feel calmer.

'Conor?' called Liv. 'Come on, I'll show you where you're sleeping.'

He stood up and slid his phone back into his pocket.

NOT SPEAKING IS AS
VALID AS SPEAKING

T HE MUSIC BEGAN as a muffled bass beat that pulsed through the floor joists as if welling up from underwater. Liv, crouching in the attic beneath the eaves, guessed it was coming from Conor's phone in the bedroom directly beneath her. She didn't know what kids listened to anymore, she realised. Birdeye had been silent for too long.

The attic these days was little more than a storage nook for boxes of mildewed camping gear, old yoga mats and a lopsided double bedstead. Liv had left Conor to settle in before climbing the narrow stairs on the pretext of checking for damp along the sheathing, but she couldn't see much in the dull light from the round window and anyway, the roof was always leaking. No, up here Liv could exercise an unspoken principle of communal living: the right to disappear, if only for five minutes. Rose proved the point each time she slipped from a crowded room to an empty one, while Sonny had long ago claimed the old dining room as his study through a series of slow, deliberate acts of occupation. Even Mishti had her meditation shrine up in the woods, out of range from the house.

Liv reached into the shadows and ran her hand along a cross beam until her fingers found the grooves she sought, smooth, now, and familiar: the words I HATE carved directly above a distinctive round knot, like a bird's eye, in the timber. Mary used to hide up here when she was a teenager. To Liv, the message she had gouged was part of the Birdeye story – a fleeting impulse, a youthful act of rebellion, but also a commitment, of sorts.

The music below was getting louder. A woman's voice was singing, though not with words Liv could pick out. She sat back on her heels to listen, glad of the noise; it reminded her of the old days with Mary and Rose screaming and shouting, guitars playing and footsteps thundering on the stairs. Liv had lived here for forty-six years with Rose and Sonny and Mishti, plus Eric and Mary for the first seventeen, along with dozens of others who came and went like so many dandelion seeds, floating in and out of their lives. People sometimes asked Liv when Birdeye really began, and she told them *January 1973, when a gentleman called Roman, whose only sister had died when he was still a boy, walked into our house and was comforted by Mary's yelling.* Roman had been suffering from dementia, and somehow, the noise of children helped disrupt the constant looping of his early loss, with its terrible silence. The story formed the first chapter of *The Attentive Heart*, which had brought more people, so that for a decade or two the community had been almost famous with bedrooms turned into dormitories, with bodies sleeping top-to-toe wherever there was floor space and meals served cookout-style on trestle tables along both porches. Then came a frightening period in the mid-nineties when a couple of twenty-somethings had almost destroyed the community. Afterwards, Liv and Mishti and Sonny had glued themselves back together, and in some respects, they were stronger for it, although traces remained: in Rose's hair-pulling, for example, and Liv kneeling here under the roof, picking at scabs such as Mary's bitter message.

A thumping crescendo from below broke into Liv's thoughts. Conor was waiting. Each visitor, she'd always said, was the start of something new, so she took a deep breath and stood up with the help of the crossbeam. As the blood rushed from her head, she rested one hand on her flattened and scarred chest, aware, briefly, of the lack of tissue for gravity to tug on. She'd had the all-clear for seven years now, and while she didn't require breasts, never sought reconstruction, her body still managed to feel surprised.

Conor's door was ajar. He was bending over the old walnut bureau in front of the window, and when Liv caught sight of his face in the mirror his reflection seemed strikingly intimate, more real than actual flesh. She hoped they could start afresh, without the atmosphere from earlier.

'Everything okay?' She spoke loudly, so that he would hear her over the music. Conor removed his hand from a drawer and turned around.

'This is wild!' he said, without a trace of embarrassment, holding out a yellowed sheet of newsprint. 'The *Catskill Times*, from 1972!'

'Ah.' Liv pushed the door open wide. Conor prodded his phone where it lay on the bed, and the room fell silent. She glanced at the clothes he had scattered across the covers: a couple of t-shirts, a pair of jeans, a hooded sweatshirt, underwear. A sleeping bag sat in a heap on the floor, as if he'd just pulled it out of his backpack. On top lay a copy of *The Attentive Heart* with its cover image of Liv embracing her girls. Back then, the three of them had looked quite similar with their coppery hair, bright brown eyes and those teeth with her grandmother's gap at the front. The book's pages were well-thumbed, she noticed. The spine was concave and broken. 'That's the year we moved in. It was more like camping, really. Sonny stripped out everything, fixed the floors, replastered walls. We learned by doing.' She smiled, remembering her first sight of the house, so at ease in its wooded surroundings. They'd arrived in the fall, and she could still picture Mary sitting on the porch steps, holding out chubby fingers to catch leaves next to a row of pumpkins carved with peace symbols and letters spelling 'Dump Nixon!' How young they'd been: Eric, at twenty-four the eldest, did plumbing work for cash in Apollonia; Sonny taught himself house maintenance from a manual, and Mishti, barely eighteen, spent the winter dreaming up a garden that would feed them. Liv, meanwhile, had her hands full with Rose and Mary, yo-yoing between surprise and acceptance, discovering the different things her girls could do, or might one day do, or possibly not do, ever.

'Then,' prompted Conor, 'you helped that dementia guy. Word got around. You had a vibe, here.'

Liv noticed the way he had marked certain pages of her book with a fold in the corner. She pointed to the newspaper. 'What's the lead story?'

'Something about a burn ban. And anglers.'

Liv smiled. 'Us Catskill folk are nothing if not consistent. I used to do some fly-fishing myself when I was young, before I thought about the killing. It's an English invention, although the Catskills like to claim it.'

'You've still got a British accent,' said Conor. 'I mean, you speak the way they do in that movie about Jackie O, or that old black and white actress, kind of snooty . . .' His voice trailed off as he realised what he had implied. Again Liv was struck again by the mix of outspokenness and nerves.

'Katherine Hepburn?' She sucked in her cheeks to make her cheekbones look sharper. 'You're not the first person to say so. It's my privileged vowels. Can't shake 'em.' Conor's charger and earbuds, she noticed, sat on the nightstand beside a rolled-up necktie. He was still wearing his white shirt, as if he'd come straight from an office job – or a judge. If he'd been in trouble, he wouldn't be the first. 'We're in a dead zone,' she went on, 'as you've probably discovered. No cell signal, just Wi-Fi. Sonny can give you the code. The best place for reception is next to the router outside the study.'

Conor clicked his tongue, then waved around at the mossy green walls with hand-painted flowers and vines that curled across the ceiling. 'Who usually sleeps here? Is it always for visitors?'

Liv moved across to the window. 'It's Mary's old room. When she was young, and her dad and Rose and I also slept in here, she used to make signs for visitors and hang them above the porch so that you could see them from that bend in the track – welcome signs, goodbye signs . . .' She pictured her daughter with her forehead against the glass, sobbing when a favourite visitor left. It only lasted until she latched on to someone new, usually female – a big sister she could follow around, copying how they walked or fixed their hair.

'What does she do?'

'She's a lawyer. In London.'

'Sounds intense.'

Conor's tone was a little dismissive, in a way that made Liv wish she'd not said anything. Mary was due to fly out from London for her joint birthday with Rose the following week, and it had been a year since Liv last hugged her. Some of Sonny's defensiveness slid under her skin and she closed her eyes for a moment, focusing on her toes, the balls of her feet, her heels, the solid weight of herself pressing into the floor – an old habit, these days re-branded by Mishti as mindfulness.

'Hey are you okay?' Conor's voice broke through behind her.

She nodded. 'When you're ready, come downstairs. We're glad you're here.'

✿

City of London, 5 p.m. BST

Mary was speed-reading a client review at her desk when she heard the shivery tinkle of wine glasses. Frowning, she looked up from her computer screen as someone rolled the drinks trolley past the frosted glass wall of her office. She had forgotten that one of the departmental managers was leaving. Bottles jiggled as the wheels hit a wrinkle in the carpet.

Mary paused the clock on her timesheet, stood up and slipped her phone into her jacket pocket. Keep this brief, she told herself, as she stepped out into the corridor. She was making her annual trip to the States in a few days and, as well as fund managers to placate, she was waiting for a call from the solicitor who was handling the conveyancing for the house she was buying up in Highgate. The purchase had been planned for the past year and a half, but she had worked absurdly hard to afford it. The stress had caused an itchy rash to break out across her fingers.

Several PAs were already crowding in the boardroom doorway. Mary edged inside, looking around for other partners, but the afternoon sunlight was glancing off the steel-framed chairs, so she slipped past a trio of fresh-faced associates and reached for a glass.

'Here.' Martin, the department's most senior equity partner, stood waggling an open bottle of prosecco.

'Thank you.' Predictably, it wasn't chilled. Martin always said that the booze shouldn't be too enticing. He'd be out of the building by half past five, heading to one of the drinking holes down in Canary Wharf.

'*Sláinte* from the dinosaurs!' He raised his glass in the associates' direction, as if he and Mary were the same generation, when in fact he was mid-sixties and she was forty-eight. He was like a hippopotamus: wallowing, thick-skinned, a killer. 'I'm off,' he murmured, leaning towards her ear. 'Say a few words, won't you.'

Mary's phone vibrated briefly against her hip – her solicitor, she assumed, with his usual impeccable timing. She waited until Martin had retreated, then made her way towards the huge floor-to-ceiling window where clients were brought to view the Tower of London far below, and the yachts lining St Katherine's Dock. The screen was tricky to read in the brightness and she had to shield it with her hand, still awkwardly clutching her glass. *Everyone is fine but I need to tell you something. Please call later.* It wasn't the solicitor. It was Sonny.

Mary was entirely used to stepping out of one world and into the other, but unexpected overlaps were another thing altogether. She closed her eyes to suppress the vertigo, then peered again as Birdeye swung towards her. Sonny wouldn't be coy if Rose was unwell. No, this was almost certainly about Liv, or a money problem, or both. Not an emergency, but something that couldn't wait until her visit.

Okay, she messaged.

'Nice of you to come,' said a woman's voice close by. The departing manager was hovering.

Mary frowned. A few words, Martin had said. She tapped the rim of her phone against her glass and cleared her throat.

SPECIALS

SONNY WORKED CONOR hard for the rest of the morning. First they went to hook the racoon's body from the pipe, and when they returned, Sonny held the ladder while Conor cleared the porch gutters. Liv, glancing from the parlour window, saw that Conor had swapped his smart clothes for jeans and a hoodie. Sonny's manner seemed warmer as he leaned in to show Conor how to do things, what to look for, and why. He was a good teacher, she knew – thoughtful and generous with his knowledge when the need or the opportunity arose. Countless young wanderers had learned how to paint a window frame or bake a rye loaf or perfect a shoulder stand under his guidance, but these things took time.

Once the ladder was stowed away, Sonny decided that the crap in the crawl space beneath the steps ought to be cleared, so Conor borrowed a pair of gloves, then hauled out three sodden mattresses, full of mice nests and spattered with droppings, from an era when visitors pitched up on a Friday and camped in the yard. When Liv came outside with Rose for their lunchtime walk, he was still dragging them down to the roadside. Sonny had told him to stack them next to the remains of the farm stand where they used to sell produce.

'Good job!' she called, hoping to sound encouraging. 'They'd have been a fire hazard come the summer!'

Conor stared at her for a moment, dropping the corner he was holding. 'Well, they've been there quite a while.' He pushed his sleeves up to his elbows. 'Where are you two headed?'

Liv took in the smoothness of his inner arms, automatically checking for bruising or track marks. 'To the diner in town. Our Monday treat. You like a trip to Caspar's, don't you, Rose?'

'Nice!' said Conor, in a way that made clear his preference for a burger over working with Sonny. 'Is that your main job here? I mean,' he nodded towards Rose, 'caring for your daughter, now that this place is quiet?' Rose, however, was already moving off, so Liv trotted after her with a wave towards Sonny who was brushing dirt off the porch steps.

'You'd better ask him – Rose and I do what we're told, mostly! We've plenty to keep us busy.'

Rose began pulling at her gloves when they reached the bend in the road, rubbing them against her hips until they fell off. In really cold weather Liv wrapped her daughter's hands in Sonny's old ski mitts, Velcroing the straps around as tightly as she dared, but Gunther had recently chewed the lining out of them, so now she tried to persuade Rose to use her coat pockets instead. It didn't work. Rose's bare hands flapped and gestured until Liv's own enfolded hers and her fingers could rest there. It meant they walked slowly, as if they carried something precious between them.

As they neared the junction with its left turn onto the old truss bridge, two people came out of a driveway. Susan Kinney and her youngest boy, Kason – five years old, if Liv remembered correctly. His mother had never been particularly friendly. Liv had tried, over the years, to be a good neighbour, taking eggs when Sonny had kept hens and leaving a card on the Kinney porch with an offer of free reiki when Susan's husband AJ lost his job. But some folk never warmed to their way of being. That was how it was.

Susan was holding a bunch of papers – flyers, maybe. She turned left towards Birdeye, but almost straight away she spotted Liv and whipped around, walking quickly in the opposite direction. Such pettiness seemed absurd to Liv, and she almost called out, but Susan hugged her flyers close to her chest, her padded nylon jacket tight across her shoulders, so Liv watched her son instead. Kason, dawdling behind his mother, bent to pick something out of a stubborn lump of snow beside the fire hydrant. As he straightened up, he looked over his shoulder, his gaze open and briefly curious before he skipped on. To Liv, his legs and spine seemed fluid, as if his bones hadn't hardened, as if all the energy it would take a lifetime to expend was bubbling away inside him.

Children's bodies were marvellous things; she had always thought so, ever since she first came to New York, before she'd met Eric, when she was barely eighteen and only half-formed herself. Take those children in her care at Camp Pine Crest – that one she had pulled from the lake – a girl of about nine, with breasts already and sombre eyes and a round, soft belly. Oh that had been another time, back then. All Liv had to do was get on a plane, they'd told her. Get the bus to the Port Authority in Manhattan, and another to Poughkeepsie. We'll meet you, they'd said, and they did – two sweating, wide-hipped matrons who scooped her up along with a few other virgin counsellors from a parking lot behind a gas station and drove them in a bright green bus all the way upstate. Fattie Farm, the locals called it, for kids sent up from Flatbush or Queens for six weeks of dieting and exercise and a daily weigh-in and a weekly check-up at which their bodies were measured in twenty-one different places. Wrists, rib cages, inner thighs. Liv had been made a swim counsellor on account of her unfamiliarity with softball. This meant that in addition to her 'dorm mother' duties and sitting with her group at mealtimes and noting down any recalcitrant behaviour, she herded them like ducklings down to the lake and made sure none of them drowned. She wore her pineapple print bikini every day and burnt in the sunshine – the slender red-headed English girl in a camp full of indoor-bred city kids who ran into the restrooms to stick their fingers down their throats or swooned over pictures of burgers and sundaes instead of singers and movie stars. No one had heard of bulimia back then. No one considered the life sentences they were doling out with the lettuce leaves and the tape measures and the scales. The nine-year-old had wriggled away at measuring time and jumped into the water. Her strength as she fought to get away had taken Liv by surprise. Of course, back then, most things had surprised her, but it was always momentary, each new sensation quickly absorbed and forgotten. Only later, after she became a mother, did such things revisit her.

Rose made a humming sound as she veered into the ragged verge. Kason in front of them had by now turned around and was marching backwards, staring at them, taking his time, keeping each foot in the air a little longer before stamping it down, seemingly enjoying the reverse perspective.

His mother paused at the entrance to another property, in front of a mailbox from which a small Stars and Stripes flag drooped. She opened the flap and pushed in a flyer, then glanced over her shoulder. 'Don't gape!' she scolded, reaching for Kason's arm.

Liv steered Rose back to the asphalt and tucked the loose end of her scarf inside her coat. The little girl who jumped into the water at camp had been nicknamed Nellie the Elephant by the other children. After all these years, Liv could still hear the tannoy, piping 'Food, Glorious Food' over the parade ground, down to the shore and out across the smooth, milky surface of the lake.

'Come on, Rose,' she murmured. 'Let's get pancakes.' And maybe a little weed.

❦

Rose banged her hand against the glass outside Caspar's, eager to be let in. When Liv pushed the door, the old-fashioned bell tinkled and the warm fug of grilled bacon and donuts greeted them, as it always did.

'Good afternoon, ladies!' The server was a round-shouldered, light-skinned teenager in a black t-shirt. Liv hadn't seen him before. 'I'm Thomas. Take a seat and I'll fetch a menu.'

Liv looked about. The place was quiet, out of season. The booths at the far end were almost in darkness where no one had flicked on the electric light. A few people sat near the bar: the girl from the gas station over the road, a couple of strangers in jeans and denim jackets, and Liv's elderly friend Dolores, eyes shut beneath the peak of her red 'This Machine Kills Fascists' cap, napping at her usual table by the news stand.

Rose sat down heavily in the nearest booth.

'What can I get you?' asked Thomas, bringing over two glasses of water.

'Is Jenna working today?' Liv guided Rose's arms out of her coat, then slid into the seat opposite and shrugged off her own. Rose reached out and touched Thomas's leg. He stepped back a little.

'She's checking a delivery.'

'She's been visiting her mother,' said a smoke-raddled voice behind Liv. 'In Saugerties. "Assisted living" they call it. My ass!'

Liv twisted in her seat. 'Hello, Dolores. How are you doing?'

Dolores rolled her rheumy eyes. She wore a thick padded coat, but Liv knew she was skin and bone beneath it. Her hands shook as she pushed her half-eaten slice of pizza to the other side of her plate.

'I'm cold. This is cold! Thomas! Heat this up a little for me, would ya? I have two vests on. I can feel the dampness.' She tapped her fingers on the table. 'O-Livia! You want to think about Rose's chest.'

A little girl came running out from behind the counter. A braid of hair was clamped in her mouth and the waistband of her leggings had slipped below the curve of her belly.

'Hi Cherry,' said Liv, smiling. Cherry was Jenna's daughter, a longed-for, long-awaited child, although her father hadn't stuck around much after. 'You remember Rose, don't you? Rose is my daughter.'

Cherry scrunched up her face. 'She is *not*.'

Now Jenna appeared in the doorway by the sandwich maker – a heavy-set woman in her late forties wearing jeans and a Caspar's t-shirt.

'Good to see you, Liv. And Rose! How you doing, honey? What are you having?'

24

'Soup!' said Dolores, lifting her chin to appraise Jenna from beneath the peak of her cap. 'They have all the soups here.'

'Do you want to see the specials?' asked Jenna.

'These are them,' said Dolores, patting the plastic menu by her plate. 'Today's a good day for soup. Tomato, lentil, but not the curry. I can't take the curry.'

'No curry,' agreed Liv. 'But you'd like some pancakes, would you Rose?'

'Oh pancakes!' scoffed Dolores. 'I got one word I tell ya. In-di-gestion!'

Liv watched her daughter's face, checking for any tension, but Rose's mouth was relaxed and her eyes were half-shut – her 'water off of a swan's back look', Eric called it. 'And my usual, please, Jenna,' she added.

When Rose's pancakes arrived, Liv cut them up and poured syrup and handed her daughter a fork. Jenna came over with the coffee pot and a basket of serviettes and sat down opposite.

'You want to make triangles?' she asked Cherry, pulling her up into her lap.

'No.'

'Okay, let's go fancy.'

She showed her daughter how to fold down two corners and bring one behind the other so that the serviette stood up by itself, restaurant style.

'Old school,' said Dolores, glancing over. 'That's how we did 'em at Marlon's. You got beef stew in a bread bowl. Or sometimes just a bowl. Rose would like it up there I betcha. But, O-Livia – you gotta wipe that crap off her chin.'

After a while, when Rose had finished eating, and Cherry had hopped down and was occupied tipping sweetener from pink sachets into Dolores' glass of Alka Seltzer, Jenna pulled a mini Ziploc bag from her sleeve and tucked it deep into one of the serviettes. She pushed it across the table to Liv, who stared down at it for a moment. The fold reminded her of the cleft cut by the Esopus around Slide Mountain.

'I'm cold,' complained Dolores. 'Put this in a box for me, Thomas. I got a nice microwave at home. Hey girls, don't forget it's Tuesday tomorrow! You better come see me!'

Liv covered the serviette with her hand. 'We'll be there, Dolores!'

'You gotta pay me,' Jenna mouthed over Cherry's head.

'I will.'

❧

Sonny was exiting the downstairs bathroom when Liv and Rose arrived home. The end of his belt wasn't tucked into the belt loop and it stuck out a little comically beneath his t-shirt. The old cistern filled behind him.

'Is Karin here yet?' Liv asked, rejuvenated by the fresh air and the tiny stash in her jeans pocket; hopeful they could smooth out any residual tension. 'Did you get lunch already? How did it go with Conor?'

'Not now.' Sonny glanced over his shoulder. His arms drooped; he seemed done in, but cleaning out gutters was strenuous work. Liv checked along the passageway. Conor was eating something in the kitchen, tipping back in his chair, his plate on his lap. Rose, meanwhile, had already slipped into the parlour; she was pacing the strip of carpet Eric had laid at the room's edges to keep her feet warm in winter.

'Hello, Liv!' A familiar voice floated down from upstairs.

Liv leaned over the banister as Karin's purple Crocs and rounded calves descended. Karin was a benign presence in the house: a born-again Christian in her early thirties whose heart was big enough to love Jesus and everyone else. Her aunt had lived at Birdeye for a year in the late eighties, and now Karin, who had an unshakeable faith in the power of community, balanced visits alongside looking out for her girlfriend, who was diabetic. Today she clutched an armful of Rose's laundry against the bib of her cut-off dungarees as she shook out her newly dip-dyed hair.

'Spring green!' Liv remarked, appreciatively.

'Thanks. Alondra did it for me.'

'Liv,' murmured Sonny, 'before you go into the kitchen . . .' He fell silent, waiting until Karin had squeezed past and disappeared down the cellar steps.

Liv saw his frown and touched his arm. 'Hey, it's me! Don't be mad. If something is bothering you, let's talk it out.'

'Well, that's it, nail on,' said Sonny, keeping his voice down. 'We're Sharing tonight, and that boy – can we trust him? I messaged Mishti, but her phone is still off. She doesn't know he's here.'

'Mishti's not a grump like you.' Liv tugged gently on the end of his belt to show she meant it fondly. The trip to the diner, coupled with Conor's arrival, had made her feel reconnected to the world; she wanted Sonny to feel the same way. 'All are welcome at our Sharing. If you won't say what's bothering you in front of Conor, then tell me now.'

'Later.' Sonny jerked his head sideways. 'Speaking of which, has he said why he's come? He's not a big talker, but he asked a couple of weird questions. Wanted to know where we'd buried Pinto! Told him to mind his own beeswax.'

Liv didn't care to hear any second-hand talk about Pinto. She missed the nudge of her dog's cold nose, the tap of her sharp claws across the floorboards. When she looked around Sonny's shoulder, she saw that Conor was rising from his seat in the kitchen, adjusting his jeans, wiping his mouth on the back of his hand.

Conor caught her looking. 'Did you have a good time at the diner? I thought maybe you were avoiding me.'

Liv suppressed a smile. Was this young man trying to *shame* her?

'Put your boots on,' she told him. 'We're taking a hike.'

THIS TRAIL IS OF
MEDIUM DIFFICULTY

L IV AND CONOR set off from the trailhead beyond the Kinney house. Liv walked in front, climbing swiftly, with Conor's hard new boots thudding on the rocks behind. Gunther followed for a short distance, but where a branch had fallen across the path he sank down on his haunches. Liv knew better than to urge him on; he would wait there or wander back home. She hoped the Kinneys were in school or at work so that they didn't spot Gunther off his leash so close to their property. They weren't dog people. She didn't want a confrontation.

Soon the Esopus was no more than a shush in the distance. The pock-pock of a woodpecker drifted up from below and a chain saw whined from across the river, but these, too, quickly faded. Liv felt light-footed, pleasantly aware of the pull in her legs and the stretch in her lungs, hopeful that the long winter was passing. Watery sunshine leaked through breaks in the cloud, catching the few brown leaves that still clung to beech saplings and backlighting them like drips of honey. The trees weren't in bud yet, but with a few more days of thaw the woods would be transformed. Just in time for Mary, she thought. She wanted the spring for her returning daughter.

After twenty minutes or so they reached a fork in the trail. To their left, a broad stream of snowmelt trickled downhill, its arteries forking and re-joining under fallen logs, under leaves, deceptively boggy. Liv turned right and continued climbing, but as the path levelled off and widened, she glanced over her shoulder and saw that Conor had paused in front of the route sign and was taking a picture. She waited for him to catch up.

'Are you worried we'll get lost?'

'No – you know the way, right?'

They walked abreast now. Conor put away his phone, then began to swing his arms exaggeratedly, as if testing the sensation.

'Do you bring everyone up here? People like me, I mean.'

Liv looked sideways at him. 'Not everyone. But yes, quite a few. Sonny calls it my meet-and-greet. I call it walking. How are you feeling?'

'Okay – mostly. It's kind of creepy out here though. All these trees.'

Liv peered at the trees and wondered what he saw lurking. Maybe he was anxious about bears, but they were making too much noise for any surprise encounters.

'So, you're up from the city. What part?'

'Rego Park, Queens. I moved there last year. A room in a walk up. It's cool, the other guys are cool, but we don't know each other.'

'That can take a bit of time.'

'Right. You've been here forever.'

Liv laughed, amused. 'Sometimes it feels that way.'

'I couldn't do that. I mean, stay in one place for so long.'

'No?'

'I don't want to get trapped.'

'Me neither. But sometimes – well, it's a state of mind. When I had the girls—' Liv mentally checked on Rose's whereabouts, as happened so many times each day: yes, safe with Sonny in the kitchen where he said he'd prep a batch of sourdough. 'When we first came here, I knew that Rose especially needed stability and routine. That's when I started hiking. I used to walk around with the two of them wedged in a big backpack.'

'Huh.' Conor wobbled on a rock before hopping over a little gulley. 'You were at Woodstock, weren't you? The festival, I mean.'

'Along with fifty thousand other people.'

'Then you met Eric, your ex.'

'Yep.'

'But he's not the twins' natural father.'

'Hey now . . . Eric's their dad. He adopted them.'

'So you married an American to stay in the US, then founded a commune to help care for your disabled child.'

Liv paused, frowning at the rocky path in front of them. She was used to the curiosity, understood it, even. Conor was hardly the first guest to pitch up with an unusual focus or fixation, but he was stating things, and drawing conclusions, as if there was nothing left to discover.

'Careful here. It's slippery. Birdeye grew from the deep longings we recognised in ourselves and others.'

'Sorry – that was stupid.' Conor continued on for a couple of steps, then stopped again. 'But you didn't go back. To begin with, I mean. To England. To your family.'

Liv looked up at him. Ferrars was an unusual surname, and she supposed stuff would show up if you googled it. The story had been in the British newspapers. Her parents, Colin and Diane – two travel writers seemingly blessed with every advantage of self-confidence and physical beauty and an unfailing absorption in each other – had gone trekking in the Karakoram without her when she was eight, and never came back. She still saw them sometimes, fleeting shadows at the edge of the yard or beneath the trees, stealing out of her life and their own. Their shapes were tricks of the mind, electrical impulses arcing across the chasm of childhood trauma. No ghosts, just gaps.

'Come on,' she said. 'You must know how this works. I want to discover more about you, seeing as you plan on staying in our home tonight. What brings you to Birdeye?'

Conor was looking back down the path, and in the soft shaft of sunshine his irises appeared pale and clear as spring water.

'I was owed some time,' he said, matter-of-factly. 'My dad died a while back. My mom – she's in Idaho.' His face seemed to fall, for a moment; it took on a blankness before he turned his head away.

Liv had noticed how he didn't check his phone constantly like most visitors did, although that morning she had seen him whispering into it, in the kitchen, before Sonny had given him the Plusnet code. She would need to probe gently, talk at the edges, leave plenty of space.

'So you decided to come all the way up here . . .'

'To see you. Do this. Feel better about stuff.'

He reeled off the words as if reciting one of those wristband manifestos young people sometimes wore. All the visitors who'd flowed through the house down the years – most would say they'd come to Birdeye for the reasons Conor stated, although perhaps not so plainly. They hoped to throw off their troubles, then found they had to sit down with them first.

'How did you find the work this morning?' she asked.

'Fine, but Sonny doesn't like me. I thought he was into Zen shit and all.'

'It's not you, although I can see how you'd feel that way. He just wasn't expecting anyone. When I saw you two out of the window, you seemed to be having an interesting conversation.'

'Well, he was talking about leaves, mainly.' Conor started picking at a patch of grey lichen on the boulder beside him. 'Do you think Rose remembers anything?'

'What do you mean?'

'I mean like stuff that's happened. From way back. Like dogs or people when they are no longer there.'

Liv was well aware of Rose's difficulty each time a favourite visitor left, and how distressed she became whenever Mary went away. With the dogs it was less obvious. Rose rarely petted any animal, but lately Liv had noticed how, in the kitchen, she leaned in her chair, twisting her head to check under the table, unwilling to greet the loss.

'Yes, she misses dogs and people. She loves them, and when they go, she grieves, the same as anyone else.'

'Same as Gunther.'

'Same as me and you.'

'Huh.' Conor flicked away a shred of lichen. 'So I asked Sonny about your dog that died. He didn't like that, but maybe you'll tell me. Did you get her cremated? Or is she buried? Did you bury her out here?'

Liv remained composed, her face neutral. Sonny had been right about the weird dog stuff, but Conor wasn't to know which nerve he'd touched. Every visitor was unusual in some way. It would be the thing that she remembered after they moved on.

'I don't know why you are interested,' she said. 'Tell me. It would help to know.'

'Oh, well wouldn't you want people to know where you were buried? It's about helping those you leave behind – nothing creepy! *"Many of our visitors are grieving. They may have lost a partner, or a relative, or a home, or a dream. At Birdeye we acknowledge this pain, we talk about it, draw it, sing it, walk with it. Sometimes we build a bonfire and burn it, or we cast it into the river and let it flow down to the ocean."'*

He was quoting directly from *The Attentive Heart*. His dad had died, he'd said. Liv gazed into the bare trees that gripped the slope below them. They stood so upright, each in their own space, trunks and branches giving nothing away, full of sap, waiting and waiting.

A woodpecker's insistent knock started up again, reminding her of Rose's pull.

'We should get back. Why don't you come with me to fetch Mishti from school? You can run into the store for some tahini.'

'Wait! I'm serious! Where's Pinto's grave?' Conor was standing in one of the little streams of water that flowed between the rocks on the trail.

'You've got wet feet,' Liv said, turning away. 'And you don't need to see it.'

⚘

Every so often, the Birdeye household, or Liv specifically, would receive a letter, or an email, or a card – like an SOS stuffed into a bottle and set adrift, but in reverse. These messages came from all corners of the US, and sometimes, the world: 'Thank you for everything,' or 'Things had gotten crazy. You saved my life.' Sometimes they recalled a specific moment, or an act: 'I was helping Rose take her boots off, and she touched my head and I just knew . . .' or 'You made me hike, every single day, and somehow I learned to breathe again.' Often, they mentioned a wish to return to Birdeye, although, in reality, this rarely occurred. Liv wondered what sparked the desire to get in touch after years or decades of silence. She also wondered about those who didn't write. Some left just as hurt, just as angry as when they arrived. A few, even more so.

She was thinking about this as she sat in the pickup with Conor, waiting for Mishti. Across the school yard in front of her, teenagers kept pushing through the double doors, letting them swing back so the next students had to lean in even harder. Most were still pulling on their jackets, breath clouding above their heads, but there was one kid, tall, with red cheeks and thick, shuffling legs and she noticed how he laughed with the others around him. He reminded her of – oh, what was his name, something old-fashioned like Joe or John. Anyway, he'd stayed at Birdeye ten or twelve years before and filled the whole house with his deep chuckle. He'd had a difficult childhood, she recalled. During his stay he formed a particular attachment to Mishti, who understood what it meant to have controlling, authoritarian parents. They used to sit in her snug and weave together.

'Mind if I turn on the radio?' Conor asked, reaching for the button.

'Go ahead.' Liv switched the ignition key to first position. 'But don't you have your own music?'

'I like the radio sometimes – knowing other people are listening, too – family maybe, or random strangers.'

Liv smiled, sorry that she had cut him off in the woods, earlier.

Conor jumped through some stations – fast-talking ads and news and some generic-sounding rock – before settling on a crooning, syncopated soul track that might have been Luther Vandross or Al Green. She nodded her head in recognition and wound down her window. The road to her left dipped then rose with a comfortable symmetry; if she nudged up her glasses, she could see the long summit of Cross Mountain with its fuzz of pines like a five-day old beard. It was a good view, and waiting for Mishti was usually something Liv liked to savour. Mary had always ridden the bus to and from school when she was a teenager.

She reached forward over the steering wheel and wiped the misted windscreen with the back of her glove.

'Is she coming?' Conor was lounging, knees up, boots on the dashboard, waggling his shoulders to the music.

'She won't be long. She likes to tidy up, talk to the kids.' Liv sat back and watched a gaunt-faced girl in her wing mirror. The girl had long brown hair and was rummaging in a Costco tote near the rear bumper.

'Does Mishti like working? I mean, she must be nearly as old as—'

Liv turned to Conor and pulled a pretend-shocked face. 'So old you'll let her sit up front, won't you? Go on. Hop in the back with Gunther.'

Mishti appeared a couple of minutes later. Liv spotted her pink ear warmers above her short, plump form draped in her knitted green poncho. She was making her way along the path that led from the rear of the building, but then she paused and stooped to study the base of a bare young sapling that looked recently planted. When a couple of students walked up to her, she opened her arms and they hugged, all three of them in a huddle with Mishti's dark head and bright ear muffs in the middle.

Conor, Liv realised, wasn't moving. 'Hey, scoot!'

As he slid into the back and settled down next to Gunther, the gaunt-faced girl started tapping on her side window. Liv opened it all the way so that she could hear her.

'Got any cash?' asked the girl.

'What for?'

The girl shrugged. She had deep-set eyes and long, swooping eyelashes.

'Need a ride?'

A nod.

'Hop in. This side. There's a dog but he won't bite you.'

'I don't bite either,' chipped in Conor, but this seemed to alarm the girl; before Liv could release the door lock, she had disappeared into the knot of kids on the sidewalk. Liv hoped she had a safe place to go to.

When Mishti reached the pickup she opened the door and heaved her bulging shoulder bag into the foot well. Liv reached forward to help her.

'This is Conor, behind me. He arrived this morning. He's staying the night – if that's all right?'

Mishti climbed in and twisted round. 'Nice to meet you, and welcome,' she said with her soft, pillowy lisp.

'Thanks for having me!'

Nevertheless, Liv could tell that something had upset Mishti; she wasn't her usual chatty self on the drive home. She asked Conor where he'd come from, and how he liked the Catskills, but then she fell into silence, her child-like hands clutching the seatbelt where it crossed her chest as if she couldn't bear to let it go. A man's voice was babbling about some promotion or other, so Liv switched off the radio. It was starting to sleet; the earlier brightness had been swallowed by a dull, draining grey and the truck in front spattered the windscreen with filth. As they left the town and climbed the hill towards the mountains, it seemed to Liv as if winter was starting over. Trees hung back, black and bare. Headlights wavered, sickly yellow.

'Bad day?' she tried, as they waited at some lights.

Mishti frowned and pushed her hair back from her eyes. 'They plant trees. To remember the dead students. That's the third in two years.'

'By the chain link,' murmured Liv. 'I saw you looking.'

Conor leaned forward, his chin nearly level with Liv's ear. 'Hey,' he said. 'Did someone at the school die by suicide?'

'Oh hush.' Liv wished now that she had Mishti to herself, but Conor wasn't listening.

'A tree isn't the best idea when you think about it,' he went on. 'People forget to water them. They should think of something more unique, something that means you'll never forget that person. A massive mural, or a mountain named after them, or a satellite they shoot into space.'

Mishti made a sound like a sob or a hiccup. 'They need to do something. Stop it from happening. Those poor kids, all that pressure from their phones, not able to switch off, hurting themselves—' She was close to tears. 'That girl was fourteen. She had her whole life ahead – her whole life!'

Liv let her hand rest on Mishti's thigh, reminded of how young Mishti had been the day she'd first met her – a mini-skirted seventeen-year-old. Mishti grasped her fingers briefly, but when Liv turned to look at her, she found Conor's face between them. He really needed to sit back a little, be more sensitive to private moments. He didn't budge until Liv nudged him with her elbow.

'Tahini!' he exclaimed suddenly, making her jump as the sign for the wholefood store flashed past. 'Sorry – Mother Earth ahead – you asked me to remind you.'

Liv braked and flicked on the indicator. Jenna's baggie was still tucked into her jeans pocket. She'd save it for after the Sharing. With a bit of persuasion, Mishti might join her.

KARMA CLEANSING

I F LIV WAS the roof and floor of the Birdeye house, and Rose, the air within it, then Sonny and Mishti were its four walls, holding everything together. Born in Detroit to a white mother and a father from West Bengal, the pair had long ago fled their parents' unremitting domestic war and oppressive expectations and constructed their own refuge within the counterculture. Mishti, with her hugs and her handicrafts and her aversion to conflict of any kind, exuded a generous, sponge-like sensitivity that over the years had drawn countless troubled souls to seek her out in her vegetable garden or join her for morning asanas, then drink herbal tea and commiserate over the planet's struggle with its own dysfunction. She'd had plenty of boyfriends, each one a wanderer, and while several had stuck around for a while, the serial nature of her relationships seemed to be something she accepted. Sonny was the organiser, the teacher, the record keeper. He kept his eye on local politics and attended Town Boards, he filed their taxes and filled albums with thank you letters and photographs, each scrupulously labelled and dated. For decades Liv had watched him cut clippings from the *Catskill News* or, less frequently, the *Washington Post*. He annotated newspaper articles in the same way he peeled an apple or cleaned his fingernails: with a deep meticulousness that Liv might have found irritating if she hadn't made a conscious choice to cherish him for it. Sonny, with his love for sharing knowledge, his prickly tenderness, and his distinctively cerebral approach to his adopted Zen practice kept visitors interested and alert, while his passion for locally sourced, organic vegetarian food sustained them. On this particular evening he had prepared an entrée of honey-roasted root vegetables with a yoghurt and tahini dressing, and a pan of comforting khichdi. The dish was one of Liv's favourites, intended, she understood, as a peace offering.

At six o'clock they gathered around the table with its bowls of bright food and stubs of candle.

'Looks delicious!' said Karin, who was staying for the Sharing. Sonny nodded, and with the familiarity that came with decades of repetition he held both palms out. Karin on his right took one in hers, while Mishti on his left clasped the other. Liv offered her left hand to Rose, then lightly rested it on her daughter's fingers, while her right hand reached for Conor's. He looked momentarily perplexed before nodding his realisation that this was a kind of grace. Soon they were all joined in the circle.

'We give thanks to each other for this meal,' Liv said. 'We thank the Earth, we thank the Sky, we thank the Mountains and the River.' She paused.

'That was nice!' said Conor. 'I mean, short – and nice.'

Liv gave his fingers the gentlest of squeezes before she let go. 'We take it in turns,' she said.

'Right.' He reached for a slice of sourdough. 'So I could do it tomorrow?'

Liv tried not to react, but Sonny looked at her pointedly. 'Tomorrow? One night, you said.'

Karin, smiling, picked up a bowl of wilted winter greens. 'This looks so tasty! What are you planning for the veggie garden this year, Mishti? Purple chard, I hope. I want some colour for my Insta! Have you got seedlings already?'

'The weather,' said Mishti, vaguely. 'It's been too cold. I'm keeping the pots in my bedroom until the frosts are over.'

It was that memorial tree at the school, thought Liv, as she spooned carrots onto Rose's plate, then cut them up into manageable pieces. A young person's death was especially tough. Mishti's feelings often fluttered near the surface, and the few hours before a Sharing could feel a little raw, a little rarified as they gathered themselves in. Karin, always empathetic, changed the subject for the second time and Liv was grateful to listen to her chat with Conor about the city, the cheapest rental areas, a concert she wished she'd gone to, and how she had studied for a year at Binghamton then transferred out to New Palz.

'Why would you trade Binghamton?' asked Conor, a little loudly.

'Well, I'm taking some time out from study, in actual fact.' Karin was blushing. 'Personal reasons. Coming here helps.'

Conor wiped his plate with a hunk of bread. 'Like how? I mean I get *The Attentive Heart* stuff, but how does coming here help you personally?'

'Uh – I feel calmer, I guess. Birdeye exists whether I'm here or not, but it makes a space for me. It's reassuring in that way.' Karin nudged her shoulder against Rose and smiled. 'And I'm with friends.'

Rose leaned away and began to drop pieces of carrot to the floor.

'Must you do that, Rose?' asked Sonny. 'Aren't you hungry?'

'You had pancakes for brunch, didn't you,' said Liv, to her daughter. 'We saw Dolores and Jenna and Cherry.'

'Oh jeez,' said Sonny. 'All those trans-fats . . . Besides which, Liv, there's no cash in the box. Rose's cheque comes in tomorrow, but we've got bills to pay. Let's be ship-shape for Mary.' He stopped and swept a hand across the dome of his head as if he'd caught himself out somehow. Mishti murmured sympathetically, and Liv remembered the money she owed Jenna, but already Sonny was pushing back his chair and muttering about needing to get gas for the pickup before the Sharing so he could drive Mishti to school in the morning.

He was being dramatic. She tossed him the keys. 'We ordered extra maple syrup!'

Mary took the lift from her flat down to the basement wearing her swimsuit beneath her robe. She didn't want to bump into any other residents, but there was no point in trying to sleep. Her brain was fizzing.

She had spent the evening working, as usual, in her muted, softly lit living room, drafting emails, amending documents, peering at spreadsheets. Then at 10 p.m. she had called Sonny as promised; they had spoken briefly before he said he had to go check on dinner. His news was good, in a way – it justified her plans and prompted her to look again at the Long Service Leave clause in her own partner contract. She knew her mom would be distressed, however, and this chastened her.

She stepped out of the lift and opened the door in front of her with a key code before feeling around for the light switch. In her younger years she'd been a promising swimmer. Liv had taught her, decades before – the ex-swimming counsellor who knew exactly how girls' bodies moved in water – and Mary had chosen her flat because of the pool access. She hadn't used it for a while, though. When the lights came up, her senses were briefly overwhelmed by the electric blueness of the water and the shadowy patterns on the ceiling. A generator hummed somewhere, and a chemical smell caught the back of her throat. She stepped out of her slides, lay her robe across a chair, then sat down on the cold tile where she could lower herself in.

The pool was a little cooler than she remembered. She didn't plunge straight away but stood there, circling her lower arms so that the water lapped at her breasts. Liv used to tell people that her daughter was good at delaying gratification, and this was certainly true right now, because there was a thing in her head, triggered by the water: something she would make herself revisit – *endure* – before she swam.

Her junior prom.

Mary had often thought about that evening over the decades. Each time, any extraneous or peripheral memory was stripped away to expose the same stark sequence of cause and effect. First, a visitor went for a hike from Birdeye on the day of the prom and got lost on a remote mountain path. The adults had formed a search party. Mary, left at home with Rose, longed more than anything for a studio portrait in her borrowed puffball dress and home perm, so she took her sister and hitched a ride to school, ignoring all the stares and comments. But Rose didn't want to be in the cramped photographer's booth. She knocked over a studio light, and the photographer, whose younger brother was a senior, told Mary she had to pay for the damage. Mary had no more money, and when he said he'd tell the school authorities, she submitted to sex with him behind the swimming-pool-blue backdrop while Rose stared at the ceiling and several prom couples queued impatiently outside. It was Mary's first time, and it was horrible, but by the end of the night – in fact, by the time she'd wiped her thighs and pulled down her skirt – the whole school knew her as the girl you could fuck for ten bucks.

One week later, the photograph had arrived in its waxed paper envelope.

'Quite the circus,' Liv had remarked, oblivious, glancing at it over Mary's shoulder. 'Please don't tell me you paid good money for that.'

In the pool, Mary's arms were no longer circling. On the far side, in the shadows, a door opened. A man's head appeared, then his body in a dark jacket and trousers. He walked towards her wearing cartoonish plastic shoe covers.

'Hello?' she said, her voice echoing across the water.

'I'm sorry.' It was one of the concièrges. 'No swimming until further notice. There's a problem with the filters.'

'Oh.' Mary felt a rush of embarrassment, caught there, half immersed. Then she frowned. The water seemed fine. Perhaps this was a ruse to get her to go back to her apartment.

'There's no sign,' she said. 'If the water isn't safe, we should be told.'

The concièrge looked down at his feet, as if he knew that she knew that it was only a matter of time.

'You'll get a letter in the morning. Everyone will get a letter.'

Mary did not want to swim in unhygienic water. She climbed out with as much dignity as she could muster and reached for her robe. 'Well, I hope so. Goodnight.'

⁂

Mishti rang the cowbell out in the passageway. Its blunt clang carried up the stairs and along to Rose's bedroom on the west side of the house. Liv, sitting on the bed, waited until Rose had swallowed her anticonvulsant followed by the Lioresal she had crushed into her oat milk. Then she wiped her daughter's mouth and chin with a hand towel and nodded towards the doorway.

'Let's boogie,' she said, reaching for Rose's hand.

Downstairs in the parlour, Mishti was arranging chairs around the knarly hand-woven rug.

'Six tonight,' she murmured, pushing her hair back over her shoulder. She rested her fingers on the padded vinyl back of the seat favoured by her brother. 'Karin's here, and there's Conor.'

'Did you take a nap?' asked Liv, opening the corner cupboard and rummaging for a candle. The windows were hung with yellowed drapes, but no one had closed them; she could see Mishti's reflection in the glass.

Mishti sighed. 'I couldn't sleep. I hoped we might talk on the way home, but then—'

Liv turned around. Karin was standing in the doorway. Conor appeared behind her, bobbing over her shoulder.

'Sorry to interrupt,' said Karin. She blew a kiss towards Rose. 'Where's Sonny?'

'He's still getting gas.' Mishti beckoned Conor in. 'Here, Conor. Leave the blue chair for Rose, but otherwise sit where you like.'

'Not the black chair, though!' warned Karin. 'I sat there once, and Sonny huffed all evening.'

Conor obediently avoided the two proscribed seats and sat down in the old Boston armchair – a low-slung, tattered thing that Liv always avoided because of the effort it took to haul herself out again. He crossed his legs and rested his hands flat on the worn upholstery.

'You'll doze off in that,' said Karin, sitting opposite him. 'And when you fall asleep you miss all the good stuff.'

'She's teasing,' murmured Liv. 'What is shared here, stays here. As soon as that candle is lit, we all enter a place of trust.'

Conor scratched his neck. 'Sure.'

Once Sonny had returned from the gas station, taken off his coat, then found his moccasins and visited the downstairs bathroom, they were ready. Mishti put a match to a candle in an earthenware holder and set it in the middle of the rug while Karin flicked off the electric light. Liv, seated between her daughter and Conor, closed her eyes and took a series of slow breaths. In through the nose, out through the mouth. When she looked again the room was transformed, as it always was, into shadows and silence. She stared into the darkness on the far side of the little flame. Here they were, once more letting go of the day's minor hurts and accommodations. She could feel Rose sitting beside her, straight-backed, her body tense, always on the point of standing, the core or root from which they had all grown. She could hear Conor's stomach gurgling. She focused on the floor and let gravity settle her bones. You breathe in, you breathe out, and when your thoughts have loosened, you begin.

'It's been a while,' she said, speaking slowly. 'We've not shared for a week. Pinto's gone, and I miss her.' She paused, needing to sift everything; taste it to see where the bitterness lay. 'I know Sonny wanted a few weeks' quiet time with no visitors, and that's been important – we've not welcomed anyone since October. Then, when Conor showed up this morning, he spooked me a little with his questions, but now, frankly, I'm glad of it. Birdeye calls us to listen; to be in the moment and accept each other for who we truly are.

It's not easy, but it's what we believe. I'm grateful he's been drawn to our rhythms. It's good to have him here.'

Liv could see the tips of Conor's sneakers. He was tapping one foot – a nervous gesture. She closed her eyes again. She'd not been wholly candid, but any new thoughts weren't in focus yet, and for some reason she felt like weeping, which was tiredness and background pain and something else, an old hurt, disturbed by Sonny's crankiness, and also Conor's probing. There had been a time when Sonny and Mishti had struggled to stand with her, when Birdeye had been threatened by the disruptor, Wren. Wren had arrived one summer with her partner Tyler and their little daughter, named after a river. Shenandoah. Tyler was a veteran who'd fought in Iraq and had PTSD or Gulf War Syndrome or maybe both, and Wren was super-protective of him, to the point of being obsessive. For the first few weeks Liv hoped that Birdeye might be the salve that eased their problems. Then things turned. The Sharings became a place for accusations and denunciations, and Birdeye was almost defeated by the lies. Oh, Liv didn't want to think about it, but Wren's mark remained in the circumspection she felt – a wariness at odds with the streams of pure feeling that used to flow like rapture in the years when the girls were young, when Sharings often took place outside in the woods, when looping circles of people held hands among the lightning bugs and touched each other's spirits beneath the trees. Back then, people talked of channelling their inner *id*. They had visions. They wailed to the heavens. Nowadays things were a little more prosaic. It was just how it was.

'That's me,' she said, trying not to sigh.

'Who's next?' Conor asked.

'Shh,' hushed Karin. 'It's Rose.'

Liv reached out and touched her daughter on the shoulder. 'We're listening,' she murmured, for Conor's benefit. Rose never spoke. She didn't have the capacity, if you believed her physiatrist Dr Khaw, although she made sounds sometimes – sucking noises, and a soft 'awah!' cry when something interested her. Mainly she used her body to communicate. She knew it was her turn; she understood that the attention of everyone was upon her and usually she got up and paced her carpeted path behind the chairs or stood at the window and bounced her long nose gently against the glass. Occasionally she would leave the parlour and then they all sat and listened to the slap of her slippers on the stairs, followed by the creak of the floorboard outside the bathroom before she padded along the landing to perch on her own bed.

Tonight, however, she remained seated, so Liv tried to focus on her breathing. She imagined the soft rush of air as it entered her daughter's chest, the passing of oxygen into the blood, the steady clench, clench of her heart. This simple meditation had saved Liv in the days after Rose was born. It still did.

After ten minutes or so Sonny coughed, and Liv nodded her head to let Karin know it was her turn to speak.

'Oh, sure,' said Karin. Liv couldn't quite see, but she imagined her twirling a strand of her green hair: a comforting habit, like Sonny's moccasins or Mishti's poncho. 'I had another fight with Alondra. She wants me to go back to college. Same old stuff. I'm not going but it tires me out. Her blood pressure and iron levels are okay, and she thinks it'll be good for me, but that makes me feel like a kid. She says I'm not her mom, but she's not mine! She won't *begin* to discuss starting a family, but I want kids – I know it's God's plan. I'm thirty-one, my eggs are cooking, so why wait? The sooner the better . . .'

Liv looked down at the floor. Conor's foot had stopped jiggling. His hand rested on the arm of the chair, and she was suddenly aware of how still he had become. No young man's twitching, no sniffing or scratching, and she felt certain that he was waiting to speak, that he had something he wanted to say. As Karin talked on, she became increasingly distracted by his presence beside her in this strange theatre of unburdening which, every so often, pulled her away to a point where she stopped being a participant and became an observer: curious, objective, oddly heartless.

'. . . And she denies it, every time I ask, but I think a part of her resents me coming up here: the Sharings, you know, talking to all of you. We've got work to do in our relationship, and hustling me off to New Palz won't help that.' Karin folded her arms, another habit. The others gave her a respectful minute.

'Who's next?' Conor asked.

Sonny uncrossed his legs.

'It's Mishti now,' warned Liv, gently. 'We move around the circle, from one to another.'

Mishti, however, was flapping her hand, waving things on. 'Not me. I'm too tired. Sonny'll go next.'

'Are you okay?' Liv couldn't remember Mishti ever skipping a Sharing. Sometimes she spoke for fifteen or twenty minutes as she picked over a worry or a feeling.

'No. No, I'm not okay. Sonny can speak. Please, for once, let him speak for me.'

Liv frowned across at Mishti's dim form before turning to Sonny. A premonition, like a sheet of clear, cold glass, pressed up against her. *Don't*, she thought, even as she nodded.

Sonny sat up and leaned into the light, his hands clasped in a gesture that seemed profoundly out of character and which did nothing to ease the foreboding in Liv's chest. He took a breath and raised his eyes to meet hers.

'We're leaving,' he said quickly. 'Next month. To a place up near Buffalo. We want to move on, Liv. While we still can.'

The silence that followed filled Liv's head with its harsh rushing. Then she heard a shriek as Rose swung her arm out and grabbed a fistful of Karin's hair just as Conor dropped something – his cell phone, the little red 'record' light glowing – and he leaned down and grasped it while Mishti jumped up to help Karin, and the words that came out of Liv's mouth were *no no no*.

CHILDREN OF THE
REVOLUTION

B IRDEYE ONLY HAPPENED because of Mishti and Sonny. Liv didn't put this in her book, but it was there: the real reason, for when she needed it.

The pair stepped into her life on a sweltering June afternoon in 1972. Liv was toiling up Tinker Street in Woodstock while Liv's husband Eric went to the store to buy ice or cold beer or something. Rose was restless in the baby carrier and Mary toddled along, grizzling, but as Liv approached the bench where a tree threw a patch of shade, she saw a couple sprawled there. The girl was clearly pregnant – six, seven months, maybe; she was leaning back against the young man's shoulder as he held a can of soda, her eyes closed, legs parted, a child-sized palm pressed against the swelling of her belly. Liv smiled as she drew level, remembering the kicks of her own babies, content to find a spot to sit a little further along. The soda looked good, she thought, as the man raised it to the girl's lips. But something wasn't right; the girl moaned, then pushed the can away. Her head tipped forward so that her long black hair swung across her bump, and Liv stared, momentarily transfixed by the liquid that trickled between the slats of the bench towards a dusty patch of pigweed on the sidewalk.

'Mommy.' Mary had seen it too. 'Pee-pee.'

A man with a jacket slung over one shoulder muttered 'Goddam hippies' as he passed by.

'Hey.' Liv stepped closer. 'Are you okay?'

The girl moved a shaking hand between her thighs. Her

companion scrabbled to his feet. Anxiety distorted his features.

'She needs help. I don't know what to do.'

Liv, unsure, glanced back down the hill. 'Do you need a ride to the hospital?'

The girl's head shot up. 'No!' she managed, before her face tightened and she pulled in her lips so that they disappeared. The skin around her eyes looked purplish and puffy from crying, and one strap of her mini dress, missing its button, had fallen from her shoulder.

Liv reached for Mary, gathering her in.

'No doctors.' The young man pushed his hand through his hair, then rubbed his palm against his jeans. There was sweat on his top lip and his cheesecloth shirt was grimy. 'They freak her out. No one helped us before, and now she's too far gone.'

An abortion, thought Liv, immediately. Women came from all over to New York, where it was legal.

'*Not here!*' gasped the girl, with what might have been determination, or despair.

'It's okay,' murmured the young man, reaching to support her, his eyes widening as she struggled to twist and bend over the bench. 'Oh god, I think it's coming . . .'

Liv looked down the hill again, and this time saw Eric's sturdy green Wagonaire rising towards them. She stepped up to the kerb, then waved the couple over.

'Hey ladies!' said Eric when Liv yanked open the door. His face changed when he saw the strangers behind her. The girl was moaning as her companion helped her across the sidewalk. Liv didn't say much, just hurried everyone inside, the young couple in the back, herself in the front passenger seat with Mary on the floor hugging her legs, and the carrier with Rose in it clasped to her chest.

'Keep your eyes on the road,' she told Eric, while the girl twisted onto her knees and hooked herself over the rear seat, panting and straining. No one knew where they were headed, but it didn't matter, because five minutes out of town the young man's frantic pleading forced Eric to stop on a quiet stretch beside a field. Eric took charge of the twins, while Liv nervously tugged at the girl's sodden underwear, peering for the baby's head, but with no idea what she was supposed to see or do about anything. The girl by now was shuddering almost continuously, biting her lips until they split and bled. Then, after several minutes or maybe a quarter of an hour, she made a sound that seemed too bleak for her small frame, and with one prolonged, awful contraction a grey mite – a boy – slid out into Liv's cupped hands. It looked dead. She knew it was dead.

When Eric mentioned the hospital again, the girl was craning over her shoulder, staring at the body Liv held, reaching for the young man's hand.

'Our baby . . .' No more than a whisper.

'Shit – hush, Mishti!' The young man was weeping, pressing his finger to the girl's lips. 'I thought you were gonna die . . .'

'Maybe they're illegals,' Eric murmured, as Liv, trembling, tried to wrap the body with its grisly cord in one of Rose's diapers. There was blood, too, and more thick stuff coming that she guessed was the placenta. Liv stole a glance at her toddlers dozing off together on the front bench seat, faces flushed, arms thrown wide, and for a moment she pictured their births as if she were outside her own body, gazing down as the doctor delivered her tiny daughters.

'She needs medical attention,' she whispered, but as she turned back to the terrified pair, she caught the look they gave each other, and the resemblance that she'd failed to notice earlier: a certain bow shape to their top lips, the same curve of their nose and brows, too aligned to be anything but close blood family.

'You're the father, right?' she murmured, to the young man.

He shook his head, but Mishti's eyes filled with tears, and although the afterpains were coming and her face was twisting, the tenderness in her eyes put it all together.

It took a few days for the fragments of their story to emerge. Mishti was seventeen, Sonny, eighteen. They hadn't meant for it to happen; they'd been messing around; it never happened again. Then morning sickness struck, and when the doctor was called, the pregnancy was discovered. Mishti refused to talk, but the doctor must have guessed somehow, because suddenly she and Sonny were no longer stupid lazy teenagers; they had done an unspeakable, unthinkable, irreversible thing, but most of all, they had blown up their family's future. Within half an hour they were kicked out of the house, their mom screaming, their baba punching his own head. A termination, they learned, was the only option, but they had to find their way to New York, and by the time they reached the city they were too late; the pregnancy was tipping twenty-four weeks. That had been almost a month before, and they'd gotten nowhere, until the stress and sleeping rough and barely eating had done the job and Mishti went into labour.

Liv, still only twenty years old herself, could not make sense of it and didn't want to. But on that hot June afternoon, as Mishti gripped her brother's hand, Liv witnessed the bond between them and felt it drawing her in. Eric was frowning, not understanding, so she told him they could either drive the pair to a hospital and abandon them, or they could all go home to their cramped place on the turkey farm for a decent meal and some sleep.

'You'll need antibiotics,' said Liv, thinking aloud as Eric drove. 'I'll say the twins have got a strep infection.'

'What about the – you know?' Eric motioned towards the pitiful bundle in Liv's lap.

'His name is Sebastian,' said Mishti, in a soft, lisping voice behind them. 'Please, will you bury him?'

Ten days after digging a hole on the mountainside and laying that little body to rest, Liv turned twenty-one and gained access to her trust money. A fortnight later, she bought a big old house to the west of Apollonia, on a rise above the river.

SAFETY TIPS

L IV SLIPPED OUT early in the morning after the Sharing, with Gunther padding softly behind her. She sat on the porch steps to pull on her waders, then stood up again to tug them past her thighs and ease her arms through the shoulder straps. The musty smell of rubber rose up from the bib across her chest; the canvas lining was split and frayed, but she barely noticed. Her head felt dull and her limbs were heavy as she set off down the track.

Once she had crossed the road, she skidded most of the way down the slope towards the rocks that lined the river. The Kinneys' red pickup flickered between the trusses of the bridge downstream, and a twist of woodsmoke rose up from one of the holiday cabins to join the low cloud clinging to Mount Sheridan. The air was full of moisture; Liv could feel it on her skin.

'Come here, Gunther!' she called, raising her voice above the rush of the water. The old dog, sitting at the edge of the road, watched her. The shaggy tan and grey fur beneath his ears looked like peeling bark. He was probably whining, although Liv couldn't hear him. He'd never been much of a swimmer.

As she stepped into the shallows between two flat stones, she had to grasp an overhanging branch to steady herself. The river was still in spate with snow melt and debris tumbling down from Slide Mountain and Hunter. It had been a while since she'd last waded out into the river and ten years since she'd cast a fly, but as the water pushed around her, she set her sights on the spot beside the turtle-shaped rock where the bed was relatively level. She didn't want a rod. What she needed was to stand firm against the push of surging water in a place where no one could reach her.

Sonny had a word for this kind of behaviour. Aloof. Of all the traits in each other they had named and dissected over the years, this one stung the most. Sonny had used it again in the long night just past, after Karin had gone home and Conor had slunk off to bed, and even Mishti had retired once she'd settled Rose and finished crying. Sonny had told Liv that things had got too fixed, that he and Mishti needed to breathe, that he'd been in touch with a project for kids affected by narcoid addiction up near Buffalo on Lake Erie. The project needed live-in house parents. It was only six hours up the Thruway. He made it sound so normal, like picking out a used car or driving up to Hunter for a hike. Liv had gone outside then, for a solitary toke, and he'd said this was what made it so hard, her shutting off. The truth though was that she couldn't bring herself to state the blindingly obvious – that his sudden announcement meant the end of Birdeye, the end of their life together.

The icy cold was making Liv's ankles ache. If her feet went numb, she might lose her footing. She rested her hand on a jutting boulder and found herself out of breath. A bough of paper birch lay wedged against the far side of the rock and the water slapped against it, splashing her face. If she did slip, she calculated, the blockage would catch her. She looked over her shoulder. Gunther hadn't moved.

'Coward,' she muttered.

The water was halfway up her thighs now. She turned so that it pressed into the backs of her knees. Sonny used to tease her for her habit of standing in the river; he said that she got off on the swell, but of course they'd each said a lot of things down the decades. He had kept his tongue sharp during her cancer years, and for that she was grateful, even as they'd whispered about death in the long hours before dawn. When she went into remission, she and Mishti and Sonny had relied on each other more than ever, feeling their way towards their third age with cautious hope. Sonny could be tetchy, for sure, but she had never questioned his commitment. Lately, though, his temper had turned inwards. She had assumed he would share when he was ready. Leaving was something else.

'Gunther!' she yelled helplessly as she tried to move back towards the shallows, her shins hurting with cold.

'Liv! What are you doing?'

Liv raised her head. Her glasses were foggy, but she recognised Mishti's voice.

'Come out, you'll go hypothermic! Wait, I'll help you!'

'I can manage . . .' muttered Liv, using a finger to wipe her lenses. Mishti, she now saw, was closer than she'd realised, balancing on a flattish stone. She was wearing her gum boots beneath her dressing gown and her hair hung loose and limp around her face. 'Don't you slip,' Liv said more clearly. 'I'm coming.'

The two of them held hands until they were both safely on the riverbank. Gunther swung his tail once or twice as they approached.

'He won't come down to the water without Pinto,' said Liv, puffing after her exertions.

'Oh, Liv, let's talk. I'm so sorry—'

'Have you changed your mind?'

Mishti was silent for a moment. She bent down to stroke Gunther's ears. 'No.'

'Well then, you're not sorry. But I don't know why you couldn't tell me.'

'We did!'

'I mean before. When you first decided.'

'We decided the day before yesterday, but we thought it best to wait until we came together for the Sharing so that Rose and Karin could hear it too . . .'

'We . . .' Liv let the word hang between them. 'But when you were thinking about it – you didn't discuss it with me.'

'No.'

Liv sat awkwardly on the guide rail. Her legs were still encased in her waders so she swung them over one at a time, her hips obedient where her shoulders so often failed. She wanted to be inside now, in the warm fug of Rose's room, massaging her daughter's belly, cutting her toenails, finding her socks.

'You look like a toad,' Mishti murmured, brushing back a strand of Liv's damp hair. The intimacy broke Liv's resolve. She stood up and felt a kind of madness then. It wasn't anger. She had seen anger come to Birdeye as the righteous fury of resistance with its red-hot burn for change, but also the incandescence of the impotent, the wail of the wronged and the stealthy, gnawing rage of those who were afraid. What she felt now was something else – something she could not name or recognise. As she stumbled across the road and back up to the house, she felt as if she were two people, or three, or four – not a single entity but a consciousness that floated between bodies, between versions of herself, noticing everything but moving on past, acknowledging nothing. She heard Mishti call out after her. She saw that Conor's curtains were still drawn. Then, as she entered the house, she heard Sonny splashing in the bathroom. Be calm, she told herself as she kicked off the waders at the bottom of the stairs. Think of Rose.

'Hey, Birdie.'

Liv used Rose's nickname as she pushed open her bedroom door. The scent of urine greeted her with its familiar pungency. For Rose's safety and comfort, the room contained little more than a bed, a chest of drawers and a cupboard for clean sheets and stores of personal hygiene items. It was bright and homely nevertheless, with a crocheted coverlet, an old-style rag rug and a mural of Birdeye painted by Mishti across one wall. Visitors had added extra people down the years: stick figures in yoga poses or leaning on spades in the veggie garden or waving from the porch.

Rose was standing at the window, by the curtain. Her hair, faded to coppery gold, lay flattened above her ears. She looked away as Liv entered, but her lips stretched into the wide, beneficent smile that had once belonged to Liv's grandmother. Her morning routine was important for her equanimity. It was change of any kind that troubled her.

'Did you have sweet dreams?' Liv asked, touching her daughter's cheek before stooping down to catch the hem of her nightdress and pulling it up over her head. When Rose raised her elbows, the loose skin of her underarms stretched into pale, crêpey hanks. Liv pushed away the question about how she'd cope as they both grew older and instead removed the bulky diaper. Then she wrapped her in her dressing gown and led her to the bathroom.

Once Rose was washed and dry and had swallowed her pills, they returned to the bedroom and Rose lay down without prompting on the bed so that Liv could massage her lower abdomen. Of all Rose's health concerns - her stiffening joints, her brittle bones and her epilepsy - her constipation was the issue that seemed to cause her most distress. Dr Khaw, whose gloomy office in downtown Kingston they visited every three months, favoured suppositories, but Liv saw how they caused more suffering than relief. Instead, Rose fixed her dark eyes on the ceiling while Liv rubbed her hands to take off the chill, then used her fingers to follow the course of her daughter's large intestine, gently probing the impaction. These movements were Liv's ritual, her morning meditation, and for a few moments her disturbed thoughts settled and were still.

She stopped massaging. Someone was thumping up the stairs - Sonny - his old moccasins slapping.

'Liv!' he called from the landing. 'Mary's on Skype.'

꿇

When Mary was five, she had pushed a small clear plastic bead up her twin sister's nose. One swift act led to a trip to the Emergency Room, bright lights and a full-on meltdown, with strangers restraining Rose and some questionable sedation. Yet Liv hadn't scolded Mary, despite the nurse's urging. She had always made a point of encouraging both girls to use their senses and explore their physical surroundings, whether by pressing Rose's hands into the mud after a rainstorm or showing Mary how to leap into the dark brown water at the swim hole. Liv thought of those times now as Mary's face moved forward on the computer screen in the study, her features distorted by the camera, her lips moving out of synch with the fractured audio.

'Mom!' said her voice. 'Can you hear me?'

'I can hear you.' Liv peered closely; forgetting, for a moment, that Mary could see her too. Her daughter's hair was an unfamiliar colour – this time a deep auburn, not Rose's pale copper or the flaming shade they'd both shared when they'd been younger. It was styled in a sort of layered bob that swung forward as Mary leaned towards her screen. 'Why are you calling me now? Aren't you at work?'

'You look worried, Mom. Please try not to worry. Yes, I'm at work. I'll be out on a morning flight on Friday.'

'I'm not worried. I left my glasses upstairs.' Liv frowned again. 'That's two days earlier than you told me before.'

'I talked to Sonny yesterday. God, it's been quite a week, and now this – Mom, listen, it's all right. I've got a plan.'

Once more, Liv had the sense of other selves at her shoulder. The fact that Sonny had already spoken with Mary was another blow she would pick over later.

'I don't need a plan. And before you say another word, I'm not moving back.'

'Don't worry, Mom. We'll sort this. We'll talk—'

'They're not serious,' interrupted Liv, although she knew it wasn't true. 'Sonny and Mishti. It's a blip.'

Mary closed her eyes for half a second too long. 'Look, I think you should listen to what's going on there. It's high time I took care of you and Rose.'

'So come visit more often.'

'I'm coming on Friday.' They stared at each other. Mary's hair still drooped forwards and Liv had to stop herself from touching the screen to tuck it behind her ears. As if she could read her mother's mind, Mary leaned back suddenly, put her fingers to her lips and blew a goodbye kiss. But Liv wasn't ready to be dismissed.

'Do you remember that time you pushed a bead up Rose's nose?'

'What?' Now it was Mary's turn to frown.

'You remember – when you pushed a bead up Rose's nostril and we went to the Emergency Room.'

A pause. 'That was stupid of me.'

'No,' Liv said. 'Not stupid. You were five. You were curious. I've never forgotten it.'

'What are you trying to tell me, Mom?'

'Nothing! Just that I remember you being curious. Not knowing stuff.'

Mary shifted sideways, so that Liv could see the books on the shelf behind her and a box of pastel-coloured tissues. 'And now I'm a know-it-all, right?'

'Don't second-guess things, honey.'

'Don't try to tell me what kind of person I am.'

When Mary ended the call, Liv sat quiet for a minute, staring at the blank screen. She longed to see her daughter, to touch her, to watch her move through Birdeye. Nevertheless, her visits could be fraught. While Liv had almost no insight into her daughter's London life, Mary could be critical of things she noticed in her childhood home. Liv hoped she wasn't going to confront her about Rose's care. Mary had once said that Liv needed her fresh eyes – that it was fortuitous, in a way, that she didn't see her sister for several months at a time, because this meant she was more attuned to subtle changes.

Liv checked her wristwatch. After breakfast she and Rose were due at Dolores'. When they got back, she would make things ready for Mary.

'Gunther!' she called out, and as the old dog wandered in and settled his pale, doleful eyes upon her, she felt his loss, because it was her own.

BRING OUT YOUR DEAD

AFTER MISHTI AND Sonny lost their baby, Liv did everything to enfold them in her love. Sometimes this meant weeping with them. Sometimes this meant watching from afar or leaving them to walk in the woods where they could lose themselves among the rocks and the trees. Sonny held tight to his pain for a while, but Liv saw that Mishti longed to evaporate like the steam on the road after a summer thunderstorm or be carried away down the river and wash up somewhere else that was clean and empty and ignorant of love.

A visitor once insisted that there were five stages of grief. Yet loss, Liv knew, wasn't linear; it wouldn't run its course or close a circle or withdraw to some tidy, demure grave. There would always be a cavity within the scaffolding of acceptance: a hollow, waiting for a wight to slip in.

Liv sat at the kitchen table with a cup of strong black coffee while Rose ate a fruit yoghurt. In front of her, in a bowl, lay the remains of the salad Sonny had prepared for his sister's bag lunch. Orzo and shredded kale with a lemon and caper dressing. Too summery for Liv. Too acidic. She wondered how Mishti could stomach it.

'We could pick up some bagels for Dolores,' she said to Rose. 'With cream cheese.'

'That sounds good! Who's Dolores?'

Startled, Liv twisted round to see Conor leaning against the doorway. She had almost forgotten that he was in the house.

'Some things are private,' she murmured, then checked herself. 'Did you sleep okay? Has Sonny given you a job to do?'

'He's not expecting me to stick around.' Conor didn't sound too perturbed. 'I think he's taken Mishti somewhere. But you and Sonny stayed up late!'

Liv pushed the salad bowl away. Conor's room was above the parlour. Her heart pumped a little harder as she tried to recall the things she and Sonny had said, but she didn't think they'd gone too far back – nothing incriminating anyway.

'Why were you recording us at the Sharing?' she asked as he strolled up to the sink and twisted the faucet to stop it dripping. He was wearing the same clothes as yesterday, and she caught a whiff of his body odour. Perhaps she hadn't told him he could take a shower.

'I wasn't recording you,' said Conor.

'Oh sure. I saw the red light.'

Conor hesitated, then pulled his cell phone from his jeans pocket and put it down on the table.

'Well, I apologise. I'd forgotten to switch it off.' He glanced across at Rose, who was gazing at something on the floor. 'I mean, I hadn't realised. When it was Rose's turn – it was her *not* speaking that interested me. Nothing else.'

'What?' Liv shook her head. He seemed to be making it up as he went along. 'It's all private! Me talking, Rose's silence – what's the difference?'

'I know that now. I thought about it. Look.' He picked up his phone, scrolled briefly, then showed her a sound file labelled *Birdeye #1*. 'I'm deleting it. See?'

'You told Sonny you weren't a reporter.'

'I'm not. Please – I'm only trying to listen. I mean, *really* listen, like you talk about in your book. I screwed up last night – I was nervous – but I'm learning. I want to stay longer, if you'll let me.'

Liv looked at Conor, saw the pink flush across his cheek as she heard the need in his voice. He'd been stupid, that much was obvious, but since when had Birdeye been too precious for stupid?

'If I – if we let you stay – and we haven't decided! – don't you ever record around Rose, or any of us again.'

'I won't.'

'All right then.'

She removed her glasses and rubbed one eye. Perhaps she was making a mistake, but she didn't like the way caution made her feel mean. She would take him to meet Dolores, she decided. She could keep an eye on him there. Besides, Dolores worked her own brand of bullshit, which made her quite the expert at sniffing it out.

Dolores lived in an old holiday cabin on the southern flank of Mount Tremper. She didn't drive anymore and instead relied on rides from neighbours to get her to and from Apollonia when she wanted company at the diner or felt like going to Mass. Liv had tried taking her plates of food that she could heat up in her microwave, but Dolores made it clear that she preferred take-outs from Caspar's – 'chow I can chew on!' – to Sonny's kabocha and courgettes. Today's visit was purely social.

The track up to Dolores' place was steep and rutted, with a precipitous incline on one side where a stream had cut deep into the rock from which sprouted thin trunks of beech and green ash and white oak. As the pickup approached her little property, its clearing strewn with plastic junk and empty mealworm buckets and a couple of rotten Adirondack chairs and some old rope hanging in mournful loops from a wire, Conor whistled from the back seat.

'It's a dump!'

'Hush,' said Liv, pulling up next to the cabin's front door. She flicked on the parking brake. 'It looks different in the summer. The trees make you feel like you're underwater, and the hummingbirds – you should see them swarm at Dolores' feeders.' She glanced at Rose, sitting quietly in the front seat beside her. Mary would say that Rose should not have her routine disrupted, that measured thinking was the way to go. Well, here they were, doing what they always did, visiting Dolores on a Tuesday for a cup of coffee and a game of go-fish or Cat-Opoly, as if nothing had changed, as if, a few hours before, her oldest friends had not tossed everything she believed up in the air, then stood back to watch it fall. She wished she had called Dolores to tell her something had come up, but it was too late now.

She helped Rose out of the pickup, then tapped on the cabin door before pushing it open.

'Enter!' called Dolores, regally, from the low-ceilinged interior. 'Who've you brought?'

'Rose is with me,' said Liv, sniffing the damp. She stepped aside to let Rose move past. Dolores sat in her easy chair near the front window, red cap pulled down snug as usual and wrapped up in her dressing gown with a nylon sleeping bag pulled over her knees. 'And this is Conor. He's staying with us for a few days. Up from the city, like you.'

Conor said hello, but he was staring around the cramped space with its two-bar electric heater and a little table and a kitchenette at the far end with a sink and a mini-refrigerator and a microwave that doubled as a grill.

'Tell me you don't climb up there?' He nodded towards the ladder stairs that led to Dolores' mezzanine bedroom under the eaves. Photographs were dotted up the wall, faded images of relatives from way back mixed with pictures of cats and one or two old-time celebrities.

Dolores snorted. 'At my age? I sleep down here in my chair. I've been thinking, O-Livia, that you could get me on that Air Bee thing on your computer and rent out my bed. Everybody's doing it. Jonathan tells me there's gonna be an item about it at the next Town Board. I could be like you and Rose here, taking in nice young men to keep me warm!'

Rose had brushed past Liv and was pacing the room, hands behind her back. She smiled when Dolores said her name.

'Rose likes that idea,' said Conor. He checked himself. 'I mean, do you like it, Rose?'

Liv moved to the kitchenette, eyes scanning as usual for any tell-tale leaks or mouse droppings. On the tiny counter she noticed a flyer announcing a meeting of the town Beautification Committee: 'Make Apollonia Beautiful Again! #MABA'. Hadn't Susan Kinney been holding a bunch of flyers the day before? Liv pushed this one under the microwave.

'I'll get some coffee going. We've brought bagels. Conor, tell Dolores about the city. Tell her what's new.'

Dolores made a wheezing noise. 'To hell with the city! I want tittle-tattle. What's up at Birdeye?' She raised her eyebrows at Conor. 'Huh?'

'Mary's coming Friday,' said Liv, quickly. She shook her head at Conor, willing him not to mention Sonny and Mishti's announcement. She wasn't ready to have it broadcast around the valley.

'Well, same as always!' Dolores pointed a finger at Rose. 'It's your birthday soon sweetie, I know that, and I hope Sonny's baking you girls a proper cake – vanilla frosting is all I'm sayin'. But I heard something else, Liv – that your dog Pinto died. I was sorry to hear it, not that I'm a dog person. I'm more of a no-dog person if you know what I mean.'

'It was her time,' Liv murmured, hunting for cups.

'But her grave is a secret,' said Conor.

'Oh Jesus,' said Dolores. 'I hope you gave her a good send-off.'

Forty minutes later, once they'd finished their coffee and Rose had decided to sit down and a game of Crazy Eights was reaching its climax with Dolores the likely winner, Liv heard a call outside. It was hollow and tinny, like an old recording. The words were hard to decipher if you hadn't heard them before, but Liv recognised the old joke: 'Bring out your dead! Bring out your dead!'

Conor, who had seemed happy to indulge Dolores' not-so-subtle cheating, glanced out of the window and immediately sat up straight.

'What a ride! It's got a bullhorn on the roof!'

'Well, that's Jonathan,' said Dolores, with satisfaction, and when Liv looked, there he was in the yard, climbing out of his ancient station wagon with his long legs and long face and his cowboy boots, immaculate as ever.

'Is he your son?' asked Conor.

Dolores laughed silently, her tiny shoulders bobbing up and down. 'My son? Sure as hell hope not. He's got a store down on Main Street – "Hope Springs Eternal", of all the dumb names – he sells the crap he picks up from folk round here. Dumps it with me first. I sort out the stuff that oughta get incinerated and O-Livia here sends it up to Tanners Ridge. Sweated labour, I'm telling ya. Every week he comes – every damn week.'

'Dolores!' Liv rolled her eyes, because everyone knew that Jonathan took care of Dolores – he brought her clothes and cushions and beef stew when she wanted it, and he cleaned her windows and refilled the bird feeders and cleared a pathway down the track after each new fall of snow. Not that he went out of his way to tell anyone. His store was 'vintage', for the summer tourists, although it was mainly junk. He ran his signature call through the bullhorn on a loop to drum up business, but while the Town Board had censured him for it and second-homers complained, Liv had never minded. The perambulations he made reminded her of the tradesmen's vans coming up to her childhood house: the fishmonger with his slabs of white cod and the kippers on hooks at the back, the milkman jumping out of his float with an extra bottle on a Friday and, in the summer holidays, the ice cream van that parked on the verge at the end of the drive and blasted 'Teddy Bears' Picnic' in staccato bursts across the village. Her grandfather had been a big fan of ice cream. He said it made any sorrow a little better.

Conor got up and opened the door, but Jonathan wouldn't come inside.

'You got company,' he mouthed to Dolores, scrunching his face up as he peered in through the front window. He raised a bulging refuse sack to show her. 'I'll be back later.'

'Leave the bag!' yelled Dolores. 'Jeez that man's meek. You're meek, y'know, Jonathan!'

Conor looked surprised. 'He can't be meek if he drives around playing shit through that bullhorn.'

Dolores raised her chin. 'Oh, and you'd know?' She nodded to Liv as he blushed a little. 'We'll see about that.'

Once Jonathan had driven off, Dolores directed Conor to empty the sack's contents onto the floor. There were working clothes, mainly, with the bodies' odours still on them. Jeans and plaid shirts in washed out shades, stretch pants, a couple of jackets, a teeny bra. Liv's eye was drawn to a shiny, maroon-coloured thing – a prom dress, perhaps – stiff, crease-free, without straps.

Conor fished out a pair of pink knitted baby bootees and placed them carefully on the windowsill. Then he rummaged some more, and Liv watched, curious about his enthusiasm for the task, the way he held up items, smoothing them out for Dolores to admire or dismiss. The older woman basked in the attention, and even Rose stooped down to hook out a fluffy primrose yellow cardigan, as if she, too, wanted to catch Conor's eye.

'You take that, sweetie,' Dolores told her.

Conor had found a pale blue t-shirt with a woman's portrait printed on it in faded black.

'Can I keep this? It's Karen Carpenter. My dad loved her!' He began to croon, swaying his hips in an exaggerated fashion. '"Calling Occ-upants of Interplanet-ary Craft." Freakin' goddess. She died of anorexia. Her brother was addicted to Quaaludes. You can hear it in that song.'

'Try it on,' said Dolores.

Conor glanced quickly at Liv. Then, with a swift, practised movement he pulled his hoodie over his head so that Liv once again caught the scent of his skin. His arms slipped into the t-shirt; he eased it down across his chest with a lithe wriggle, but not before the three women had seen his narrow white torso, and the hollows of his hips and the dark whorls of hair beneath his arms and below his belly button. Rose made a humming sound as Liv closed her eyes, stirred by the proximity of youth and other things she was trying not to think about. When she peeped again, he had pulled out his phone and was taking a selfie. He stuck his chest out and posed with his hand behind his head.

'It's kinda feminine, dontcha think?' said Dolores. 'Not that I'm complaining, but you know Jonathan oughta have it. Retro sells.'

Conor glanced at the image he'd taken. 'Maybe I'll buy it.'

'Whaat? Are you a Trump or something? I'm kidding you. Go on, you take it.'

⚜

Karin didn't come up to Birdeye that day. She messaged to say she had a migraine. Liv and Rose made a visit to the dental hygienist, and dinner that evening was an uncharacteristically hurried affair: a spinach dhal that Sonny dug out of the freezer in the basement, and some chewy, underdone brown rice. He and Mishti were going out to a talk on zazen meditation in the community room at the Methodist church in Apollonia, and while they'd mentioned it several days before, Liv knew it suited them to be out. They hadn't spoken about the fact that Conor was still there.

'Can I catch a ride?' Conor asked, pushing away his half-eaten meal.

Mishti looked up, surprised. 'To the talk?'

'To the bus drop,' said Sonny. He caught Liv's eye. Liv frowned and checked her wristwatch. The last bus to New York would have passed through already.

'I thought you wanted to stay another night,' she said to Conor.

Conor flashed a quick smile. 'If you'll have me, but I'd like to look around, maybe check out the diner.' He nodded towards the rice he'd left on his plate. 'I mean, no offence.'

He was sitting opposite Liv, still wearing the t-shirt he'd put on at Dolores'. The t-shirt stretched tight across his ribs and what struck her now was the image that stared back at her: Karen Carpenter's almost skeletal face; that pointed chin and those bright, pleading eyes, same as Pinto's. It seemed so intimate, somehow – a kind of homage worn close to the heart, even if Conor didn't mean it in that way. She wanted to do something, she realised – something that had nothing to do with Sonny and Mishti.

Several things, actually.

AREA OF DETAIL #2

ADOPT-A-HIGHWAY
PROGRAM
NEXT 2 MILES

HOPE SPRINGS ETERNAL ANTIQUES

CONOR STOOD ON the verge in front of the sign. A truck rushed past, its cold slipstream pressing into his back.

He'd noticed the signs elsewhere, spattered with dirt, a few of them 'vacant' or missing a mileage number. They were all over the state, dotted along main routes like this one and quieter roads too. Some of them bore the names of businesses or organisations. Some of them said 'In Memoriam' followed by a person's name.

He wondered what you had to do to become an adopter, and how much it cost, and whether Liv or Sonny would know, but he'd seen how they stressed out when he asked a bunch of questions. He'd search online when he got back to Birdeye, although Wi-Fi there was intermittent.

A silver saloon shot past, flashing its lights. People didn't walk along this stretch of highway. When he'd left the diner and crossed the town bridge, he'd had to hop over a guide rail and find his way in the near dark. Not that this bothered him. Sometimes you had to see a thing in front of you to be sure you'd remembered it right.

He checked over his shoulder before stepping off the verge to take a picture.

REFUGEES WELCOME HERE

B ACK IN THE late seventies and eighties, when Liv and Eric were still married, when the community was still growing into itself and no one had worried about how it might end, they all agreed that the winters felt special. Visitors dwindled in the fall, and the ones who remained – the ones who didn't pack up and head to college or hitch south for a warmer vibe – believed themselves to be the real Birdeyers. They understood what it meant to say *I'm here*, and *I'm staying.*

Of course, they did still leave, eventually. But each winter, Liv, Eric, Sonny, Mishti and the twins were joined by six or seven stalwarts, hardy enough or needy enough to see it through. They chopped logs and wore moth-infested sweaters; they hunkered around the smoking stove in the parlour and told their parents this wasn't a phase; they gave notice on their old jobs and registered their cars in the state and they wove placemats to sell at the summer flea markets and dated local people. The Sharings took on the character of a saga; each participant groped inwards and pulled out stories about themselves, adding new details, old backstory, revising and refining as the need arose. For Liv, the winter was a time of reciprocity, where surprises were fewer, but the rewards were richer, more sustaining. Eric used to say you got to really know a person when you sat with them in the kitchen while they made soup, or cut each other's hair, or bickered or read silently, and the snow lay deep and the sky was dark outside, and no one was going anywhere.

'I need to go out for an hour or two by myself,' said Liv the next morning. She sat beside Rose, cutting up her daughter's French toast.

Mishti was preoccupied, opening cupboards, rummaging for something. 'You're not taking Rose with you? I don't think we're expecting Karin today.' She straightened up and checked her wristwatch. 'Oh okay, there's time, I guess, if you're back by ten-thirty. I have to be up in Tanners Ridge by eleven.'

Mishti didn't ask Liv where she was going, which was a relief, but also out of character. Liv almost told her anyway, but then an image came to mind, prompted by that Carpenters song of Conor's from the day before: a grainy spacecraft suspended above the Earth, a service capsule decoupling from the passenger pod, floating away. She fished the keys out of the bowl on the table and waved goodbye to her daughter.

In the pickup, the grey forest kept drawing Liv's gaze as she crossed the town bridge, then took the back road around Mount Tobias. She'd not driven this way in a while, and scanned the trees for signs of greening, but the forecast on the radio threatened sleet or maybe an inch of snow and there was nothing new to note on the half-hour drive, even as she approached Woodstock with its neat white houses in tended plots and its signs for art galleries. Mishti always said that spring came to the east side of Ulster County a few days before it reached Birdeye, borne up the Hudson on a warm breeze from the city.

In actual fact, Woodstock looked a little harried, out of season. A brisk wind blew down Rock City Road as Liv parked up, and the flag opposite the Reformed Church flapped irritably. She thrust her hands into the pockets of her fleece jacket and buried her chin in her scarf as a couple scooted past clutching bagged pastries from the deli. She knew this place, but she didn't know these people. The old hangouts had been reinvented as chic minimalist boutiques and the head shops on Tinker Street sold fridge magnets and Jimi Hendrix wigs. A printed notice in the window of a taco place said 'Refugees welcome here' beneath the 'Closed until spring' sign. Woodstock had been Liv and Eric's town before it became a museum, before they'd followed the Esopus upstream into the high Catskills where the real estate was cheaper, and people still thought hippies were all draft dodgers and bums.

Axel's Tats was tucked behind an organic cosmetics store near the Millstream. The reception area was empty when Liv pushed open the door, but an alarm rang out back with a surprising blast of organ music.

'Hi.' A man in a watermelon-pink t-shirt pushed aside a curtain made of thin strips of leather. He looked mid-forties, Latino, and had black and grey inking over his muscular arms and neck – delicate Victoriana with cobbled streets and gaslights like nothing else Liv had ever seen.

'Axel?' she asked, taking in the old pine desk, the silver laptop, and the photographs in frames around the dark green walls. 'Do you do animals – photo realist? Any discount for seniors?'

The man smiled. He had bright white teeth and his skin creased across the top of his cheekbones. 'All of the above. Is it for you? You had a tattoo before?'

'A long time ago.' Liv pulled up her jacket and showed him the outline above her hip. 'It's faded.'

Axel put his head on one side, appraising. 'Oleander, right?'

'Rosemary,' said Liv, remembering the run-down studio in Tanners Ridge where she'd asked for two stems growing from a single root when the girls started kindergarten. Rose had been placed in the special unit where she'd managed all of three days. 'It blew out straight away.'

'Shame,' said Axel. 'All my tats are custom, but more complicated requests can't be guaranteed. Senior skin takes a little longer – depends what you want.'

'I want two dogs,' said Liv, as a high-pitched buzzing started up in the room beyond the curtain. She glimpsed a client's bare soles hanging over the edge of the consulting bed.

'We do a lot of dogs. Where do you want them?'

71

'On my chest. I've had a double mastectomy, and there's scarring.'

Axel nodded. 'You still got feeling there? Nerves? If they're gone, you'll be fine but sometimes sensitivity is worse.'

'Some. A little. Can you take a look?'

'That won't be necessary until I fix the transfers.'

'Please. I need to know this will work.'

As Axel led Liv through to the other room and pointed to a screen behind which she could undress, doubt flickered briefly in the pit of her stomach. A heavily built man lay on the bed, his face buried in his crossed arms. An elaborate design had been stencilled across his lower back – an eagle with spread wings and a snake in its talons. A youngish woman wearing tight blue gloves worked at one wingtip where the skin looked shiny and inflamed. Neither client nor artist looked up as Liv stepped behind the screen to take off her jacket and shirt.

Axel's hands felt cool and light, even though he pulled on gloves before touching her. He ran his palm over the puckered fold of flesh on her left side, where the flaps hadn't knitted so well. The tips of his fingers rested in the groove behind a pale, shiny ridge as his thumb plucked at the skin to test its elasticity. He didn't speak for a minute and Liv found herself wondering who had last touched her naked body. A nurse, maybe, at a cancer check. She didn't mind the intimacy. On the contrary, Axel's attention was oddly comforting until the other tattoo artist suddenly laughed at something and she remembered that this was a business arrangement.

'Okay,' he said, once she had dressed and re-joined him at the front desk. 'We can do this, but mature skin can mean more bruising. You got pictures?'

Liv pulled a photograph out of her back pocket and set it on the desk. It was a little creased, but she didn't keep many photos for herself and hadn't wanted to ask Sonny. This one showed Pinto and Gunther looking directly at the camera. 'Just their heads and shoulders. I want Gunther, the German Shepherd on my left, and Pinto on my right.'

Axel picked up the photograph and scrutinised it.

'What kind of dog is Pinto?'

'Oh, she's – she was a mutt. Some kind of terrier cross. She had a beautiful brindled coat, like old velvet. A white flash down her nose.' Liv paused. 'She died last week. Gunther is really missing her.'

'Tats make great memorials,' said Axel. 'Leave the picture with me. I'll make up the stencils and you can see how you like them. Friday suit? And I'll need two hundred down payment. Fifty an hour after that.'

He opened his laptop, ready for her details. Liv, however, was staring at the photo.

'Do you reverse the image?' she asked.

'Not unless the client wants it. The process—'

'I want it reversed. I want it so that when I look in the mirror, I see the dogs I know.'

'Most people don't think about it that way. You sure?'

Liv nodded. 'No one else is going to look at them. Only me.'

⚜

'Liv!' yelled Sonny, hurrying down the steps as she eased the pickup into the front yard and cracked her window. 'Where the hell have you been?'

Liv turned off the ignition and rested her forearms across the steering wheel, reminding herself of the pain in her shoulders, waking up the inflammation and her attention to the present. Eric's blue Silverado was parked up by the porch and with a stab of dismay she remembered Mishti. Wednesday was Mishti's day up at Tanners Ridge, where she helped out in the thrift shop at the community centre and volunteered as an addiction counsellor. She needed a ride.

'I'll run her up now,' she said.

Sonny yanked open the door. He was still in his kimono, which he wore as a kind of dressing gown; it hung open, revealing his jeans and his leathery chest with a few grey hairs and the skin loose across his ribs.

'It's eleven-thirty already! I'm taking her. Rose had an upset while you were gone, and we need to discuss how we're going to manage our transition, but right now I'd be grateful if you went inside and told Conor he can't stay another day – he's been here two nights already.'

'I suppose you called Eric?' Liv retaliated, deciding there and then that he didn't need to know about the two hundred dollars she had just withdrawn from Rose's account. 'Like you called Mary?'

'I didn't know where you were! Mishti needed a ride.'

Liv got out and tossed Sonny the keys. The front door of the house was open; she could see Gunther's head through the fly screen, the mesh making him seem like a ghost.

'I'm getting somewhere with Conor,' she told him. 'Anyway, seeing as you've chosen to leave, I think these kinds of decisions are up to me from now on, and I'm going to need the extra pair of hands. He could help me with the veggie garden. You said it yourself – the fence has a hole in it, and we've got compost to dig in.' It seemed so reasonable, as she said it, but Sonny was shaking his head.

'We're going up to Buffalo this summer, Liv. Don't get stuck in denial. You can't carry on like before, even with Eric and Karin coming by. Hey, don't scowl at me like that. I know we should have talked sooner.' He reached out to put a hand on her arm, and in that moment, Liv felt like pushing her face up to his and shouting that he was not the man she thought he was.

'You're mad at me,' he added, stepping back a little. 'I get it. But Mishti and I needed to decide this by ourselves. We're tired. All three of us! We need to cut loose, keep on growing. Maybe you don't feel that yet, but I know you will.'

'And Rose?'

Finally, Sonny had the grace to look uncomfortable. 'Talk to Mary, Liv. Talk to Eric. We're not leaving before the girls' birthdays, and we don't stop being a family when we no longer live here.'

A memory came to Liv then – green leaves at the open window, she and Mishti weak with laughter as Sonny slid across the floor-boards in his socks, trying to moonwalk. Liv and Sonny had peered into each other's hearts, fought often and cherished each other all the more for the difficulties they had been through, but last night Sonny had dragged this from under her and dumped it like the mattresses down by the road. Now she felt that with Sonny she might say anything, do anything and it wouldn't make a difference.

'Please, Liv.' Sonny ran his hand across the top of his head. 'At least tell that boy to go. Don't you think it's weird that he's still here? Eric's inside with him now.'

'Maybe he's got nowhere else to go,' Liv said, pointedly, just as the fly screen banged open. She looked up and saw Mishti dragging out two big laundry bags for the community centre, as if she was clearing out her stuff already. The thought made Liv shut her eyes for a second, but then she walked towards the house, up the steps, and helped Mishti with her burdens because this was the way they had always been with each other and neither woman knew yet how to do it differently.

The first time Liv saw Eric she was four and half months' pregnant and eating a slice of pizza in a hostel room in Albany. Her room-mate was a willowy Argentinian girl, another misfit who would soon depart on the rainbow trail to Oregon. It was December, the chain-link fence outside the window glistened with ice and Eric was in the hallway searching for the room with the frozen pipe.

'Not us,' Liv said. 'Try next door.'

'Hey!' Eric stopped on his long legs and leaned backwards in a comical, exaggerated fashion to look into the room. 'Is that a British accent?' Liv saw him take in her thickening waistline, the pizza, the bras drying on the heater. 'I heard you girls know how to party.'

Later that night, when Eric put his face against the curve of her belly, she teased his hair between her fingers and told him she thought there might be two babies.

'Cool,' he said, after a few seconds' silence. 'Instant family.'

There was attraction, without a doubt, but Liv and Eric also saw a fix for their respective problems, and they seized it. Vietnam was a shitstorm, and fatherly responsibilities would make it easier for Eric to escape the draft, given that he didn't care to hop to Canada, or dress in women's underwear. Liv's visa was about to expire, but she had already made up her mind to return to New York somehow. They married one frosty morning in downtown Kingston, to the soundtrack of an anti-war march outside City Hall. She wore pale blue dungarees and a long Afghan coat she'd borrowed but couldn't button across her middle, and Eric presented her with a bunch of winter jasmine that he'd hopped over someone's fence to pick. A couple of months later she flew alone to London, and the girls were born at St George's, care of the NHS. Doctors made grim predictions in the days that followed. There was talk of a cord around the neck, and brain damage, and when Liv finally telephoned Eric, her hands shook so much she could barely dial the number.

'They don't know what Rose will be like,' she whispered. 'They're not giving her much of a chance, but I'm bringing the babies over and I want you to know that as soon as we get settled you can divorce me.'

'Divorce you? We just got hitched!' said Eric, astonished, and for a minute or two afterwards Liv had rested the receiver against her cheek and pictured his smiling face while her tears splashed on the linoleum.

That first year had been gruelling: two rooms plus a shared bathroom on the turkey farm, the hospital visits, the early seizures, the feeding problems and the way Rose never slept for more than one or two hours at a stretch. Fortunately, Eric turned out to be a natural parent – practical, calm and kind. He made up bottles, he drove around the mountains with the babies tucked up in an apple crate on the back seat, and in all ways possible he cared for Rose and Mary as if he'd made them himself. Two decades later, when he left Liv, he didn't go far but raised a new family down in Tukesville. He still looked out for Birdeye, for the girls' sake, and, Liv believed, for her.

'You've heard, then,' she said as she walked into the house and found Eric in the kitchen with Rose.

Eric's thick grey hair stuck out beneath his fleece-lined fishing cap. As he stepped across to kiss Liv on the cheek, she sniffed engine oil on his faded plaid shirt.

Rose wandered out to the passageway, as if three in one room were too many.

'Do you think they'll change their minds?' Eric asked. He leaned back against the sink, a hand on each side of the counter, making a square with his arms and shoulders.

'Do *you*?' Liv moved up beside him. 'We built Birdeye, the four of us and the girls. I know you needed to leave – Mary too – but it's different with Sonny and Mishti. They made a promise.'

'What did they promise?'

His tone was gentle, but Liv felt put on the spot.

'They're my family! We did all of this together! Why *now*?'

'You'll work it out.' Eric put his arm around Liv. 'Mary's coming soon, and I'm nearby. No one is abandoning you and Rose.'

Liv pressed her forehead into Eric's shoulder. She could feel the warm weight of his hand above her hip, and she almost laughed at the disorientation, the sudden giddiness she felt. When a new thought appeared, she grabbed hold before it had fully formed.

'Why don't you move back in?'

'What?'

'I mean – you and Dawn and the kids.' She raised her head and looked up at him. 'We'll have space now. You'd be rent free. Harrison has his licence and Cori will too, and it's only a little further for Dawn to get into Kingston.'

'Liv,' murmured Eric, carefully lifting his hand away. 'You're not thinking straight.'

'Yes, I am!' She could see it all so clearly, the simplicity and the rightness of it. 'It makes perfect sense – you'll save money, you'll see Rose every day, I can move up to the attic so you have the main bedrooms to yourselves – this was always your house too – it still is . . .'

Eric stood up straight, a puzzled, sad look on his face. 'No,' he said. 'You know Dawn couldn't do that.'

They stared at each other, and in the silence, Liv longed for him to put his arm back around her. They had been lovers, once. They had learned everything together; they had always, she imagined, understood each other's desires.

'Eric,' she murmured, as he turned to glance out of the window, but in that same moment, she realised there was something else – an absence of sound around them, a vacancy in the house, above and behind. She raised her head and focused on the ceiling. No footsteps. No shuffling. Eric took a breath, about to speak, as a sudden, ferocious panic seized her. She turned and ran along the passageway, yanking open the front door and straining to see down the track beyond Eric's Silverado.

'It's okay!' shouted Eric. 'She's in the yard with Conor!'

Liv hurried back to the kitchen and saw for herself. There they were, through the window, in the gloomy north-west corner of the yard, Rose in her padded coat and Conor in his blue rain jacket. Conor was holding her hand, leading her beneath the trees. A memory swept over Liv like a cold, dark fog: Wren, out there with Rose.

'Conor!' She stepped through the yard door and strode across the dirt. 'Stop. What are you doing?'

Conor looked around. Rose did too. He didn't let go of her hand.

'We're just going for a stroll. I thought Rose wanted to.'

'No,' said Liv, out of breath. She caught up and studied Rose's face, checking for signs of distress. 'Rose doesn't like to walk in the trees. She stays in the yard or goes down the road with me or Mishti or someone.'

'Oh.' Conor glanced at Rose as she twisted her head towards the river. He released her hand.

'She gets frightened in the woods. She's fine in the yard, but up the trail – absolutely no.'

'No damage done,' said Eric, as he caught up with them.

'Well, I apologise.' Conor was looking at Liv strangely. 'But it's not my fault if you don't tell me stuff. It's like you guys want me to screw up! I mean, I was hoping you'd let me stay for a week or so. If you ask me to stay, I'll work hard, I'll learn. You're going to want extra help.'

'Then I suppose you heard what I said to Sonny earlier,' Liv said. She had to admit that Rose hadn't entered the woods willingly for years and now here she was, calmly shuffling through the leaf litter and tolerating the drips from the cedars above their heads. 'There are things you don't know – things that hurt us. Let's take it one day at a time. If you're not sure about anything, come and find me.'

Conor nodded earnestly. 'You're the boss.'

HUMAN BE-IN

BIRDEYE WAS WAITING for Mary. Both Eric and Sonny had said as much, and Liv felt it too – a phoney kind of peace as each went about their tasks, treading carefully, being mindful and considerate in their movements and their habits in a way that felt coolly unfamiliar. No one suggested another Sharing, and even the temperature refused to lift itself out of its wintry depression. On Thursday Mishti went in early to school, keeping busy where she felt she was needed. Sonny worked outside, raking debris from the yard and fixing fly screens, only coming indoors to prepare food with Rose for company, or huddle over the computer in the study, the door half closed, making plans for a new life. Conor, meanwhile, threw himself into any task he was given. Liv, trying to thread a needle at her bedroom window, gave up and watched him down in the polytunnel. He was checking the ground ties, and while she could barely see him through the cloudy plastic, every so often his head or his spine would press against it like a pupa in its cocoon. She had told him he could stay the week, which infuriated Sonny, who was barely speaking to her. It meant that Conor would meet Mary, but Liv tried not to second guess what they'd make of each other.

Rose wandered in and began to shuffle the three and half steps between the chest of drawers and Liv's bed. Back and forth, back and forth. It was nearly time for their walk. Liv knew that the atmosphere in the house was affecting her.

'Look what I've got,' she said, jabbing the needle into a pincushion so that she could pick up the pair of smooth river pebbles she kept on her nightstand. She weighed one in each palm, then sat down on the bed and placed them both on the counterpane. 'You remember, don't you? Your hand-stones.'

Rose came to a stop. She had pushed both arms behind her back, one hand clasping the other arm at the elbow. Without letting go, she bent down low over the bed until her face almost touched the nearer stone. Then, just as quickly, she straightened herself up. Liv reached out and gently unlocked her daughter's arms. She picked up the larger stone and placed it in Rose's palm.

'This one's Mary's,' she murmured. When the girls were about seven Mary had picked it out of the creek one day and set it on a rock to dry. After a short while, she had brought it over to Liv, who was helping Rose dabble her feet in the water, and said, 'Feel how warm this is!' Liv had taken it from her and thought how similar it was to her daughter's own hand – it had its own weight, its own smoothness. When she told Mary this, the child had fetched another and dried that one too and explained that Liv would now be able to hold each of their hands, even if they weren't there.

'I'll always be able to hold your real hand though,' reasoned Liv.

'Yes,' Mary had said, solemnly. 'But we don't know about Rose, do we.'

Liv pushed back her glasses and glanced out of the window again. She had intended to move Conor to the attic so that Mary could have her usual room at the front of the house, but now she had a better idea. Mary could have Liv's room, and Liv would take the attic instead, which meant Conor wouldn't have to switch. She imagined Mary putting her glass of water on the nightstand, hanging her dressing gown on the nail behind the door, sitting on Liv's bed and feeling a renewed bond as she saw how those two hand-stones were the last things her mother looked at before she fell asleep each night.

Too late, Liv turned around and saw that Rose had pulled herself in tight. Then she swung her arm and let go so that the stone flew out and smashed through the windowpane.

'Whoaa!' Conor's disembodied voice floated up from the polytunnel.

Liv stared at a long, lethal finger of glass that now dangled from the ancient putty.

'Oh Rose,' she said, suddenly frightened. 'Don't do that when Mary is here.'

※

Liv braced herself for some choice words from Sonny, but Sonny stayed tight-lipped as he removed the shattered pane and fitted some ply as a temporary replacement. He didn't come into Rose's room very often, and he took his time, gazing down at the yard through the window before pulling on his thick gloves, placing the shards on several sheets of newspaper he'd laid out, then wrapping them over and over. When he'd finished, Liv took the package out to the glass recycling crate in the donkey barn, then asked Conor to help her find the hand-stone.

'Ahead of you there,' he said, pulling it out of his jeans pocket. 'I guess it's special, right? She nearly got me.'

They were standing by the front porch steps. Liv still felt a little shaky, and she put her hand out to grasp the handrail. 'It wasn't you – she wasn't aiming at you.'

'I'm joking.' Conor leaned sideways to look past her shoulder. 'I think you've got another visitor. I'll get back to work.'

Another visitor. Liv turned around, but it was only Karin walking up the track with Susan Kinney. Liv was relieved to see Karin with her wide, calm face and her green hair and her unflustered ways. She was less sure about Susan Kinney.

'Hello,' said Susan, stiffly. She took her hand out of her pocket and pushed her pale hair behind her ear. Liv knew why Susan didn't like her. It wasn't so much that Birdeye welcomed every stranger who wandered up along Dutchman's, or that they didn't fly the Stars and Stripes on the fourth of July. It was because once, about seven years ago, Susan had come across Liv relieving herself in the woods beside the trail with her underwear round her ankles. Susan's eldest boy had been with her and while Liv had smiled and said oops, she had yelled at her boy not to look.

'Hi,' Liv said. 'Karin, how are you feeling now?'

'Better – much better thanks.' Karin glanced at Susan. 'I'll go say hi to Rose,' she added, diplomatically.

Liv watched Karin climb the porch steps and disappear indoors.

'How are you, Susan?' she asked. 'How can I help?'

'I heard you're thinking of moving out.' Susan's voice was polite. 'I wondered if that was the reason for all that garbage piled up on the road.'

Liv frowned. 'A couple of mattresses? We're not moving. Who told you that?'

'Three . . .' Susan glanced over at Eric's giant squatting Artemis. 'Three mattresses. Someone heard from a young man you've got staying.'

'Well, that person got it wrong,' said Liv, dismayed that Conor should be talking about their recent problems in town. 'We're not moving.'

'All right then, but that mess is outside your property's boundary.'

'Who says? I'm guessing you are speaking for the Beautification Committee. I've seen your flyers, although you didn't bring one up here.' Liv felt her anger rising.

'We're taking it to the Town Board,' said Susan. 'I thought you should know. I'm trying to be neighbourly . . .'

'We live at a dead end. There's no one else. Who cares?'

'We do.' Susan's face had hardened, but as she turned to leave, she looked down at her feet. 'Your dog poops in the woods. It's just dirty, okay?' she murmured, in a way that said she didn't want a fight, and that she had screwed up some courage inside of herself to make the trip up from the road.

※

Mishti didn't want a fight, either, but to Liv, her silence was beginning to seem like cowardice. That afternoon, after Sonny had fetched her from another shift at the community centre, Mishti took the pine cleaner into the bathroom, saying she'd spruce it up for Mary, and stayed in there for nearly an hour with the door locked. Liv tried to imagine what she'd say if brother and sister changed their minds about leaving. *All is forgiven*, or *Nothing is forgiven*. Her own responses, as well as Mishti's, were a mystery to her.

It came as a surprise, then, when Mishti seized the initiative. Liv had been shaking out Gunther's bed in the yard, beating it with a stick so that the dust and dog hair flew up into the light from the kitchen window. When she tried to step back inside, something was blocking the door. She gave it a shove with her elbow, cursing as pain shot through her shoulder.

'I'm here!' protested Mishti from the other side. Liv leaned in, then stuck her head through the gap and spied two baggy-trousered legs in the space between the yard door and the kitchen. Mishti was sitting on the floor with her knees pulled up to her chin, surrounded by the abandoned sneakers, the flip flops, the desert boots and the cork-soled slides the house had accumulated over the years.

'Did you fall?'

'No—'

'What then?' Liv kept her voice neutral and used her hip this time, pushing until Mishti shifted. Mishti didn't look up as Liv squeezed in, but it was obvious from the damp wadge of bathroom tissue in her hand that she'd been crying.

'It's kind of overwhelming,' said Mishti, her voice shaky. 'You don't want to talk to me, but I'm still here, you know, and I was thinking, I've been sweeping this floor for four decades. I know every knot in the wood, every scratch and stain.' She pointed her toe towards a small grey lump stuck to the wooden baseboard. 'That's a ball of Patrice's gum – the piece we said we wouldn't touch. It's part of the house now.'

Liv, standing over her, had to admire the deflection. She peered down at the gum. Patrice had lived at Birdeye for two or three years in the late nineties. He'd been a taxi driver until his license got revoked. There were many ways he'd not been smart in his life, but he was humble, and unhurried in his outlook, and while a couple of the young ones thought him irritating, they made space for him. He'd had the teenager's habit of leaving pellets of chewing gum around the house, stuck to saucers or above lintels or the underside of the bathroom sink, as if leaving a trail for himself – something to find again when he needed it. Rose had been fond of him, and he'd had a thing for Mishti, which made it all the more shocking when he picked up his coat one day, walked out and didn't come back. Mishti was particularly upset, so the gum remained with the other scuffs and stains. Seams of feeling, Liv knew, ran through Birdeye's walls: Sonny's moods, his frustrations and his insecurities; the monthly wrinkle in Karin's otherwise even temper; Rose's rituals and outbursts, and Mishti's tears, shed every other day over the climate catastrophe or child migrants or a dead robin on the porch because her heart was warm and full but also, perhaps, because such tenderness padded the pin of steel within her.

Mishti leaned her head against Liv's leg, as if her pain wasn't self-inflicted, as if she hadn't forfeited the right to get nostalgic about indelible marks. Liv stared down at her, in a kind of wonder. She felt so foolish, suddenly, and might have pushed her away, but the cast-off shoes were all around so instead she nudged a child-sized moccasin with her toe.

'We really ought to bag these up,' she said, 'before Mary tells us someone's going to break their neck.'

FORMER SITE OF OLIVE

L IV WOKE EARLY that Friday, roused by a streak of electric blue that seared the darkness behind her eyes and made her fling her arm out with a jolt that left her breathless. She lay still, waiting for her heart to steady, feeling the rucked sheet beneath her calves and listening to the rain tapping on the window. At least it hadn't snowed for Mary, who'd be mid-Atlantic by now, eating airline food or catching up on emails, or asleep with a mask over her eyes. Liv longed to see her, but the longing sat heavily on her chest, and it was a few minutes before she felt like moving, even though she had a million things to do. Once Sonny was back from dropping off Mishti, she'd tell him she was going to take Rose to visit Eric over in Tukesville. This wasn't a lie, exactly. Nor was it the whole truth. Sometimes a lie-by-omission was necessary for harmony in communal living. You drew your silence down like a blind at a window, you did your thing, and when you raised it again you often found that your heart was more attentive.

Something like that, anyway.

By the time Liv made it to Woodstock, her mood had changed. She parked on the street, impatient now, shaking the raindrops from her hair as she entered Axel's shop. The bell played its organ cascade, and when Axel appeared through the curtain of leather ribbons, she was relieved to see that the room beyond was empty.

'Ready?' Axel brought out two sheets of paper from under the counter. 'I drew these.' He laid the sheets flat and Liv frowned at the drawings of two dogs, each a little larger than her handspan. They were good drawings, she could see that. 'If you're happy, I'll make the transfers. Try looking in the mirror. You'll see them how you wanted.'

Liv took the sheets and held them up to the mirror near the door, placing them over the two breast pockets of her shirt. 'Yes,' she said, not certain, now, what she'd been expecting, and wishing it was done already. 'I understand. That's what I want.'

'Which one first?' he asked. 'Don't forget you'll need three weeks to heal before I start on the other side.'

Liv had thought about this. She'd pretty much decided she didn't want an inking of Gunther while he was still alive, but she wouldn't mention it until she was certain. 'This one.' She raised Pinto's drawing and felt the need to say something more. 'I loved her, and my other dog loved her, and my daughter. She wasn't a cuddly kind of dog, but she was real, and if she didn't like a person, she'd show it. My neighbour said she was aggressive, but it wasn't that. All she needed was a little respect.'

Axel nodded sympathetically. 'Which side?'

'Oh – the right.'

'Okay, let's do it.'

Liv sat on a little chair in the back room with a paper cup of matcha tea while Axel made the first transfer. The room was lit thoughtfully, with lamps as well as the bright lights over the workstation and the black tattooing couch. A large mirror reflected Axel's face and upper body as he cut around the drawing, then fed thermographic transfer paper into a small machine. She studied the tattoos on his arms and neck, and noticed the way he worked quickly, efficiently, putting on a pair of clear-framed glasses and frowning in concentration. She appreciated having something to admire.

Once the transfer was ready, she stood up and took off her shirt and vest while he pulled on some blue gloves, then rubbed a stick of clear stuff all over the right side of her chest. It felt cold, as he'd told her it would, and she saw the way he frowned as he positioned the transfer. He was firm and unafraid. She liked that.

When Liv checked the result in the mirror, she was relieved to see Pinto as she remembered her, her good ear tucked in close to her armpit. It wasn't until she looked down at herself that she had a shock. Now Pinto's snagged ear was on the left side of her head, which wasn't the real Pinto at all.

Liv covered the marks with her hand. Her fingers ached to touch something alive. 'I've got this wrong,' she said. 'I don't want her that way round.'

'You overthought it,' said Axel, stooping down to rummage beneath the counter. 'It's okay. We can fix this.'

⚙

After twenty minutes of inking, the noise began to get to Liv. The stop-start whirring reminded her of the chain saws and leaf blowers that whined in the valleys around Apollonia, and she was beginning to perspire. She could feel each hot jab of the needle, and in the lower area, at the base of her ribcage, her sensitivity was even greater.

'I like that airship on your arm,' she said, seeking distraction. 'Amazing detail. Is that Big Ben below? Have you been to London?'

Axel shifted position above her, wiped a spot and started to work on a new section. 'I'm planning on going,' he said. 'I love all that stuff. Jules Verne, Sherlock Holmes. I've got a three-sixty panorama of Baker Street on my leg.'

'I was born in England,' said Liv, surprising herself.

'No shit! I thought you had an accent. What part?'

So Liv told him about Winchester with its chalk downs, its cathedral and its quaint old buildings with their flint walls and rose gardens. She described the countryside of her long-buried A-level texts with its villages and churchyards, and she made it sound like a beautiful place that anyone with a drop of romance in them would love to visit. Axel, she thought, would like to hear about that.

'Why'd you leave?' he asked as he twisted round for more ink.

Liv stared at the shadowy face of a man in a bowler hat near Axel's elbow. Conor had asked the same question, and she didn't feel like explaining that sometimes you had to run as soon as you were able. Her parents had driven off without her and she never saw them again. She couldn't recall their actual departure; her final memory of them was when she'd peeped into her parents' bedroom the night before and watched her mother, laughing, rub Vaseline into her father's heels. Weeks later, when they failed to return from their adventures, her grandparents became her guardians, until her grandmother died of bowel cancer. A few days after the funeral, her grandfather stepped out for some fresh air. It was Liv who found his body beneath the willow by the mill stream, his polished shoes kicked off, his stockinged feet dangling among the cow parsley and the nettles that stung her legs as she struggled to lift him. She was fifteen: packed off to boarding school until she was old enough to catch a plane to the first country that seemed to want her.

The air was too thick, suddenly, too cloying with the smell of the disinfectant and the sound of the machine and the bright light above her. She couldn't breathe.

'Hey, you need to take a break!' Axel laid down the needle and helped her sit up. 'I mean, I can tell you've got plenty of nerves in that section. You're a strong lady – you survived the Big C!'

Liv was careful not to look down. She didn't want to catch sight of her chest in its unfinished state, so she focused instead on a wooden carving that hung on the wall above the mirror – a mask of some sort in pale, unpainted wood, with exaggerated flaps of skin that reminded her a little of Dolores.

'I'm okay,' she said, lying back again. 'I need this done. Give me a minute.'

⚜

Liv eased herself back into the pickup and headed south out of

Woodstock where she joined the county road. The rain had stopped and the sky was brightening so that the nickel-grey reservoir to her left glinted between the trees. She was thankful for the drive, for the half-hour it gave her to readjust to present realities. Mary's plane would have touched down by now. She'd probably be queueing in Arrivals. Another hour at the airport, picking up a car, then two hours up the Thruway, maybe more on a Friday. Liv felt the flutter of nerves through her belly. Perhaps, if the weather turned a little warmer, they'd pack a picnic and come down here for the girls' birthdays the following week. The reservoir had always been one of Mary's favourite places, especially as a teenager when her tastes began to shift towards environments that were tidy, suburban, man-made – the start of her revolt against Birdeye's earthiness. The dam had been built more than a hundred years before, and a dozen or so villages were lost or re-located when the Esopus flooded the valley. Its waters served New York City, and Mary would get furious if anyone peed or spat in it. 'Someone has to drink that!' she'd yell as her friends messed about on one of its little beaches.

On impulse, Liv indicated left and took the road that bisected the reservoir via a long strip of bridge. This way she could loop around, then approach Tukesville from the opposite shore. She'd been gone for several hours already, so an extra fifteen minutes hardly seemed to matter. A couple of vehicles passed her in a sudden rush as the road left the trees and the sky stretched out above her, but soon she was advancing across the bridge quite alone, with the calm water on either side and the gentle humps of the mountains edging the horizon like a trim of grey ric rac. When she reached the middle, she took her foot off the gas, the feeling coming over her of being safe somehow, or at least unreachable, when surrounded by water. She took several deep breaths, then continued on, into the trees on the far side, past the cement slab of the dam itself and then round to where the reservoir disappeared and there was nothing but bends in the road and the silent trunks of cedars and pines.

As Liv passed a sign announcing 'Former Site of Olive', something flashed on the asphalt ahead. She heard a dull thump as the Sierra's passenger wing made contact. Her head jolted back then forward as she slammed on the brakes. *Shit.* She pulled over and checked in her rear-view mirror, but she knew what it was already. Her heart thumping hard, she opened her door and slid out onto the verge.

The deer, a female whitetail, lay on its side by the guide rail. She stepped towards it, then stopped, stricken. It was still breathing, shallow and fast; its eyes were open and rolling, its thick tongue lolling. There was blood, too, near its hind leg. It wasn't going to survive, and the kindest thing would be to smother it, but Liv couldn't do it – she couldn't. She glanced at its belly, guessing it was probably pregnant, and sickness rose in her throat when its body began to shudder. Short spasms seemed to ripple across the tight barrel of skin. Just like Pinto. *Die quickly* was her only thought as she ran back to the pickup. She spun her wheels off the verge in her haste to reach Tukesville, aghast at her inability to put a helpless creature out of its misery.

Eric's home was in a clearing along a track in the woods. As she pulled up she could see his silvery head in the trailer's big end window. Dawn would be at work and the kids were in high school, and he was probably talking to Rose about the cartoon on the TV in the background, or about what he was building in his workshop, showing her pictures of Cori and Harrison on his phone, and maybe making her a snack. He was good at filling time like that. He was a good dad.

She knocked and pushed open the door, calming herself as she saw Rose who stood in the little corridor that led to the bedrooms.

'Eric,' she said. 'I've hit a deer. I didn't kill it.'

'Oh, Liv.' Eric grabbed his jacket and stepped outside with her. 'Are you okay? Is the pickup damaged?' Then, once he'd ascertained what she wanted him to do, he fetched his welding gloves and a ball-peen hammer before climbing into the Silverado. As he cranked the ignition, she knocked on his window.

'Will you call up for a tag?' she asked. Roadkill was legal gain if he called out a State Trooper, and Eric was a carnivore these days – he'd switched back when he moved in with Dawn. Sonny called them carcass-eaters, although Eric was never a senseless killer.

'I'll see how mashed it is. Tagging takes too long, and I'd need to hang it quick. No one saw you, right?'

Liv swallowed down the sour taste in her mouth. 'Maybe you could bring over a couple of pounds for Gunther. He's got a gut problem. Some minced venison might settle it.'

'Sure,' said Eric, with his sad smile.

Liv nodded. 'Just – you know, keep it to yourself.'

THIS IS NOT A BRIDGE

MARY FOUND THE correct queue in Immigration, then switched on her phone. The familiar image of her sister Rose stared from the screensaver for a moment before messages flashed up: missed calls and pings from her assistant, a couple of updates from her solicitor, an invitation to a client's box at the opera. She tapped on a message from GlennNevis66 via the dating site she'd signed up with, then went back and scrutinised his picture. The sailing-club type, she thought. Salty stubble and sunglasses on a brightly coloured string, someone with a work-life balance. He wanted to meet. No chance of that, not for the next fortnight. She frowned as relief rippled through her, wondering yet again what it was she thought she needed.

In the line to her left, a toddler, hanging over its mother's shoulder, started to bawl. Mary was no good with children. For a while she'd wondered if she might like one, but it never happened, which was just as well as they made her feel inadequate, with their limpid gazes and uncensored remarks. She wanted to use the bathroom and she wanted to sit down, but there were too many people in front of her and most of them were elderly or pregnant or carried infants or silently and stoically broadcast some other reason why they were more deserving than she. At least she didn't have to queue for two or three hours like the non-US arrivals. There were some advantages to dual citizenship.

She distracted herself by returning to her phone to scroll through restaurants in the Hudson Valley. Her mother would resist the notion of a day out, good food, a little sightseeing, but it meant they could talk in private, away from the others. Anyway, she wanted to spoil her. Liv was facing a crisis, and the thought helped Mary forgive her harsh words on their Skype call the other night. Her mother needed her full attention.

As she raised her head to take in the oily light that shone in through the big windows, as she absorbed the blend of anticipation, frustration and resignation that percolated all around her, she let go a little of her London life and inched towards the small fold in the Catskills that her mother still insisted was Mary's home.

⁂

At five o'clock, when Sonny shouted that Mary had arrived, Liv felt momentarily dizzy. The long hours of waiting, the butterflies in her stomach and the unfamiliar dressing on her chest meant she hadn't eaten all day. She put her hand on the porch rail as her first-born daughter climbed out of the SUV she'd rented and reached in for her shoulder purse and her coat while remarking on the unseasonable cold.

'Mom,' said Mary, turning. 'You look tired.'

Mary looked the same to Liv: those familiar dark eyes, the gap between the teeth, dabs of make-up that would never disguise the frown lines between her brows.

'Come here,' she murmured, and as they embraced Liv felt Mary's bones and her car warmth. She felt her smooth hair against her cheek and smelled the flowery perfume that Mary must have reapplied after her flight, and she held her for as long as she could, before words were spoken, before positions were assumed.

Rose was there too, bobbing on the porch. Her arms remained stiffly at her sides when Mary hurried up the steps and hugged her, but she smiled and made a quick noise, high and bright.

'I love you too,' said Mary, eyes shining with emotion, and Liv would have given anything to preserve that moment – her two daughters, both where they belonged, two parts of one whole.

The kitchen after nightfall produced a particular kind of glow – a warmth that eluded it in daylight. Perhaps it was the lamplight against the orange walls that reflected in the window, or the sense of being battened and caulked against the darkness outside. Mishti had placed green and purple candles across the table and away from Rose, who now paced quietly between the sink and the door to the passageway, her hands behind her back, her stooped profile casting fractured shadows across the storage jars on the shelves. The others remained seated: Liv, Sonny, Mishti, along with Mary and Conor, and Eric, who'd driven over. Sonny had laboured all day over the food, creating an intercontinental menu of empanadillas filled with the last of the kabocha squash, an entrée of rice noodles with bean sprouts and cashews in a dark soy sauce, and pretty dishes of cardamom-scented payesh for dessert. The talk was of Mary's jet lag, the latest presidential bullshit, a new sculpture Eric was working on and how they might celebrate the twins' upcoming birthday. Liv watched Mary watching Rose, each drinking in the other in the way that only a prolonged period of proximity can satisfy. No one spoke of Sonny and Mishti's decision. Certainly, Liv had no desire to spoil this first evening. Conor, she noted, was being particularly attentive, passing round the water jug and standing up to fetch an extra spoon. He'd been working remarkably hard over the past couple of days, digging compost into the veggie garden and replacing rotten posts along the fence. Sonny must have noticed.

'One, two, three, lots!' murmured Liv, when Mary served her some noodles.

Mary shook her head, smiling. 'I can't believe you still say that, Mom.'

'Is that like a family thing?' asked Conor.

'It's because I couldn't count. When I was little.'

'The house was always full,' Liv said. 'Mary used to sit right where you are now, on the highchair Eric made, sprinkling us with water from her beaker like a bishop and shouting "One, two, three, lots!" at dinner.'

'The girls' chairs!' Mishti put her hand to her mouth. 'Mary's had a yellow rabbit I stencilled on the seat, and Rose's rabbit was lavender. The girls got too big for them, but at mealtimes you still used to say "go sit on your bunnies!"'

'Roman loved that,' said Sonny. 'Our first visitor. He was always happy around the girls. Rose and Mary, we salute you. You helped an elderly man forget what he couldn't remember.'

'And then we had that wedding for his son!' Eric waved his chopsticks. 'I'd forgotten. You were quite something, Liv, officiating.'

Conor looked puzzled, so Mishti put him straight. 'It wasn't legal, nothing like that. But we had a wedding party for Roman's son Paul and his girlfriend Betsy because Roman liked weddings. Everyone got dressed up, and oh my gosh the liquor, but it was so beautiful, and Liv wore Eric's high school tux and read out a special blessing.'

'I meant every word,' Liv said, thinking of the love.

Conor reached for the water jug. 'You didn't put that in *The Attentive Heart*.'

'No.' Mary's eyebrows were raised. 'There's quite a few things she left out.'

'Right,' said Conor, and Liv realised he was watching her. He leaned forward and set the water jug back down on the table. 'You can't put everything that happens in a book like that, but you remember it, so that's cool. In point of fact, I was wondering – does anyone know what this means?' He had his cell phone in his hand. The screen was lit up with a photograph of something.

'How funny!' exclaimed Mishti, peering. 'Must have been there twenty years!'

'What?' asked Liv, as they all leaned in, and when Conor held out his phone, she saw an image of a tree trunk with a postcard pinned to it. The postcard was encased in a clear plastic bag, but she could still make out the brown and black picture of a tobacco pipe and she knew what the words said without reading them. She passed it every time she hiked the Garfield Mountain trail. Conor must have wandered up there, too, though she couldn't think when he'd had the time.

'"Ceci n'est pas une pipe",' said Mary. 'Except someone has crossed out "une pipe" and written "un pont".'

Conor frowned. 'What does that mean?'

'It means "This is not a bridge",' explained Mary. 'The original meant "This is not a pipe" – it's a seminal artwork by Magritte called *The Treachery of Images*. The image of the pipe doesn't actually—'

'It's a joke,' interrupted Liv. 'About the slippery log we used as a bridge to cross the stream where you saw the sign. We've had some jokers staying here, over the years. You'd be surprised at how often they'd leave a reminder behind.'

'And weren't they all hilarious,' Sonny deadpanned. 'Burn marks on the sofa. That huge bong in the basement. Condoms in the polytunnel . . .'

'We used to have a sign that read 'No sex in the yard!' said Eric, grinning at Liv. 'Didn't stop 'em. Or us.'

'Oh, enough now,' murmured Mishti, as Liv remembered the young bodies, the noise and the bright hair and the laughter.

'It wasn't always funny,' said Mary, sounding put out. 'All that supposed democracy. Each visitor got a vote, even if they'd only been here an afternoon. We had that old tin with Mount Rushmore on, and you used to make me count the papers like some puppet presiding officer.'

'It was important,' said Sonny. 'We voted for sanctions against apartheid, against funding the Contras . . .'

Mary snorted. 'And nonsense like "Birdeye votes in favour of optional nudity." "Birdeye votes to boycott the misogynist cashier in Hannaford." Wasn't there some insane ban on honey-based products at one point, because of cruelty to bees? Honestly, think of all the stuff poor Rose has had to put up with. Some of it was crazy. People could be selfish and destructive.'

Mary meant it in a general way, Liv knew, but Mishti and Sonny exchanged glances, and in the silence that followed she saw Conor sit forward. There had been one autumn in particular, '94, no, '95, when philosophies had clashed and arguments had escalated to the point of no return. Wren, with her secretive, manipulative personality, had made a point of winkling out each person's weakness to open wounds and sow division. Yes, people could be selfish and destructive. It made Liv queasy to think of it and she didn't want Conor asking questions. Mary had never heard the full story – she had been doing a law conversion course in London at the time, the start of her permanent uprooting.

Liv turned to Rose, who was still circling the room behind them. 'Ready for dessert?' she asked, but it was too late, the mood had shifted. Rose was nodding to herself, her thoughts elsewhere, and in the pause that followed, they all heard an unpleasant retching sound from beneath the table.

'Is that Gunther?' asked Mishti. Liv grabbed a candle and bent down to look, but Conor had beaten her to it.

'Gunther's thrown up his dinner,' he said, straightening up and pushing back his chair.

Liv could make out Gunther wagging his tail guiltily against Sonny's legs. The old dog's pale eyes regarded her, almost luminous in the light of the flame.

Then Sonny's face appeared under the tablecloth and Liv caught the force of his glare before he saw the foul mess near Mary's foot. 'What the hell has that dog been eating? Oh what the fuck . . . Is that – is that *meat*?'

※

Liv lay on her back and stared into the darkness of the eaves up in the attic. The weight of the night pressed down on her eyes, and her pillow smelled damp and mouldy. Mary had seemed less than thrilled about sleeping in her mother's room. Now Liv thought that maybe she should have moved Conor instead.

She shifted onto her side, then rolled over again as pain jabbed in her shoulder. Cramp, arthritis and a tetchy bladder all contributed to stretches of wakefulness at night, and once her thoughts were rattled, she knew it would be a long one. Her mind was like static, pricking and tingling: Mary, always; Conor, who she wasn't making time for, despite his persistent questions; Sonny and Mishti's departure, and the old bitterness over Wren. There was something else, too – an emptiness. She felt it in this old bed with its dips and folds and the corner by her foot with the broken spring.

Eric. He had grinned at her in the way he used to, across the table.

She knew she should push the feeling aside or fill it with a meditation on the night sounds or a list for tomorrow's trip to the drugstore. Instead, when she closed her eyes, she saw him working on one of his sculptures, his broad hand selecting a piece of solder, his back as he hunched over. She imagined the weight of him, not on top of her, but beside her in the mattress's warm hollow. Eric had been with his second wife, Dawn for longer than he'd ever shared Liv's bed, but it didn't stop her wanting him. Something solid, familiar – someone who wanted her. They were all pairs, circulating and separating like drops of quicksilver. Mary and Rose. Liv and Eric. Mishti and Sonny. Gunther and Pinto. She'd explored almost every nook, every angle of this narrative in her Sharings over the years. There was little left to say – only the space in which she now lay.

A siren wailed briefly along the valley beyond the round window. Liv rocked herself into a sitting position and listened. Gunther was alone also, in the kitchen. She fumbled for her cardigan and wrapped it around her. Her own sorrow over Pinto still burrowed inside, but Gunther had lost her too and his suffering spoke to her now with all the clarity of the night hours. She stood up and felt her way down two flights of stairs.

'Gunther,' she whispered as she shuffled from the passageway towards his bed by the stove. He was dreaming; she could hear his breath catching, ragged in his throat, one paw quivering and scraping. Levering herself down, one hand on the cold stove top, she reached out to touch his head. 'Hey, old buddy. It's only me. Come and sleep upstairs.'

Gunther stirred and buried his nose beneath his tail. She stroked an ear until he raised his head and licked her hand. His tongue felt warm and comforting, so she slipped down to the floor and tugged up her t-shirt.

'Here's your friend,' she murmured. Gunther nudged at her. He could probably smell the hemp oil she'd applied across her chest, and when he began to lick the red, still-raised skin, she didn't stop him. A dog's saliva was anti-bacterial.

When he was done, she gave his side a push with her palm. 'Come with me,' she murmured, but he wouldn't move. He'd never slept anywhere but the kitchen. Mishti had argued for latitude on this point, but it was one of Liv's last remaining English traits drawn from a childhood full of dogs and cats and horses. Dogs didn't sleep on beds. You loved them fiercely, not sentimentally. How wrong she'd been, she thought.

She waited for a moment, then hauled herself back to standing and reached for Gunther's leash on its hook by the door. He sat up as she quickly fastened it to his collar. With the leash on, he rose and followed her out into the passageway, his claws clicking on the wooden boards.

'Old buddy,' she repeated, as they reached the bottom of the stairs. 'Soon be there.'

Gunther dutifully clambered to the half turn, then hung his head and sank down on his haunches.

'Come on, Gunth. It's cold.' Liv tugged at the leash. She had never used force with her dogs, and any visitor who couldn't accept this didn't stay very long. The Birdeye way was one of empathy and understanding, but while poor old Gunther was bound by the habits of a lifetime, Liv could finally see a way to help him; his need was her need. She stepped behind him and put her arms around his belly, gently pushing him towards the step. His hips slid a couple of inches across the floorboards, but when he tried to stand, Liv's shoulder joint got stuck. She fell against the wall, treading on Gunther's tail so that he yipped, high and quick.

A door opened. Two doors. The stair light snapped on.

'Mom!' Mary peered down from the first-floor landing. 'For goodness' sake! What are you doing?'

'I'm fine. Go back to bed.'

Mary was already hurrying down the stairs though, her robe pulled tightly around her. 'What's the matter?'

'Nothing. I heard Gunther whimpering. He needed company.' Liv could feel her face reddening. Gunther shook himself and raised his head towards Conor, who stood illuminated in his doorway.

'Are you hurt?' persisted Mary. She put out her arm to link with her mother's.

'No! And now you'll wake Rose with all this noise. I was seeing to Gunther . . .'

'He's fine – he should stay in the kitchen. Why's he got his leash on? You weren't taking him for a walk, were you? It's three a.m., Mom!'

Liv steadied herself against the wall and let go of her daughter's elbow. 'I'm going to bed,' she said. 'And so should you.'

As she closed the attic door behind her, she heard whispers on the landing below.

'I'm sorry you had to see this. She's not herself. Thank god I've been able to visit.'

Then Conor's voice. 'Why should she be herself? Her other dog died. People are leaving. It's grief.'

PURSUANT TO A JUDGEMENT
OF FORECLOSURE

Liv WAS BEING taken out for lunch. They were going to a nice place in Hudson, Mary told her, just the two of them; Sonny would stay home with Rose. They could talk, catch up, and Mary would pay for her mother to get her hair cut.

Mary's rental car, some kind of hybrid, was roomy and swish. It had deep leather seats, it made soft, discreet bleeps and it didn't smell of dog. Liv sat beside her daughter and thought about how close they were in that space, but also how far away. She resisted the urge to reach out and touch Mary's arm, and instead leaned her head back against the headrest and watched the mountains recede in the wing mirror: Tremper, Wittenberg, Cornell, their summits dappled in the morning sunshine. Soon they passed the turnoff for the reservoir, then the high school and the farm stands and the half-built houses clad in Tyvek. A few more miles and they cruised down the hill past the Tibetan Centre and the orange roof of Kenco Outfitters, after which they joined the looping ribbon of traffic that encircled Kingston with its malls and linked them to the Thruway and up the Hudson Valley. Mary chatted as she drove, recounting snippets of her English life: the cat that she'd left with her neighbour; a story about her PA who was getting married, then called it off; the way the countryside was changing and not always for the better because of the Tories or the trains or something. The words floated around the interior of the car, attaching to nothing. Mary was merely filling the space until they were settled in the restaurant she had picked out and they could 'talk properly'. Liv tried to appreciate the sound of her daughter's voice with its measured intonation, its tall vowels and its sense of a full life. Here they were, mother and daughter, gliding along like all the other people she could see in their vehicles – that man in the collar and tie, that child asleep in its car seat, those teenagers with their mouths opening and shutting, heads turning, hands gesturing. Being driven induced an unfamiliar passivity. Liv had another daughter along with a dog and other people she called family, but they were tucked away in the valley behind her, and she didn't need to worry about them now.

As they turned off the Thruway, Liv twisted in her seat for another glimpse of the Catskills escarpment, distant now, where it rose up from the fields and farmsteads and disappeared behind a band of pale cloud.

'Let's go by the Mountain Top on our way back,' she said, thinking it would be more scenic and the views from Hunter would do them both good.

'All right,' said Mary, reaching for some coins as they entered the toll to cross the Hudson River. 'I mean, this is your day,' and in that twist of a moment as the lights switched from red to green and they accelerated away, Liv remembered that it wasn't her day at all. Her mood sank then. Her daughter was like a sheep dog, separating her from the fold. She would single her out and isolate her until Liv gave herself away.

As they drove across the bridge, the sun broke through the clouds on Liv's side. Someone had tied a cellophane-wrapped rose to the guide rail – dried up now, a token of some sort, a small memorial, as dead as the lost life it echoed. It made her think of Mishti, and also Conor's questions about Pinto.

Mary put on her sunglasses. 'Pull your visor over, Mom,' she said, but Liv didn't move; she kept staring and staring at the grey-blue water as the iron struts flashed their shadows across her eyes.

❦

They parked in a gated lot that led out onto the vintage shops and quaint red bricks of Warren Street in Hudson's historic quarter. Mary, it transpired, had booked everything while she had queued in Immigration the previous day, and their first stop was a hair salon opposite the church. Liv sat there like a child under the too-bright spotlights as Mary and the stylist discussed her bone structure.

'I won't take it too short,' said the stylist, standing behind and tugging Liv's hair down around her jawline. 'The face isn't elfin, but it is defined. She needs more shaping at the front, to soften.'

Liv didn't care what she looked like, but she told herself she could do this for her daughter. It would steady them both and soften any blow that might come later. Someone fastened a slippery black gown around her, and she was glad at least that this covered any sign of her still-healing tattoo beneath her shirt. She lay back and let a teenaged girl wash her hair. The girl's fingers were surprisingly assertive, and Liv thought about how this was the second time in a couple of days that a stranger had been intimate with her. Was this how Rose felt when Liv massaged her daughter's belly? She wanted to tell the girl that she was good at her work, but Mary was nearby, sipping a glass of water.

One hour later Liv emerged with smoothed, svelte hair, scalp tingling, smelling of lemongrass and ginger. It made her feel light-headed, and she almost laughed to herself at the thought that Sonny, with his cook's nose, would sniff her. Then she caught sight of her reflection in a window and pulled a face. Fuck Sonny.

Next stop was lunch, but Mary wasn't in any hurry. She seemed excited as they walked along the sidewalk, tapping Liv's arm, saying look at this, oh isn't that sweet, and pointing into windows. Liv tried to admire the artisan cheeses, the ceramic workshops, the handcrafted promise of exclusivity and the extortionate prices. Store signs, she saw, were tasteful and witty. Passers-by seemed painstakingly assembled with their soft car coats and glossy fingernails and faces like polished pennies. Liv touched her own head and understood how clever Mary had been to take her to the salon first, so that she would fit here. Before she could comment though they reached an archway and Mary ducked into a boutique, pulling Liv along behind her. The store sold clothes made of especially fine linen and Mary took out her credit card and paid for a long collarless shirt in pale pink for Rose. 'Perfect for the summer, when it finally arrives,' she said. 'Cool and fresh with long sleeves to protect her in the sun.'

'Is it a gift?' asked the shop assistant.

'Yes,' answered Mary the bountiful. Mary, who had somehow persuaded Liv to leave Rose behind for the day.

Mary, the deserter.

৺

'Think about it, Mom. I'm entitled to up to three months' long-service leave. I'll use it to settle you both in.'

Mary had been talking for a while. A few minutes earlier she had opened up her shoulder bag and pulled out a brochure for a house she said she was buying. Liv saw pictures of a fancy kitchen island and a curving staircase, a striped lawn with a copper beech tree at the bottom, and a pond stocked with orange koi. The house was somewhere in north London. The brochure was printed on stiff card and took up a lot of space on the table.

She looked down at the plate of food in front of her and poked sceptically at the okra. What would Sonny and Mishti make of this restaurant, she wondered, with its organic vegan menu, all locally sourced, apparently. Mary had told her about a rave review in the *New York Times*. The walls were exposed brick, the paintings were original, and the cutlery and glassware gleamed in the soft sunlight that flooded through the window. Two young women at a table behind Mary put away their phones and talked earnestly about the foraged ramps they'd just ordered. The waiter next to them looked happy in his work, his apron tied in a particular way around his hips, expressing his delight with their choices. Doubt had been excluded here, it seemed. All those people who'd come up to Birdeye over the years, seeking peace, or grace – they might as well have come to Hudson instead and been absorbed into this beautiful, contented bubble.

'Mom, are you actually listening?' Mary took a sip of her water.

'Every word,' said Liv, pulling her feet underneath her chair as she remembered there was no Gunther or Pinto here to come and sit on them.

'It's just that you seem distracted. It's taken me ages to find the right property, and I want to know what you think. See the outside space? It's all walled, so it's completely secure, and it faces south, and there's an intercom for the granny flat.' Mary kept tapping the brochure, but she was frowning, which struck Liv as odd. Indeed, the longer the brochure sat on the table between them, the more detached she felt.

'The thing is,' she found herself saying, 'when you were a girl, I knew you'd leave me one day.'

'Mom . . .'

'Let me finish. You preferred other people's houses. You wanted to go on trains. You had a mind of your own – such an independent mind – and I loved that about you and accepted what it meant.'

'This isn't about me.'

'No. This is about Rose and I.'

Mary pushed her plate away. 'So let's talk about Rose! She has her routines, yes, but she hates the winter storms, the wind through the high tops. In this house she'd be safe, but she could also walk around the garden, watch the birds—'

'Birdeye is where we belong.'

'So you always say, as if that's the last word about it, but you're not the only one to speak for her.' A wrinkle had appeared in the tablecloth and Mary tugged at the edge, trying to straighten it. 'She's my twin sister.'

Liv looked pointedly over the top of her glasses. 'Then I'll speak for you, too, if you like. You think I'm getting too old to take good care of Rose. You think you'd do a better job in England, and that

Rose and I should come and live with you in a tidy house with wall-to-wall carpet and a private nurse and a bath harness and trips to cathedral tea shops when I get moody or whimsical.'

Too late, Liv realised she'd gone too far. Mary's face had fallen.

'Why do you have to reduce everything to something mean? Do you think I haven't made sacrifices? That I'm not, potentially, putting my career on the line if I take this sabbatical? The other partners are circling like the proverbial sharks—'

'Don't, then—'

'Just face the facts, it's only going to get more difficult for both of you here. All these visitors – you can't keep scooping up strangers. Conor has got his feet nicely under the table, but what do you know about him? I can help, Mom, if you let me. Birdeye is falling down, and Sonny and Mishti know you won't do the sensible thing and sell up for as long as they continue to live with you.'

'That's not why they are leaving,' Liv said quietly. 'They are leaving because they want something else.'

'Well, what about Rose? You can't be her main carer forever – you just can't – and the longer you leave it, the harder it will be for her to adjust. Oh, and don't get me started on money. You're losing Mishti's little salary, and you'll have to pay your insurance and your town taxes somehow. You'll need to get the landline reinstated in case there's an emergency, and that's expensive, which means I'll have to pay the bill, but I can't keep propping up your life choices when they're not appropriate for my sister. Call it tough love, but you're in denial.' A muscle beneath Mary's eye twitched, as if she'd pinched herself under the table. 'My few days here is the only break I've had all year. I've worked flat out because I want to take care of you both, Mom. Let me do it properly.'

Liv studied her daughter, whose made-up face was trying so hard. She was struck by how Mary had become exactly what Sonny and Mishti used to say their father had wanted before he'd kicked them out. Successful. Respectable. Was it so hard to reach for her – to hold on to the pretence of an occasion and talk earnestly like the couple behind them? But she couldn't forget the sullen twenty-one-year-old who'd left for London on a scholarship, and then her own last trip to England, booked at Mary's insistence when she learned her mother was cancer-free. Rose had remained at Birdeye with Mishti and Sonny, which had been horrible, but what Liv remembered most was how much she hated her birth country. She'd felt strangled by the little villages and the narrow streets and the narrow houses and the narrow strips of garden and the narrowness of the people with their brittle voices and their codes that she had spent a lifetime trying to forget. She knew that English people weren't all like that, but she had turned herself into something else and she could not belong there again.

'I'm not Rose's carer. I'm her mother,' she said, her heart sagging and heavy, as it was so often lately.

'You could write another book, Mom. On that exact subject. You'd have the space you need, plenty of time, no interruption . . .'

'I should never have written the first one.'

The waiter, glancing up from his workstation, came across to check that everything was to their liking. Mary frowned again and said yes, their food was delicious.

'She'd like the check, please,' Liv told him.

'I thought you'd want some tea,' said Mary, her dark eyes pleading now, but Liv felt that if she continued to sit at that table, she would flay her daughter with guilt about leaving Rose, about leaving Eric and Sonny and Mishti and the dogs and just about everything that mattered apart from Mary herself.

⁂

Every once in a while, back when the twins were still children, Eric would get itchy to visit somewhere new. They kept a couple of tents at Birdeye, so one Labour Day weekend, when the summer visitors had mainly left, he and Liv packed up the station wagon and the four of them motored south-east across the Hudson, then along

Connecticut's sunny byways to Rocky Neck State Park, with its wide sandy paths and views across Long Island Sound all the way to the Atlantic Ocean. The change would do them good, Eric said, but Rose quickly became anxious in a space without boundaries. While Mary splashed in the surf and made a friend at the playpark, her sister sat on a towel, fists clenched, head rocking backwards and forwards as if trying to head-butt the waves. After a sleepless night of bed-wetting and shrieks and investigations by concerned fellow campers, the family packed up and returned to Birdeye. Eric winked and dug out dimes for sodas at the gas station. Liv, transfixed by the girls' diverging needs, watched in the wing mirror as Mary leaned out of the window, her glinting copper hair blowing across her eyes as she strained for one last glimpse of the beach and, perhaps, another kind of family.

Liv remembered things like this as she lay awake in the dark attic. She got up, pulled on her cardigan and went down to the middle floor.

'Mary,' she whispered, standing in her socks outside her own bedroom. The silence fizzed around her ears until she heard her daughter murmur 'Come in.'

Liv opened the door carefully and slipped through the gap. She saw straight away that the reading lamp was on: an old angle poise with the light directed across Mary's knees. Mary was sitting up against the pillow. Her laptop and some papers lay across the coverlet and she was wearing reading glasses, which for some reason took Liv by surprise. The room seemed different, too; it smelled of soap and there were clothes folded over the back of a chair.

'I didn't want to disturb you,' she said, hanging back by the door.

'Yes, you did.' Mary took off her glasses. 'But it's okay, I'm glad you're here. If you hadn't come, then at some point I'd have gotten up to find you.'

Liv wasn't sure she believed that. 'Never go to sleep on a cross word,' she murmured, glancing towards the nightstand. She wondered if Mary had noticed the hand-stones she had left there. 'Although once, as I recall, you vowed you'd never sleep again if that meant you didn't have to apologise.'

Mary frowned. 'Is that what you want me to do now, Mom? Apologise?'

'No!' Liv stepped forward, horrified by the prospect of another fight. 'No. That's my job. I'm sorry. You work so hard – I know that. Too hard!'

She sat on the bed, and almost immediately Mary smiled and moved her laptop as if to say she'd forgiven her already. Then Mary reached out an arm and Liv rested her head on her daughter's shoulder, although it gave her no relief. Her joints ached and her tattoo was sore and itchy; she felt uncomfortable and dishonest, and when she shut her eyes, she saw the ocean that lay between the two of them, strange and leaden and heaving.

AREA OF DETAIL #3

CONOR SLIPPED DOWNSTAIRS once the house had fallen quiet and no light showed beneath the other bedroom doors.

He went first to the study, then the kitchen, where he stood in the darkness in his jeans and bare feet and set his cell phone to record. The milliseconds flashed as he held it aloft, listening intently, picking out the night sounds: Gunther's breathing; the refrigerator's irregular hum; other indistinguishable ticks that might be mice or old floorboards settling. A bed creaked above him. He remained still for a few seconds, then placed the phone carefully on the draining board while he ran cold water from the faucet, cupped his palms and drank.

The splashing caused Gunther to whine a little, so he wiped his hands on his jeans, paused the sound file and tapped on the torch.

'Good boy,' he murmured. 'On your own now, aren't you? I bet you miss your friend.'

The torch was spooky, the way it reflected in the window and revealed his own blueish-white face. He flashed it quickly around the walls and was about to turn it off again when he glimpsed something unfamiliar on the counter near the yard door. A woman's purse. The leather looked new and expensive. Mary's, almost certainly. He put his hand out to touch it, but then suddenly he drew back. A fifty-dollar bill had been tucked beneath it.

Conor frowned and rubbed his phone against his chest. He guessed what this was: a test for him – unsubtle and insulting. He almost wanted to take the bill, to see what the others would do, but instead he switched to camera mode and took a picture. It didn't look much – an indistinct outline, like his reflection in the window.

He left the kitchen and went back upstairs to bed.

DO NOT PROCEED
WITHOUT CRAMPONS

L IV STOOD AT the bathroom window in the cold morning light and watched the snow falling out of the sky. It sank past her in sticky clumps that slid down the curved roof of the polytunnel or settled on the ground in uneven patches. The forecast had mentioned rain for the valleys, but with one miniscule nudge of an isobar, the house had stepped back into winter.

A trail of paw prints, she noticed, led to a small steaming mound up near the treeline. Sonny must have risen early and opened the back door to let Gunther out. Liv let her gaze run along the dripping conifers at the yard's perimeter as Susan Kinney's words about the Town Board came back to her. Where was the Birdeye boundary, exactly? She had never cared before. There were documents in the study, somewhere.

Out on the landing Liv listened for signs of life. No shuffling yet from Rose's room. No open doors or gargling cistern. Sonny often returned to bed after his dawn meditation, and when she made it down to the kitchen, she found that Gunther had followed suit. The kitchen smelt of farts; he didn't raise his head, but wagged his tail feebly as she bent down to stroke his ear.

'Hey boy,' she murmured. 'Hey old stinker.'

After refilling his water bowl, she went along to the study. Sonny's domain. They all needed access, but Sonny had worked hard to fill it with his personal preoccupations: the scrap books full of hand-written recipes; the books on Zen Buddhism; the mix tapes and CDs of Leonard Cohen and Jason Molina, and a stack of cheap photo albums that Liv knew were full of images of community cook-outs and softball competitions in Kodak candy shades, faces caught in contemplation or laughter, most out of focus, blurred and over-exposed.

In contrast, the morning light, dull and blank with snow, barely intruded through the half-drawn blind at the window. Liv flicked on the overhead bulb and looked around. On her right was the desk with the computer and a pile of junk mail – glossy invitations in search of a connection. Straight ahead, beneath the window, several untied refuse sacks full of old clothes and sleeping bags too ancient for Jonathan awaited transport up to Tanners Ridge or the recycling depot, while the shelves on the wall to her left were lined with concertina files of newspaper cuttings, each item clipped and filed under headings such as 'waste' and 'river management' and 'Catskills Reps/Alt-Right Watch'. Liv couldn't imagine Sonny and Mishti shifting all this stuff to Buffalo. They'd have to burn it or shred it, but first she needed to check on the whereabouts of certain things: correspondence about taxes and welfare; hospital details; the passwords that none of them could memorise. Also, any documents pertaining to her ownership of the house. She reached up to extract a lidded box, but as she took its weight, her shoulder refused to cooperate. The contents slid to the floor: bills, drugstore catalogues, a few clippings from *National Geographic*, all so starkly pointless without her faith that Sonny's curation would continue to the end. A dog-eared takeout menu landed on her foot and when she kicked it off, she saw Mary's face staring up at her, aged about fifteen, wearing makeup with her bright hair all curled. It looked like a prom photograph, still in its packet with its see-through window. Liv stepped back to avoid treading on it, bumping instead against the desk and knocking the computer keyboard. The last user hadn't turned it off, and now a motor whirred before an image appeared on the desktop screen: a house, biggish with three floors and a wraparound porch, not unlike Birdeye only whiter, tidier, with an SUV parked up outside. 'Esopus Realty!' proclaimed a ribbon at the bottom. 'Apollonia, five bedrooms, one acre, two wood stores, $700,000.' Sonny had been checking on local property prices. Liv pressed the power button hard, holding it down for longer than she needed to.

Mary's photo was still on the floor. *What are you looking at*, she thought, and in a sudden rush of anger she yanked up her t-shirt to expose her chest with its tattoo.

'Liv?'

Startled, she let go of her shirt and turned around. Sonny stood in the doorway, the eye mask he wore at night pushed up on his forehead, white stubble on his chin, his kimono tied loosely around his hips.

'What's going on?' He was staring at the mess on the floor.

'I dropped a box.' Liv felt caught. She stooped to pick up Mary's picture. 'I found this. Must have been her junior prom.'

Sonny stepped over the spilled papers towards the desk. He was checking to see what she'd disturbed.

'Well, I'm glad you're okay,' he said.

'Did I say I was okay?'

'Liv.' He sighed. 'This is hard. I don't want it to be hard, but if it was easy, then what would that say about our lives here? You've said this exact same thing to every visitor who has struggled to leave us. You're going to run short of money, though. You have to face that. You have to think about selling up, while you've still got the energy for the change.' He touched the pile of junk mail, straightening it a little. 'And there's another thing. I know you think Mishti and I don't deserve a say, but Conor worries me. He asks questions, but he doesn't tell us anything, doesn't seem to *want* anything.'

Liv laughed, although she couldn't keep the bitterness out of her voice. 'Maybe that's what you can't stomach.'

'Except I don't believe him! And nor do you. He jumps to any task, works hard, but he's holding back on us. It's like he's waiting for Mishti and I to leave. It's time he moved on.'

Liv imagined Sonny's finger, raised in admonishment. She wanted coffee, or painkillers, or a cherry Lifesaver or anything to take away the bad taste in her mouth. Conor wasn't the problem here. He'd come in good faith, and no wonder he acted bemused when Sonny and Mishti willingly pushed Birdeye into crisis.

'Granted, Conor's a puzzle,' she said, wanting to make Sonny see a connection. 'Like you were when I first met you, remember? You were sitting on that bench in Woodstock with Mishti about to pop.'

'Don't!' Sonny turned, putting up a hand. He looked wounded, and Liv might have drawn some satisfaction by continuing, but the memories hurt her, too. Wasn't she the one who had buried Sonny and Mishti's child one humid summer's night all those years before? Sonny had been in shock after Sebastian's birth, so, after Eric and Liv had taken them both home and cleaned up Mishti and settled her in their bed, Liv had wrapped the body in a muslin square and used Eric's metal toolbox as a coffin to protect it from racoons and bears. She'd driven up the Olderbark Mountain Road while Eric minded the twins, then dug that dreadful hole among the trees. It was what Mishti had wanted. She hadn't thought to ask Sonny.

'Liv?'

She looked down and saw that she was still holding Mary's prom photograph in its crisp waxed envelope.

'I never properly appreciated the way you looked after this stuff,' she said. 'All that labelling and filing and clipping. Our history, the history of Birdeye – you've kept everything, and I don't think I cared until now. I thought the house, and us in it, was enough.'

'You won't burn it all then.' Sonny picked up a little plastic statue of Venus on her half shell that he kept by the phone charger and set it down again on the pile of junk mail.

'No. Well, maybe the diaper catalogues. Not the photos; not the postcards and the letters.'

'I wondered if you'd get rid of it.'

'I'm not going anywhere.'

'Okay then.'

Liv propped Mary's photograph behind the basin taps and glanced at it while she bathed Rose that morning. Now that she was calmer, she appreciated how pretty Mary looked, her features soft with youth, despite the thick application of blusher and a halo of strenuously curled hair she must have permed herself. Nevertheless, there was something about Mary's expression that wasn't quite right. Perhaps it was the way she kept her mouth closed when she smiled; she had never liked the gap between her teeth. Liv tried to cast her mind back to the day in question. She couldn't recall Mary getting ready or setting off, but she supposed it had all gone smoothly. She had been proud – she felt certain about that.

'It's your birthdays on Wednesday,' she said, once Rose was settled on the toilet seat with her hair in a towel. Like an empress, Liv thought – straight-backed on her throne in her long dressing-gown. Rose wasn't keen on the toilet, but she suffered the ritual for as long as her mother stayed close by. Her early menopause had been a blessing. Liv wondered how Mary was coping. She had noticed the rising flushes on her neck, and the way she fanned herself in the kitchen. She wanted to ask if her daughter was all right, but she feared her concern would be dismissed, or misconstrued.

'We need a gift for your sister,' she added, moving to the window and rubbing at the condensation with her sleeve, but the bathroom light was reflected in the glass, making it hard for her to see. 'How about a little shopping trip of our own this morning – just you and me?'

Rose was silent, but as she twisted to face the wall her mouth widened into a smile.

'Alrighty!' Liv said, yanking on the toilet roll, skipping the usual massage, overtaken by her desire to get Rose dressed and out of the front door before she lost momentum. Better to move straight away, before another encounter with Mary could slow her down or swallow her.

THIS MACHINE KILLS FASCISTS

T HE SHUTTERS WERE down behind the door to Hope
Springs Eternal when Rose and Liv pulled up outside. A
cartoon image of a trout announced 'Gone Fishing Or Somethin'
in the darkened window. Fortunately, Liv had spotted Jonathan
ambling along the sidewalk. Jonathan presided three days a week
over the tiny thrift store's racks of second-hand clothes, its hunting
memorabilia and other pre-loved miscellany.

'I need a gift!' she called, as she helped Rose out of the pickup.
'Can you open up for a few minutes?'

Jonathan, dapper as ever in tan slacks, a black bomber jacket and
a bolo tie with silver tips, didn't look like he had anything else he
needed to be doing, but his thick eyebrows were permanently arched
at the top of his long face and gave the impression of a man peering
down from a worryingly high precipice. He studied the toes of his
cowboy boots, then the tracks of grey slush that carved up Main
Street and the speckled mountains beyond.

'I'd like to see your best stuff,' Liv threw in, as an incentive.

'Oh, that'll be everything then!' he muttered, picking through his
bunch of keys. 'I don't take in crap – not like the goodwill store up
at Tanners Ridge. Sorry. No disrespect to Mishti. Wipe your feet.'

Inside, the air smelled of old wool and damp cardboard – fusty
and homely. The curtains were drawn, but Jonathan flicked on a
light and stepped behind a red Formica kitchen unit that served
as the counter. Rose was already reaching out to touch the oily
fur of the stuffed beaver that Jonathan always swore he'd never
sell, although its tag read 'Somebody take me'. It was balanced on
a mound of fake snow on a crate in the corner, near a four-foot

black bear carved out of wood and several rummage boxes full of chipped enamel cookware, hiking maps, gloves and gaiters. Liv looked about, wondering if she'd find what she needed. Mary had expensive tastes, and while Liv could have found a cheap factory-made picture frame at CVS in Woodstock or the Dollar General in Kingston, she wanted something more distinctive, some kind of keepsake that her daughter would be glad to take back to London and place on a side table in her living room.

She pulled Mary's prom photograph from the pocket of her rain slicker and placed it in front of Jonathan. 'Do you have a nice frame for this?'

'Hm.' Jonathan picked it up and held it nearer to the light. 'Used to have a thing for Mary in high school. Lady Mary, we called her – like your British Lady Di!'

Liv suppressed a smile. Rose had her arms clasped behind her back and was eyeing Jonathan like some benign Edwardian chaperone.

'I did have a couple somewhere.' Jonathan bent down to sift through a battered suitcase of odds and ends on the floor beside him. 'Gotcha!' he muttered, yanking out two brightly coloured plastic kiddie frames – one decorated with blue dolphins and the other with orange Halloween pumpkins. He propped them up on the makeshift counter. 'Like these, Rose?'

Liv, however, had just noticed a frame on the shelf above Jonathan's head. It contained a scrap of paper with the message 'One-way service, no returns' underlined with green marker, but the incongruously ornate metal frame had a certain gleam – it might be spelter, or even silver-plated. Leaves and flowers curled around its corners and in the centre of the bottom edge sat a tarnished, bulging heart.

'How much do you want for that one?' she asked.

Jonathan fetched it down and studied it. 'Ten dollars.'

With a bit of trimming, Mary's photograph would fit.

Liv and Rose were stepping out of Hope Springs Eternal when a car splashed towards the kerb in front of them. Liv didn't recognise the vehicle until Mary swung open the door and climbed out. She was wearing a long, waxed coat with a kind of shoulder cape, and snow boots that seemed to swamp her. She left the door open, but her face had shrunk into a scowl as she picked her way through the slush, so it seemed best to wait and say nothing.

'Mom! What were you thinking? You forgot to give Rose her medication this morning!'

Liv shook her head. She never forgot Rose's pills. They were kept in a calendar box with little compartments that sat in the locked bathroom cabinet. Except Mary was holding the box in her hand, rattling it at her mother.

'You cannot forget stuff like this! It's taken years to get it right, and you know the consequences of missing the Levetiracetam - do you want her to have a seizure? It's not fair on Rose, or any of us.'

'I don't *forget*,' said Liv, dismayed, remembering now that she'd hustled Rose out of the bathroom without the routine visit to the cabinet. It was out of character; she'd slipped up and of course Mary had found her out.

'No?' Mary pulled something else out of her pocket and waggled it. A small Ziploc baggie. It still contained a few dryish shreds.

'Let's go into Caspar's,' Liv suggested. 'Rose can take her pills in there. We can get coffee. You shouldn't have come after us, Mary - we were on our way home anyway.' She turned to take Rose's hand, but Rose jerked her arm away. Her whole body had stiffened; her jaw stuck out and she was sucking her lips across her teeth.

Immediately Liv felt a pressure in her own chest. A bleeping sound had started up behind her - Mary's car, its sensors triggered by the open door. Rose froze for a second, but her eyes were huge, lids stretched open as if to draw in the entire town. Before Liv could stop her, she lunged at Mary, screaming in a way that sounded strangely flat and toneless in the damp air of the street. *Oh my girls*, Liv thought as she swooped forward. She didn't try to separate them – she couldn't – but instead wrapped her arms around both daughters, locking them more tightly together, all three.

'Hey there . . .' she murmured over and over, feeling their stiff, unyielding limbs, their heaving chests and the frailty within.

After a minute or so, Rose's clenched fists had tired sufficiently for Mary to prise them open. When they separated, Liv shuddered to see a fistful of hair. The screaming had stopped, and Jenna was peeking out of the diner's front window, while Jonathan and a couple of strangers hovered concernedly. The car was still bleeping, but no one shut the door.

Rose, as usual, appeared unmoved; she tilted her face towards the clay-coloured sky.

'Let's go home,' murmured Liv, but Mary, flushed and dishevelled, smoothed her hair down and glanced along the street.

'You came in the pickup, didn't you?'

'Well, yes, but I can come back for it later. I'll ride with you.'

'No Mom.' Mary wouldn't even look at her. 'I'll drive Rose. You take the pickup. I've got this.'

⁂

Liv couldn't bring herself to follow Mary back to Birdeye. She wanted to be alone, but her need for coffee was greater, so she stamped the slush off her boots and pushed open the door to Caspar's.

'Right with you,' said Jenna from behind the counter. She was snipping the top off a milk carton as Liv slid onto a bar stool.

'I was talking to that boy you got staying!' called Dolores, from her usual seat by the magazine stand. Liv caught Jenna's eye and mouthed a silent thank you for saying nothing about what had just occurred outside.

'I guess Mary took Rose home?' asked Jenna, quietly.

'Yep.' Liv pushed her glasses up to her forehead and rubbed her eyes. 'I'd like some coffee.'

Jenna was pouring a cup already. 'I'd forgotten Mary's visit was due. How's she doing? Tell her to call by.'

Liv nodded. She sipped the coffee, then glanced over her shoulder, but Dolores had turned to speak to a couple sitting at a neighbouring table. 'She wants me to sell up,' she said, keeping her voice low. 'Sonny and Mishti are leaving.'

'No! What the hell! I did not know that!' Jenna's outrage seemed rehearsed; she'd heard already, which meant Dolores knew, too. Conor or maybe Karin had been talking. It was hardly a secret, although the words still felt shocking to Liv when she spoke them, as if a crow had flown into the diner and every so often flapped its wings in a dark corner.

'I've got to sort some stuff out,' she said. 'But I'm staying put.'

Jenna leaned across the counter, frowning.

'It's your house – right? Where are they going? Jesus, after all you've done for them . . .'

Liv shook her head. 'Come on, don't put that on me. We share everything. They're my family. I just – I didn't see it coming.'

'Have they still got – you know – relatives? Back in India or wherever?'

Liv looked up. It was easy to forget, sometimes, that Jenna had another side she revealed only rarely. 'There is no "back". They're from Detroit. They're moving upstate to a place that takes in kids on narcoids.'

Jenna put the milk carton back in the refrigerator, making herself busy. 'They are good people.'

'Now you're telling me.'

'But Mary will take care of you and Rose, right?'

'That's what Mary would like.'

'Come on, Liv – you've got to think about Rose. Mary's a hot-shot lawyer. She's got plenty of money, whereas you don't, as I keep finding out.'

Liv pushed away her cup and stood up. 'I owe you.'

'I didn't mean it like that, but—'

'No. I owe you.' When she zipped her rain slicker, she felt the newly purchased picture frame press against the still-healing tattoo. A confrontation lay ahead; Mary was like a badger. She would never give up. It was what made her so good.

Dolores turned away from the couple next to her and started up again about Conor. 'You know I believe he is a reporter! Nose in all sorts. Asked me how long I'd known you. You wanna watch him – he'll be scouting one of them undercover movies. Hey, you going, already? You just got here.'

Liv pulled open the door and felt the cold air around her knees. 'Forgot my second vest.'

That evening, Mary said she wanted to talk with Liv and Mishti and Sonny. No Conor, she stipulated. No Rose and no Karin. They waited until Rose had gone to bed and Conor was clearing up the dinner things in the kitchen, then took their cups of tea into Mishti's cramped snug opposite the parlour; they all knew this wasn't a Sharing.

'You've got to use a chart,' said Mary as soon as the handloom had been shunted to one side and Mishti had pushed her baskets of wool into the corner. 'In the kitchen, where everyone can see it. You've got to tick off each time Rose has her medication.'

Mary was next to the lamp, perched on the high stool Mishti used when she practised her recorder. She regarded each of them gravely: Mishti and Liv squeezed onto the old blanket chest that stored three decades' worth of needlework and art materials, their hips touching, and Sonny on the floor with his back against a scratchy woven wall hanging.

Mishti started nodding.

'Good idea,' echoed Liv. She had spent the afternoon stopping leaks with a caulk gun in the attic, and it had calmed her a little. A chart was okay – fine, even. Besides, Mary looked lonely on her stool. Liv's heart was already in pieces, but Mary was hurting too.

'She needs stability,' Mary went on. 'There's been too much change. The news that Sonny and Mishti are leaving, Conor hanging around, her lack of daytime routine – yes Mom, don't shake your head . . . Things like that car alarm this morning are a trigger, but we all know her upsets come from deeper disturbances around her . . .'

Liv stayed quiet, though it was tempting to point out that the tumult might just as easily have been caused by Mary pulling up in her car and indignantly rattling the pill box. That Rose felt distress was beyond question, but Liv had always pushed back against any attempt to over-analyse her outbursts. Visitors, especially, wanted reasons – she understood this – it was human nature to look for patterns and connections, though these usually turned out to be a reflection of themselves. Rose had a right to privacy, as Liv saw it. No one could pronounce on her innermost feelings – her rage, her frustration, her curiosity, her need for attention or her boredom. Perhaps, even, her hate. Mary, the bringer of order, of explanation, sometimes chose not to acknowledge that her sister might have a long memory, or that possibly she was perfectly able to parse what was to come. Routine – that was Mary's answer to everything. Liv believed in acceptance and rootedness, not charts and timekeeping.

'You're saying you think a move to London is the only option?' Sonny had tucked his legs into a half lotus and his face was in shadow against the wall. He sounded faintly surprised; sceptical, even, but she couldn't forget that he'd been the one who'd contacted Mary, or that he'd been checking property prices online.

Mary, meanwhile, was saying something about a period of adjustment.

'I know a move will feel disruptive, but the benefits, once she's settled, will be enormous. It's the next life phase for her. She's had the most incredible experiences here, that's a given, but we've got to look ahead. These outbursts aren't good for her heart and, well, I'm her sister. Mom's not getting any younger and you and Mishti have decided to leave. The only alternative is social care and believe me, I won't let that happen. Not ever.'

Liv had often imagined Mary at work, sitting at her desk or with colleagues in a boardroom. In the early days she used to worry about her being pressured or even bullied, but of course Mary had succeeded, because when she took a view she was like a snow plough, pushing down the highway, flinging objections aside. Liv didn't think she could stand to hear any more. She couldn't bear the way her daughter had orchestrated this, almost as if she'd been waiting for her mom to slip up with the medication.

'How do you know they aren't good for her heart?' she said. 'They are part of who she is; she's often happier, more relaxed afterwards—'

'Oh yes,' interrupted Sonny, sourly. 'And we all know that sometimes you provoke them, because they make *you* feel better.'

The room fell silent. Sonny's words had nowhere to go and no one could take them back.

'Fuck off. All of you.' Liv stood up abruptly, tugging at her cardigan that was trapped beneath Mishti's bottom. 'I can manage this place on my own. Conor says he'll stay. I'll do what we've always done – welcome strangers and take care of Rose. If you really cared, Mary, then you'd live here instead of Sonny and Mishti hanging on and feeling guilty – or not guilty, or whatever it is they are feeling because you know what? I've no idea!'

She was still holding her tea, and it sloshed across her hand as she realised that she was shaking.

'Liv . . .' Mishti reached up and took her cup.

Liv looked around at Mishti, whose eyes were big and glistening, and beyond her to the music stand and the patchwork cushions and the purple candle in its hand-thrown candlestick on the shelf. Then she thought of the piles of clothes and the books and boxes in the room next door and the herb jars in the kitchen and the macramé plant holders and the Malcolm X bust in the downstairs bathroom and the wooden skis stacked against the wall in the cellar and the multitude of things that Sonny and Mishti had brought into the house, and, for the first time, she imagined them gone.

AREA OF DETAIL #4

CONOR STOOD IN the darkness of the passageway, staring down at his cell phone. The dishcloth lay draped over his shoulder. He tugged it off and carefully wiped the screen.

'Fuck off,' he murmured. Then he sucked in his cheeks and tried again. 'Fuck *orf*.'

The voices had fallen silent. He stepped back into the downstairs bathroom just as Liv emerged from Mishti's snug, but she didn't see him; instead, she yanked the front door open and was gone.

An engine started, then revved and faded as Liv drove away.

Conor's finger hovered over the red record button. A single tap.

'Exiting the Area of Detail.'

INSERT YOUR LOVED ONE'S
NAME, WHERE INDICATED

T HE OLD SIERRA'S transmission whined as Liv swung left
onto the highway. She didn't think about where she was headed;
all that mattered was the night, the gas pedal, the engine's hum. She
passed the cemetery and the recycling centre, then the inn with a
row of motorcycles lined up on the dirt strip, and when an oncoming
vehicle briefly dazzled her, she stared ahead to where the asphalt was
sucked into the darkness until the flashes faded behind her eyes.

At a farm stand she took the right fork and drove north, the road
narrowing and winding as the mountains reared around her. There
was no moon, but the dials on the instrument panel glowed companionably, and time and space spun into a wider, dimmer sphere. She
loosened her grip on the wheel, and at a sudden bend she leaned in,
momentarily closing her eyes until, like a chime ringing with soft
insistence, she recalled a game she had played with her grandfather
when she was a child of six or seven. The game involved writing
letters to each other addressed to places they had never been – a
room number, a hotel, a street, then a city, a country, a continent,
always followed by the World, the Solar System, the Galaxy and
The Universe, underlined for emphasis and surrounded by inky
stars. When Liv had asked her grandfather what was bigger than
the universe, he'd said 'infinity'. The notion of something endless
had worried her at first, but as the two of them walked down to
the post office to buy stamps for Benin or Kyrgyzstan or Patagonia
she realised it couldn't be a line, stretching on forever. Infinity was
a circle, with her grandparents' house in the middle.

At the mountaintop junction she turned right, through the ski resort, cruising past its bars and Chinese takeouts and lodges. She passed an old house, broken-backed and falling in on itself. She passed the fire station with its empty lot and its flagpole like a white pin in the night and then she turned right again, looping back down the bumpy notch road with the creek tumbling below her. Most years a car tipped on a corner here. People died on nights like this, kids driving too fast, and once a whole family of seven on a trip up to North Lake. It was heart-breaking to see the sodden teddy bears and the photographs tied to trees. The river gulley was littered with twisted metal.

Almost full circle. Liv paused on the bridge where the smaller creek merged with the Esopus. She wasn't ready to go home yet, though her tired eyes were stinging. She wanted comfort, from the one person who had known her before the girls were born, before Sonny and Mishti, before Birdeye. She swung the steering wheel to the left.

A quarter mile from Tukesville she slowed, then pulled off the road and eased onto the rough track that wound between the trees to Eric's. The tyres made popping sounds as they rolled over the rocks and the roots; she kept one hand on the steering wheel but let the pickup feel its way. The pale beams of the headlights picked out the trunks of cedars and pines, and once or twice they caught the outline of great wings or a giant head – rusting sculptures like totems, standing silent in the forest.

As the track curved to the left, Liv killed the lights and the pickup slowed to a stop ten yards or so from the long rectangle of the trailer. Eric was home; the porch light shone down on his blue Silverado parked up next to the little wood store and some stacked containers that in the summer months held black-eyed suzies and chrysanthemums. Several windows showed lights through thin curtains – Cori's bedroom, with its string of midget bulbs along the curtain rail, and the bathroom next door. The pale glow from the living area dimmed and grew bright, then dimmed again – the tv was on and Liv thought that maybe Dawn, Eric's wife, was watching it with their son. Not Eric, though. She could see the outline of his workshop a few yards to the right of the trailer, and a tell-tale strip of light showed beneath its corrugated iron door.

Liv flicked off the ignition, turned her head to one side and stared out into the dark. She didn't want to think about why she had driven here. Now that she was stationary, half hidden among the trees, a tiredness came down around her and she let her spine and haunches sink into the seat. Her hands rested in her lap, palms up and open. The night pressed against her eyelids and she let them close, accepting sleep.

※

'Liv!' A sharp rap of knuckles against the window. She sucked in her breath and stared out at her own dim reflection, then saw Eric's face beyond. When he opened the door, she almost tipped out, her shoulder stiff and aching. Shame made her shrink back as he stooped and peered in. This wasn't what she'd wanted. She had half thought to slip into his workshop and surprise him. Now she wished she had driven home.

'Are the girls okay?' Eric asked. 'Are you okay?'

Liv nodded and rubbed her eyes, wanting to erase all the scenarios Eric might be entertaining. 'What time is it?'

Eric frowned. 'Nearly midnight. You're cold. Get out. I'll find you some coffee.'

The trailer windows were dark now. Only the outside light remained, pooling over Eric's truck. Liv did as she was told and traipsed behind Eric, the chill air causing her to shiver.

The fluorescent strip in Eric's workshop made her close one eye and squint with the other. 'Woah!' she said, but Eric made no move to flick it off and rely on the softer lamp at his workbench. He stood next to his welding suit that hung like shucked-off skin from its peg. She realised straight away that he didn't want her there, that it was late and she was being unreasonable. All the same, she couldn't help herself.

'What are you working on?' she asked, looking round. Usually there was something big in the middle of the space: a time machine or a spirit guide or a figure of some kind, half human, half animal, a work-in-progress constructed from the scrap metal Eric stored in a great heap in the woods behind the trailer. She could see a bulky shape hanging in a corner, covered with a sack, but she realised with a shudder that it was the deer carcass.

'Liv, what—'

'Don't ask,' she said, quickly. 'I needed to get out, that's all. I wanted to see you.'

Eric was pouring coffee out of a flask into a small metal beaker. He turned and handed it to Liv and although his face remained slack, his eyes were full of questions.

'Do you remember,' she started, with no idea what she was going to say until her gaze rested on an old hay rake, its long metal tines bent out of shape. 'Do you remember when the twins were small, and we were still living on the farm?'

'Sure.' Eric paused. 'You were something all right. You were strong – fearless. You took care of the girls, and you fought the doctors who called Rose a retard and anyone else who said you couldn't do it.'

'We took care of them.'

'We did.'

'And do you remember one evening after we'd moved to Birdeye and we were sitting on the porch – it was early summer, I think – and you said we were both makers?'

Eric leaned against the workbench, his big hands with their white hairs pushed deep into the pockets of his jacket. He sighed. 'Did I say that?'

'You said that you made art, and I made our Birdeye family.' Liv shut her eyes for a moment, summoning the warm air of that time on her skin, the insects buzzing and Rose sitting on her lap with her stiff limbs digging into Liv's belly. They had been contemplating Eric's most recent sculpture on the grass beside the house – the huge figure of the goddess giving birth to twin girls, with a surprisingly large tunnel for her vagina. When Liv shifted a little, she could see all the way through. It had puzzled her at first, why he had made her this way, but later on she decided that the gap was his own longing.

Now Eric cleared his throat. 'Well, that was true enough. I mean, that's what you've done your whole life, Liv – the girls, Mishti and Sonny, all the people you've helped.'

'But that's not really what you meant.' Liv stepped forward beneath the strip light, realising now what she wanted to say. 'You wanted us to make a baby. You thought that would make us complete. And I said no, because it already took every ounce of my strength to keep the twins safe. We had Birdeye, and we welcomed strangers, because to shut them out was to trap our girls in. But it was always such a fragile calculation, wasn't it? Rose could take it – she was always more resilient in that way – but not Mary. She wanted us exclusively, and that was something neither of us could give.'

Eric shifted his feet. 'Why are you talking about this? It was a long time ago. Over forty years! I have another family. I've been blessed with Rose and Mary, who I've loved like they're my own, and now I have Cori and Harrison.' He spoke their names quietly, looking towards the door.

'I just needed to explain. I never did, really, and I owe you that.' Exhaustion prickled under Liv's skin. She wished Eric would hold her, but he didn't move, and in her state of agitation she perceived a certain tension, as if maybe an embrace was something he wanted, too. He had drawn in his top lip, and he looked older in the fluorescent light. She'd noticed how the lobes of his ears beneath his woollen hat were more droopy and fleshy these days.

'You *are* a maker,' she repeated, finally, and with that he seemed to brighten somehow. He turned back to his workbench.

'You want to see?'

Liv, surprised, moved alongside him.

'I'm making a birthday gift for Mary,' he went on. 'It's a ring made of washers. It's the smallest thing I've ever done.' He pulled his hinged lamp down over the dark metal of the worktop and placed a chunky, rough-looking ring the diameter of a five-cent coin in its circle of light. 'Don't worry, it's not finished. It's in three layers – two steel and the middle one's brass. I've soldered it with tin and torched the edges, and I'm ready to start on finishing.' He placed the ring in a small clamp at the end of the bench and proceeded to rub its outer surface with a heavy metal file. After a minute or two of abrasion, Liv could see a silvery sheen on the rim. Eric kept turning it, wiping away the filings, and then he adjusted the clamp and began to file down its inner surface to increase the circumference of the hole. The noise was harsh and irritating; Liv was reminded of Axel's needle when he worked on her tattoo. The concentration was the same, too; she couldn't look away and, ten minutes later, after some vigorous sanding and buffing, she was rewarded. Eric placed in her hand a small ring of bright steel, polished and lustrous, with a narrow inner band of glowing brass.

'If it doesn't fit, I can file it some more,' he said.

The ring felt solid and warm, almost hot in her palm. 'It's beautiful,' she murmured, slipping it onto her little finger without thinking – the joints on her other fingers were too big.

'Hey!' Eric said, loudly. She looked up and saw him staring towards the doorway. Dawn stood there, scrubbed and shiny in her fleecy blue dressing gown and snow boots, her arms hugging her chest.

'Hello, Dawn,' said Liv, feeling stupid. She tried to tug off the ring. 'Eric was finishing Mary's birthday present.'

'Very nice,' said Dawn, not smiling. 'It's a little late for socialising.'

Liv knew it didn't look good. Dawn was tolerant, and respectful of Eric's relationships with Rose and Mary, but where Liv was concerned, she had her limits. The ring was stuck, too.

'I'll slide it off with a little olive oil and bring it back in the morning, easy-peasy,' she said, walking out past Dawn, waving her fingers, trying to make light of it.

Nevertheless, as Liv drove off down the track, then bumped onto the main road and headed back to Birdeye, she looked again at the ring. She wished she had never put it on, wished she had never gone to the trailer. The old loneliness was waiting, and as it settled down across her shoulders, she welcomed it, because right now she needed the touch of something she understood.

WE'VE GOT YOU COVERED

MARY WOKE UP with a start. The movement nudged her laptop back to a state of alertness; its power light pulsed softly beside her in the dark. Her mother was home, she reminded herself, patting the nightstand for her phone. The display showed three forty-five. Liv had returned at around two a.m., fumbling about in the hall and flushing the toilet in the bathroom before retreating up the attic stairs. Now the house lay silent, apart from the slow ticking of a pipe along the wall. So often, as a teenager, she had lain beneath the covers and listened to the night sounds in winter – adults murmuring, beds creaking, a barred owl whooping from a high branch in the woods or, sometimes, the horrid scrabbling of vermin above her head. When Sonny found out what was frightening her, he had given her a broom and told her to bang on the ceiling whenever she heard the skitter of claws. The marks would be there still, she imagined, in the front bedroom, her room, where Conor now slept. For the life of her she couldn't understand why Liv had put Conor in there. Why wasn't he up in the attic? Mary picked her battles carefully, strategically, so she'd let this one go, but it didn't mean it hadn't hurt, in a way that seemed out of character for her mother. Liv was stubborn and sometimes downright perverse but these last few days she had seemed careless towards Mary, as if she couldn't be bothered to try.

Sonny thought so too, she reminded herself. She and Sonny and Mishti had talked, after Liv had cursed at them and driven off. They'd agreed that Conor had to go, and that Liv might come to her senses if she was left on her own with Rose for a couple of days. To this end, Mary would drive Sonny and Mishti upstate to see their new accommodation. Karin could call by in an emergency, but everything else – well, perhaps Liv would see how much she was taking for granted.

Mary felt a prickling sensation across her shoulders and a wave of heat rolled up towards her neck. Another hot flush. The backs of her knees, her shins, her ankles were sweating; she hadn't known until recently that ankles could sweat. She swung her legs out of bed, grateful for the cool air on her skin. A drink of water would help, but the glass on the nightstand was empty; unless she replenished it, she wouldn't have a hope of further sleep. What, she wondered, irritably, would GlennNevis66 make of these early-hours visitations?

Downstairs, in the kitchen, she switched on the overhead light. Gunther breathed out heavily from his bed by the stove, but otherwise he didn't stir. There was a bottle of water in the refrigerator and as she pulled open the door she thought about her purse and the money she had tucked beneath it on the counter. Her gaze was drawn to it, as perhaps she had intended all along.

The fifty-dollar bill was no longer where she'd left it. She checked around and checked the floor also, but she knew it was gone.

Mary shivered; her nightdress was clammy now against her skin. She wouldn't tell her mother – such betrayal from a visitor would be too upsetting and Liv would only argue that no one was past saving, although she never used that word. Conor, Mary decided, had to be on the bus back to New York before Liv came down for breakfast. Eric used to do this – escort a bad influence off the premises, maybe once every couple of years, but now she and Sonny would manage it.

As she flicked off the light and turned to leave the kitchen with her water, she heard something outside, from the direction of the trees. She glanced behind her, and the pot-holders hanging around the window like knotty skulls spooked her a little. Her breath quickened; her heart raced. The night was black beyond the glass, but she stood still and made herself listen, and there they were, their yips echoing across the valley, more dreadful to her than rats in the rafters – a pair of coyotes, barking.

'What are they plotting, hey Birdie?' Liv brushed the stray hairs from Rose's face and gently moved her into the morning light so that she could apply a little more Bio Oil to the dry spot she'd noticed on her daughter's shoulder. The voices below rose up through the floorboards and the rug in Rose's bedroom: Sonny's rumbling, Mary interjecting and the soft echo of Mishti, who'd had so little to say for herself lately. Liv couldn't catch the words; she wasn't sure she wanted to. Better to linger over Rose's massage, brush her hair, rearrange the sweaters in her wardrobe. The two of them could hide up there all day.

Rose turned her face to the window and flexed the fingers of her right hand, splaying them out so that bones and tendons formed ridges like the underside of a leaf. Liv took it in her own, palm to palm, and slid her fingers through the gaps. Their thumbs touched briefly, before Rose's twitched away. She followed her daughter's gaze and stared out towards the trees. The sky was brighter this morning. The low cloud had shifted and when she glanced further up the valley, she could see the conifers on the upper inclines washed in soft sunlight. Look, Rose, she almost said, see over there at the edge of the yard – two figures, vanishing: her parents, Colin and Diana, who had never come to Birdeye, who had driven off down an English country lane one spring day in 1959. Their murmurings and laughter behind carefully closed doors had similarly shut her out.

Rose wanted her breakfast. She was pulling at her dressing gown, eager to get dressed.

'Mom's a doofus,' Liv murmured, feeling the throb in her little finger where Eric's ring was still stuck beneath the joint. She dribbled Bio Oil around the edges where the skin was puffy, but it didn't budge.

Sonny wasn't one to beat about the bush.

'We're going to Lake Erie for a day or two,' he said, glancing up as Liv and Rose entered the kitchen. He sat at the table with Mary and Mishti as he sliced a thumb of root ginger, coolly practical. Liv was tempted to say *aloof*. 'Mishti and me need to take stock of our new place. It's an annexe, semi-furnished, but we don't know with what.'

'Mary has offered to take us,' added Mishti, providing the softener, the sweetener, as she always did. 'Which is very generous of her. So that you've got the pickup.'

Mary stood up and took oat milk from the refrigerator. 'We're making Thai pancakes,' she said, pulling out a chair for her sister. 'If you don't want them now, you can warm them up later. I'd like to make the trip, Mom. We'll be back tomorrow night. We'll be here for our birthdays on Wednesday, I promise.'

We're, we'll, we – Liv was being excluded, but she quickly rallied. 'You're going to drive them, then?'

'I am. I mean, if that's okay. I want to see where Sonny and Mishti are going. I don't know when I'll get another chance, and you'll have some space to think, here on your own with Rose . . .'

Liv pushed up her glasses. 'To see if we can manage, you mean – Rose and me and Conor.'

'Well—' Mary stopped and peered at her mother's hand. 'Oh, what's that?'

Dammit. The ring. Liv held up her little finger. Somehow, the glistening oil she'd applied made it look worse. 'Look what I did,' she said. 'Can't get it off. Can't be trusted. Strikes me it's a little irresponsible of you to up sticks right now.'

Rose, pacing behind her, made a grab for Liv's arm, but Liv held it up higher.

'It looks like a can pull,' said Mary, just as Liv remembered it was Eric's gift to his daughter.

'It looks painful.' Mishti leaned across to see it properly. 'Have you tried olive oil?'

Sonny, though, would not be side-tracked. 'Conor's gone,' he said. 'I gave him a ride to the bus-stop already.'

Liv lowered her arm. 'What? Without saying goodbye?'

Mary was frowning, a picture of concern, while Mishti poked at one of Sonny's slices of ginger. Squirming, thought Liv. Mishti was in on it.

'Don't tell me – you made him leave. You never wanted him here. I can't believe you think that's okay. What if he's got nowhere else to go?'

'Now listen, Liv.' Sonny pushed his chair back, as if to stand, but he seemed to change his mind. 'Turns out we had good reason. He took some money. Mary's money.'

Mary was shaking her head at Sonny. 'I'm sorry Mom, I didn't want you to find out. I – well, I left my purse in the kitchen. I suppose the note – it was fifty dollars – it was poking out. He didn't touch it for the first couple of days, but when I checked in the night, it was missing.'

'Wait,' said Liv. The room seemed too full, suddenly. 'You're telling me you tried to trap him?' She stared at Mary, whose face was mirrored by Rose directly behind her. The two women had the same high foreheads, the same damson eyes, but while Rose's gaze kept flicking down to Gunther, Mary stared straight at her.

'Mom—'

'No! How could you do that, in this house? You're a lawyer, of all people! How do you know it wasn't me who took it?' Liv's voice was raised; she couldn't look at her two friends, couldn't bear to see the evidence that they were complicit.

No one said anything for a moment.

'Was it you?' Mary asked, finally.

'That's despicable,' muttered Liv, as she walked out.

GET BACK TO THE GARDEN

I T WAS TEN o'clock by the time Mary, Mishti and Sonny
departed. Mary had climbed the stairs to kiss her sister, and she
gave Liv a quick, awkward hug, then left her standing in the window
of the front bedroom. Liv watched the car slip down the track
towards the road, soft shadows flickering across its rear windscreen.
She hadn't asked them about their arrangements, or what they would
talk about and do. It was too late now.

When Liv turned around, she could see Rose at the far end of
the house, in the bedroom where Mary had been sleeping – Liv's
bedroom – pacing past Mary's big suitcase that lay closed on a chair.

'Mary's coming back tomorrow,' she called. 'They've only gone
for one night.' Conor, she imagined, was probably just stepping off
the bus in Manhattan, absorbed once more into the noise and chaos
of the city. They had failed him, was what it amounted to. She and
Sonny and Mishti had been distracted by their own quarrels.

Conor had left the bed neat, she noticed. His backpack and blue
rain jacket were gone, but his copy of *The Attentive Heart* still
lay on the old bureau, and behind the door she found a couple of
discarded sport socks, their undersides grubby where his feet had
padded about the house. She didn't know what to do with them, so
she left them lying there and wandered along the landing, making
herself think of jobs to be done, errands in the pickup, ways to keep
busy. Karin would come up later to help her with the chores, and
maybe then she could hike up the trail to clear her head for an hour
while Rose had company.

At Mishti's door, she paused.

She didn't go into Mishti's bedroom very often these days. It had been different when they were young and everything seemed possible, available, permissible; when possessions had been irrelevant, and privacy no less so. After Eric left, she and Mishti often slept in the same bed, companionably breathing in the scent of each other's hair, and sometimes Sonny had joined them. Later, after Wren and Tyler, after Liv became ill, her own bedroom had become a place of nursing, of dressings and pills, of mint and liquorice infusions left on the windowsill until they grew floating islands of mould. Doors were shut: first to let her sleep, then to separate her from the painkillers on which she'd become dependent. Afterwards they'd remained closed, a tacit boundary, a line of disinclination.

Except now Liv felt inclined. She turned the cracked porcelain handle and pushed. Immediately a smell greeted her, earthy, like damp, punky wood. Something hanging from the back of the door flapped lightly, and as she stepped inside, she saw it was the saree that Sonny had spotted at the flea market a few years back, hand-embroidered, green and gold, now encased in a moth-proof bag. Mishti's wide bed was tidy; the counterpane with its mirrored discs was smoothed and straight. The room faced south and the dust in the air moved like specks of mica around the bright scarves, the little statues on a shelf, the tube of sooty kajal Mishti applied to her eyes on special occasions and the books for self-care and meditation that for decades she had shared with visitors. She had always been more of a nurturer than Liv or Sonny. It was impossible to walk up to the window and look out, because the floor, a low table, and the windowsill itself were covered with old yoghurt pots and trays of seedlings laid out on wads of moistened newspaper.

Liv squatted down and adjusted her glasses. 'French beans,' she murmured, reading the words written on a finger of damp card in Mishti's small, neat hand. Spinach, too, and strawberries – 'late harvest'. Some pots hadn't germinated yet, but already she could recognise the first pinnate leaves of tomato plants forming in the axis of the seed leaves. Usually, by mid-April, Mishti would have moved the trays down to the polytunnel or set them in the propagation frame on the porch, but the winter had dragged on, and her room was the sunniest of all the rooms in the house. Liv picked up a pot that had once, apparently, contained locally-made feta, and squeezed it. The moist soil pushed up, and with it emerged a fat yellow pepper seed, swollen, its first white root already groping downwards. She tried to imagine what Mishti had been thinking when she'd sown it. That she'd still be here to plant it out, and harvest it, and eat it? That Liv would now have to do all of this herself? Or, worst of all, that she'd take all these trays with her? Liv took the seed between finger and thumb and squashed it under her nail, quickly, knowing she would despise herself for this act of destruction, feeling the tears rise.

'Rose!' she called, scrabbling to her feet. 'Where are you, Rose?'

✿

Rose was looking out of the window of the front bedroom, her forehead against the glass. She opened her mouth: 'Awah.'

'Rose?' Liv stepped through the doorway. Rose's voice was rare music, clear and deeper than people tended to imagine. She wondered if her own emotion had piqued her daughter's impulse to speak, and she joined her at the window, yet all she could see when she looked out was the pickup and the trees, branches reaching up like bare grey arms to the sun, and glimpses of the river.

Then a sound from downstairs – the screen door's creak, followed by the front door opening and a cautious 'Hello!'

Rose's face opened out into a wide, toothy smile. Liv pictured an electric blue flash of a rain jacket. She sucked in her breath. It was Conor.

✿

'Want a banana?' Conor nudged his backpack nearer Liv. A generous selection of fruit lay nestled on top of his stuff: oranges, grapes and kiwis, along with a trio of bananas. The two of them were sitting on the bench in a small patch of sunlight at the rear of the house, sheltered from the breeze, watching Rose as she wandered across the backyard. The sun, Liv noticed, had some warmth in it. She lifted her face to drink it in.

'Sonny wouldn't approve,' she said. 'Not exactly seasonal.'

'What? Don't tell me you don't eat bananas!'

'I know a funny story about bananas.' Liv hesitated, knowing it might sound weird. 'Okay. Well, when I was a child my father wore Y-fronts – you know, stretchy jockey shorts. So I picked up a pair one day – I must have been five or six – and I asked what the gap was for. My father said it was for fruit – an apple, or a banana – just in case he or my mother got hungry. I believed him, of course.'

Conor raised an eyebrow. 'One for later.'

'Exactly.'

They stayed there for a while, and Conor told Liv that he'd jumped off the bus in Kingston, done a little sight-seeing around the historic part of town, then caught another bus right back to Apollonia. Liv nodded, remembering his bare torso at Dolores' place; not ready to ask him certain questions. She squinted across the yard.

'Rose loves fruit. Especially raspberries. We grow them here. See those sticks over there, poking up near the polytunnel? Should've tidied them up by now, cut out last year's dead canes. And Mishti's got pots of strawberry plants germinating in her bedroom.'

'Sounds like you'll be busy.'

'Yes.' Liv noted that he hadn't said 'we'. 'I don't think I can do it on my own. Mishti is the gardener. I'm just the summer labour.'

'Watch some YouTube,' suggested Conor. 'It can't be that hard.' He reached into his backpack and pulled out an orange. 'You know, in some ways, this place is definitely *not* what I was expecting.'

'No shit,' said Liv, drily. 'What were you hoping for?'

Conor was silent for a while, peeling the piece of fruit, releasing its bright, citrusy aroma. She thought maybe he wouldn't answer as he began to pick off the pith and flick it to the ground, but as she made to stand up, wanting coffee, he offered her a segment.

'You,' he said. 'I was hoping to meet you, and I have, but you're not what I thought. You aren't clear about things. You don't know everything.'

'No shit again!' said Liv, laughing. She couldn't help it. Conor reminded her of being young, and of not seeing the world in the way everyone else thought she ought to. 'You could stay,' she added. 'It's not up to the others. It's up to me.'

'And Rose,' said Conor, looking serious. 'Rose!' he called, as she drew nearer. 'Can I stay?'

When Rose reached them, she saw the orange and stooped forward to inspect Conor's stash of fruit.

'We could throw a birthday party. We always used to,' mused Liv, thinking of the treasure hunts they'd organised when her daughters were small. Everyone took part – children and adults, rampaging through the house, pulling everything out of drawers and cupboards, just because they could. Mishti and Liv would place wrapped candy at eye level or on the ground in Rose's path and shout 'found one!' when she passed, while Mary turned over stones and scrabbled through the woodpile, searching for treats.

Conor grinned. 'Mmm – banana cake!' He pointed to the ring on Liv's little finger, still shiny with oil. 'Looks painful.'

'It's for Mary. I can't get it off.'

'Sure you can. I'll help you.'

As he led the way to the kitchen, then found ice in the freeze box and made a cold compress and told Liv to keep it raised to reduce the swelling, Liv felt lighter, less burdened. Conor seemed brighter, too – not as pained or awkward as before. After five minutes he inspected her finger, and when he applied some dish soap and carefully wiggled off the ring, Liv noticed his touch and thought how it was warmer, more personal than the gloved hands of Axel at the tattoo parlour. They could make this work, she told herself. They could spring clean the place, invite guests, show Mary and Sonny and Mishti that Birdeye could thrive without them.

'There's one thing I need to ask you,' she said as she dried her hand. 'Did you take Mary's money?' She looked out of the window to where Rose was still standing next to Conor's backpack, and Gunther lay in the sun. 'I don't think it matters if you did – not to me, anyway. But I'd like to know, for Mary's sake—'

Conor placed Eric's ring in a saucer beside her. 'Look at this,' he said, his voice different now – oddly flat. He was pointing at Mishti's old notice board, but it wasn't until Liv had put on her glasses that she saw something skewered to its frame with a drawing pin beneath the faded word 'Communition!'

A fifty-dollar bill.

'I found it yesterday evening,' he said.

'Did you?' Liv reached forward and unpinned the money. She stared at it for a moment, wondering how they'd all missed it, then stuffed it in her pocket. 'Well, that's good. We're going to need it.'

❧

It was a six-hour drive from Birdeye to the place south of Buffalo that was to be Sonny and Mishti's new home. Mary drove at a moderate speed; they picked up coffee near Albany, then stopped for a bite to eat – her treat – at a nice-looking independent deli off the Thruway once they'd cleared Utica. The day had brightened; the air seemed clearer, the sky more blue as they cruised west. Mary kept the radio on in the background: local stations, weather and jingles mainly, soothing or irritating – she couldn't decide which until Sonny complained that his legs were getting stiff and his brain was getting fried. So Mary pulled over again, and while he swapped seats with Mishti, she reminded herself that he would turn sixty-seven next year – catching up with her mother, almost – and she ought to make allowances. She had thought they would chat about the new work with recovering addicts that Sonny and Mishti would be doing, or the training they'd need, or that they would reminisce or question Mary about how things were going in

London. Instead, Sonny shut his eyes and Mishti stared out of the window, her usually mobile face slack and a little hollow around her eyes. It occurred to Mary then that they were angry with her for some reason. Weren't they supposed to be on her side? She shifted in her seat and glanced out of her window at the ribbon of parking lots and strip malls, drive-thrus and lumber yards. When she had been a small child, she used to think she had two mothers – Mishti and Liv. She remembered staring at their legs under the kitchen table: two short tan legs and two long creamy freckled ones. One time when Eric and Liv had taken her and Rose on a camping trip to the beach, Mishti and Sonny had stayed at Birdeye, and all the way, in the car, Mary had wished that Mishti was her real mom.

Now here she was, feeling guilty again, as if she were the one who had made Sonny and Mishti leave Liv and Rose behind.

⚜

Conor, Liv and Rose were browsing the party accessories aisle at the CVS pharmacy in Woodstock. They had already stopped at Crawford's Market to pick up chocolate, eggs, butter and confectioners' sugar, along with a couple of family-sized bags of potato chips, and Liv was getting anxious about money. The other day she had withdrawn the rest of what she needed for her tattoo, and she owed Jenna. She'd been relieved to see that the pickup still had plenty of gas.

'We gotta have balloons!' said Conor. He gave a rotating stand of greetings cards a gentle twirl.

'Balloons? You're not too keen on them, are you, Rose?' Rose, taut and watchful by the party tablecloths, didn't respond. Liv frowned and referred to her list. 'We could make paper streamers though – they'd look pretty with the fairy lights. We'll need sticky tape. And a sheet of nice card.'

'Invitations?' asked Conor, flicking through the multipacks. 'Kind of retro. I bet Dolores would like a proper invite.'

145

'No time,' said Liv. 'We'll do it in person. Eric and Dawn and the kids, Jenna and Cherry. We'll see Karin this afternoon. And maybe Jonathan will bring Dolores.'

'What about your neighbours – the family with the red truck?'

'The Kinneys? I don't think so. Anyway, that's fifteen of us by my count, and this stuff adds up.'

'I'm not being much help!' Conor held up a pack of candles – the sort that re-lit when you blew them out.

'Yes, you are.'

A thin teenaged girl in a long black sweater entered the aisle, a plastic basket over her arm, looking for something. Conor stepped aside, but Rose was standing in the way, shoulders forward, her arms clasped behind her back. The girl, who seemed familiar to Liv, hesitated as she noticed Rose, and before Liv could guide her daughter to one side, Rose had reached out and grasped the edge of her basket.

'Rose,' said Liv, gently, 'let go.'

The girl tried to pull away, but Rose's grip was tight. With a sudden frown, the girl let the handle slip from her arm and the basket spilled its contents at Rose's feet. Something smashed – a glass bottle with orange liquid inside it. Rose didn't move her legs, but she dropped the basket to the floor and raised her chin, lips tight, to peer over the shelves into the next aisle.

'I'm sorry,' the girl said, staring down, her eyes wide. Then, looking at Liv, 'But it wasn't my fault. I'm not paying for that.' Now Liv remembered where she'd seen her before – outside Mishti's school the previous week, asking for money.

'Are you okay, Rose?' asked Conor, moving forward and stooping down to remove a piece of glass from her shoe. Liv, distracted, turned to watch the girl who was already hurrying towards the exit, so she wasn't quick enough to catch Rose's hand before she gripped a handful of Conor's hair and yanked it up.

Conor didn't yell. He just crouched there, the white skin at his temples stretched tight, as if this had happened to him a dozen times before.

'No, Rose,' murmured Liv, as she tried to prise open her daughter's fingers without making things worse.

Once he was freed, Conor remained calmly squatting while he picked up the other dropped items. The tips of his ears had flushed a dark pink. It wasn't until after they'd alerted someone to the spillage and were leaving the store that he seemed to want to talk about it.

'She didn't scream,' he said. 'Like she did the other times.'

Liv nodded, taking her daughter's hand. 'You like to mix it up a little, don't you, Rose? You want to see how we'll react.'

The truth was that most visitors got their hair pulled if they stuck around long enough. Some even viewed it as a rite of passage – an initiation. She wondered if Conor would ask whether he had passed Rose's test. He didn't.

⚘

They spent the afternoon back at Birdeye, scrubbing the mildewed seed propagator with Bio Kleen, securing the chicken wire around the vegetable garden and making, on Conor's insistence, a piñata from a store bag puffed out with balled up pages from the *Catskill Times* and decorated all over with coloured paper hearts. It was focused work, but companionable, and Liv found herself relishing both the labour and the unhurried silences between them, as if they'd known each other for a longer time. She messaged a few people about the party, but it was only when she started to think about dinner that Conor, bending down near the kitchen door and petting Gunther, seemed to want to talk some more.

'Why is Rose frightened in the woods?' he asked.

Liv, who was easing her feet out of her thick soled boots, looked up and followed his gaze across the backyard. He was watching Rose as she paced steadily along the north-west perimeter, a good ten feet from the tree line. The sky above the valley had been clear all day, but the sun had dipped behind the mountains and the place was entirely in shadow. Liv's cheeks burned a little, yet the air had cooled, pooling in the hollows, warning of a freeze in the coming night.

'She doesn't like the wind, and it's always worse under the trees,' she answered, pushing away an image of Rose with her wrist bleeding, wet ribbons of hair across her face. Not that, she thought, and reached further back. 'We get some pretty wild storms. There was one big one, when the girls were eight or nine, must have been May or June. An awful gale whipped along the valley, roiling through the trees. Green boughs split and cracked – more terrifying than dead wood falling in winter. Pieces of scrap metal from Eric's stash were flying around outside, and a huge white oak in the front yard practically split in two. Part of it hit the porch. Rose crawled under the kitchen table. She wouldn't go in the woods after that.'

'I hated the wind, too, when I was a kid,' said Conor, quietly. 'Used to scream like hell when my hair blew across my face, so my mother got a shaver and buzzed it straight off.'

Liv kept her eyes on her daughter who was walking with her head on one side. Rose looked as if she were listening to their conversation, although of course she couldn't possibly hear it. 'Did you mind?'

'No,' said Conor. 'I mean, it showed me I could do something about it.' He straightened up. 'Are we going to have a Sharing tonight?'

Liv, taken by surprise, gave a sort of laugh. Once again, the sensation of being unmoored took hold of her; it was as if she were separating into different versions of herself – the strong Liv, the forgiving Liv, the youthful Liv. Where were Sonny and Mishti this evening? Were they ordering their dinner with Mary in some diner, or eating with strangers at the new place? They belonged at any Sharing, and she missed them in the way she missed Pinto, with a sharpness that reminded her to keep moving, to not stand still for fear of succumbing to something too dark, too unfathomable.

'Could do,' she said, reaching down for her slippers. 'I'll see if Karin can join us.'

AREA OF DETAIL #5

C ONOR TOOK THE cowbell and his copy of *The Attentive Heart* and sat down in the black chair while Liv was upstairs with Rose. Darkness had fallen, but he didn't turn on the lamps. Instead, he placed the bell by his feet and held his book up high to catch the light that shone in from the passageway.

He flicked to a page he had marked with his thumb and began to read aloud, softly - feeling the shapes of the words with his tongue and lips.

Something happens when a person lights a candle.

Parents set them in the window when a child is born or dies. We break bread and make love in their kind, forgiving glow. Children delight in a candle on a cake, and the ritual unites us with our sisters and our brothers of many faiths and none.

A candle is lit. The cowbell has called us, and we gather, eager or weary, upset or unthinking - we bring ourselves. The circle forms, people shift, gaps are closed. There are coughs and, at first, a few sideways glances. I lift Rose to my lap and rest my arms lightly around her. Mary sits on the floor, cross-legged, leaning against someone's shin. Our shadows settle. Silence. We are ready.

It is time to listen. It is time to speak.

'That's one of my favourite parts. It's beautiful, don't you think?'

Conor twisted round. Karin was there, leaning against the door frame, her green hair loose around her face.

'I didn't know you were behind me,' he said.

'Oh – I'm sorry.' Karin moved across the room and retrieved a blackened candle in its holder from the corner cupboard – the same one they'd used the week before. She set it in the middle of the floor and squatted to light it. 'I sometimes wish I could have been at one of those early Sharings. When there were more people.'

Conor pushed the book down between the chair arm and his thigh. 'We don't need more people. I don't know how anyone could share properly with a crowd.'

'Hmm.' Karin sat down on the floor, facing him, legs crossed so that Conor noticed how her wide hips creased up and pushed out sideways beneath her dungarees. He knew Karin had been coming to Birdeye for a while, but that she lived someplace else.

'You want a baby then, do you?' he asked.

Karin looked startled.

'You said, at the last Sharing,' he went on. 'You wanted to start a family.'

'Mmm. But my partner Alondra doesn't want to. She says there's enough medical intervention in our lives already. IVF, all those drugs to stimulate egg production – I mean, okay, it's a lot, but a new life is worth whatever it takes.'

Conor shrugged. 'That's one way of putting it.'

'Don't you think so?'

'I think the people who are already here matter more than something that's just in your head. But you want a baby. That's cool.'

Karin smiled, blushing, and picked at something on the rug. 'I know when I've ovulated. My temperature rises, and I can't think about anything else.'

Conor watched her for a moment. 'Like now?'

Karin smiled again, which made her cheeks and lips look a little shiny.

'Who do you look up to most?' he asked. 'Mishti, Sonny, or Liv?'

'That's a weird question. I know what you mean though – I admire them for sure. Mishti is so creative and empathetic. She gives the best hugs, seriously! Sonny – I have huge respect for him. He doesn't do "easy"' – her forefingers double-dipped air quotes – 'you know? But Liv . . .' She pulled her face into a frown, earnest, like a children's TV show host. 'She's the one I want to notice me, I guess.'

Conor leaned forward. *Does she notice you?* he wanted to ask, but there were noises on the stairs; Rose and Liv were coming. He leaned down and picked up the cowbell.

'You don't need to ring it – we're all here!' remarked Karin.

He shook it hard, just the same.

SHOULD YOU ENCOUNTER
A BEAR WHILST HIKING

KARIN SHARED FIRST.

'. . . I get so crabby with Alondra sometimes. She's always telling me I should go back to classes at New Palz in the fall. I mean, the Inclusive Christian Alliance would support me, for sure, and Alondra's mom can drop by, and she says her routine won't be affected, but there are more important things than a Bachelor of Arts. The weird thing is she says she doesn't mind when I come up here, which is amazing and I'm so blessed, but I don't always believe her, and then I think, well, if it's true, then why is she so keen to have me out of the apartment? It's insane, the way I over-analyse, and I guess we're doing okay as a couple, but I want us to become a *family*. I cannot imagine not being a mother, and hello, Alondra! I'm thirty-one. Conceiving is just going to get harder.'

Her words circled round and round the soft halo of candlelight, hovering above the real problem, hesitating. Liv, still feeling the strangeness of a Sharing without Mishti or Sonny, tried one final time to listen carefully, attentively. Karin wanted to have a baby, and Alondra didn't. This difficulty could be teased out over coffee, over the laundry, tomorrow or the next day, another time. The Sharing wasn't the place to ask questions – its purpose was one of unburdening. There had been so much unburdening, in this room, down the years. Liv exhaled slowly, aware of the gentle rise in her diaphragm, the sinking of her ribs. The darkness held her, as it always did, and the flame bound her to Karin, to Conor, and to Rose, who was quietly circumnavigating the ring of chairs. Her mind felt for words she wanted to say out loud. *In community. Communion. Communication. Communion.* That song Conor had liked hummed in her head: 'Calling Occupants of Interplanetary Craft'. A smile twitched on her lips; she touched her mouth to hide it.

The room around Liv had fallen silent. Conor crossed his legs. 'Thank you, Karin,' she murmured.

Rose was next in the circle, but she was already slipping out; half a minute later, the creaking floorboards indicated her movements on the landing upstairs. Liv, after an appropriate pause, turned her head.

'Conor?'

When his foot moved, her heart quickened a little. She had been waiting for him to speak, she realised. More so than for Karin.

'Oh,' he said. 'Sure. Well, I didn't take my turn the last time, and I'm glad I didn't, because I was still adjusting.' He paused, catching Liv's eye, and she didn't look away. 'I didn't know what to expect, and it's pretty quiet here, right? I'm not used to quiet. Not the Catskills kind, anyhow. Then this morning I felt mad – like, totally freaking mad when Sonny said I'd taken Mary's fifty dollars, and I thought fuck you because it wasn't fair. My mom used to jack every store in Rockaway Park exactly because no one expected any different. Anyway, I was glad to leave Birdeye at first, but then I got to Kingston and I thought, don't do that, so I came back, because okay you guys have your own shit going on, but this place has got to me, and you should know, Liv, it's because of you.'

He dropped his gaze, finally, and stared down at his hands. Liv resisted the temptation to touch his arm. There was more Conor needed to share, she believed – she was ready for more – but this was a breakthrough, surely.

Conor's shoulders had slumped. 'You *noticed* me,' he finished. 'I'm so grateful for that.'

Karin made a sharp noise in her throat, but Liv waited, honouring the disclosure.

After a short while he leaned back. 'Your turn,' he murmured, once again looking directly at her.

Liv felt her stomach flutter. Her legs felt jittery as a child's. Conor had fired her up, in a way she'd not felt for a long time. Earlier she had thought she would tell a story, perhaps the story of how she had first come to this house with her babies, with Eric, with Sonny and Mishti, back when Birdeye was a half-formed dream. She didn't want to look back, though – not now. Seized by a sudden impulse, she leaned forward and grasped one each of Conor's and Karin's hands.

'Reborn,' she said, firmly. 'That's how I feel. I was knocked so low by the last Sharing. I was angry, I was bitter. But tonight – with you two here, I feel hope.' She thought of Mishti and Sonny in Mary's car as it disappeared down the track. 'Change is hard, but maybe some people are meant to move on. Birdeye still has work to do. We can keep our hearts open. We can welcome strangers and be a place not just of solace and acceptance but also green shoots and renewal.' She tasted the old words on her tongue, spat out the dust; they were words she thought she had lost beneath the compromises and the weary silences and the long winter almost past. She rose to her feet, pulling Conor and Karin with her, reading, in their surprised expressions, a lack of guile she now craved. 'This is Birdeye,' she said, to make it real and stop it fading into the shadows. 'This is us.'

That night, Liv dreamed she met a bear. It was sturdy and dark and when she saw it in the woods it turned its head and stared at her for a long time. She couldn't move. She wanted to, but she was frozen, like Mary's face over a weak connection. After a while it grew bigger, or she moved closer, and she saw the dirt and bugs and pine needles in its fur. She saw its claws. She saw surprise in its black eyes.

A noise downstairs woke Liv. She was still sleeping in the attic, but she heard voices murmuring, and the screen door's bounce. Karin and Conor had stayed up late, she knew, and now Karin was going home. Liv stared at the ceiling for a while, to steady her breathing.

Mishti, she reckoned, would have something to say about a dream with a bear in it. Mishti was good at telling people what they wanted to hear. You whispered your dream and she'd say, 'Oh that's so sad, you must be lonely,' or 'you should talk to your friend,' or 'come here, you need a bear hug!' and the person with the dream would think she had interpreted it just right. Liv had heard Mishti's shtick so often she could administer it to herself.

Outside the branches of the trees creaked and clacked and a thin rain pattered against the round attic window. The burning she'd felt at the Sharing had cooled a little, but you had to feed a fire, and that took skill, as well as hope.

She flipped her pillow over and went back to sleep.

NO CARCASS-EATERS HERE

'HEY, LIV!'

Conor's voice. It took Liv a moment to realise he wasn't in the attic bedroom with her.

'Some guy's here!' He was calling from the stairs outside her door.

She swung her legs over the side of the mattress. She couldn't use her left shoulder – not yet. Sometimes it took ten minutes of coaxing and manipulating and wincing to get it moving. She rolled herself upright and checked her phone, noting 8.52 a.m. with dismay.

'Where's Rose?' she called out. 'Is she up already? Is she okay?'

There were no messages. Nothing from Mary or Sonny or Mishti.

When Liv got herself downstairs, she glimpsed Rose on the porch in her nightdress and, beyond her, a gleaming white SUV. She pulled Rose's padded coat from its hook and stepped outside as Conor appeared beside her, dressed in his t-shirt and jeans. The air was cool and damp, and the river seemed loud. It must have rained a lot in the night.

'Hello, Liv,' said Jeff Zimet, touching the brim of his woollen cap. Jeff was Apollonia's long-standing Town Supervisor. Super Jeff, Jenna called him. He had been resting his ample rear on the bonnet of his vehicle, and although he stood up straight when Liv appeared, there was no urgency in his movement. 'Is that jacket for your daughter? Kind of chilly out here this morning. I apologise for disturbing you. That young man,' he nodded in the direction of Conor, 'said I should wait.'

Liv draped the coat across Rose's shoulders. Jeff cultivated the appearance of a relaxed man, a peacemaker, but he could also be a little pompous. Theatrical, as Mishti put it.

'It's early,' she said, aware that she was still in the threadbare leggings and sweat top she had slept in. 'What's the problem?'

'Ah!' said Jeff. He pulled a dog biscuit from the pocket of his padded jacket and squatted down to pet Gunther, who was slouching at the bottom of the steps, hips splayed. 'Who's an old boy, huh? I been hearing things about you. That you wander off unleashed, and do your business on other people's land—'

'Oh.' Liv felt a spike of irritation. 'The Kinneys.'

'Now Liv, I'm not going to say where the complaint originated, but an item has been raised for Thursday's Town Board and I'm advising you to get along.' Jeff stood up, and his soft blue eyes did their best to look concerned. 'No one wants to get a fine. You got to keep him leashed. If he starts harassing deer, on top of folk's concerns about public hygiene—'

'She rescued him,' interrupted Conor. 'She took him off the mountain. She chips them. Gets their jabs.'

Rose had walked off around the side of the house. Liv gestured after her. 'Will you go with Rose, please?' she said.

Conor nodded and did as he was asked, though she noticed he had his phone in his hand. Gunther stood up and followed them.

Jeff was smiling again, his soft chins pushing into his neck above his collar. 'You should be careful who you invite in,' he said, speaking just loud enough for Liv to hear him. 'There's been a spate of break-ins along Pine Road. When did he arrive? Where's he come from? I don't like that you don't take full ID.'

'It's a free country,' said Liv. 'When I last checked.'

'Now then, Liv, you know how it is. There's a groundswell. The Airbnb-ers mostly take ID, for everyone's sake, and we both know how people get opinionated, and they push small concerns together and start seeing them as one big problem. The Beautification Committee aren't happy about those mattresses you've left by the road.'

'This is ridiculous, right?' Liv resisted the urge to laugh.

'Well, you could just get along to the Town Board and set folks' minds at rest. Remember, no one wants to hand out fines. Have a good day now.' He fiddled with his cuff as he started back towards his car. His cell phone in a pouch attached to his belt bounced against his backside.

Liv waited as Jeff eased himself back into his vehicle. Mount Sheridan across the river was blotted with low cloud – soft clumps snagged its bare trees. She breathed in the moisture, then bent her knees and folded herself forward from the hips, dropping her arms and letting them swing to open up the space in her shoulders. Uttanasana. Rag doll pose.

'Fascist.'

Liv turned her head. Conor stood with Rose at the corner of the porch, staring after the SUV as it disappeared down the track. From upside down, the two of them looked shorter.

'He's not a fascist,' she said, pushing her knees back, feeling the stretch in her hamstrings. 'He thinks he's doing his job. It's my neighbours who made the complaint.'

'And that's okay with you?' Conor sounded a little disappointed, as if he had expected to find her raging or throwing rocks at Jeff's retreating vehicle. Liv, aware now of her sweat top slipping back along her spine and its implications for concealing what now marked her, put a hand on one of the porch supports and eased herself upright. She hadn't thought about her tattoo for a day or two. She hadn't thought about Pinto, and the realisation was as sharp as any grief.

'I meant what I said last night,' she said, as the blood rushed from her head. 'I am sixty-seven years old. I've screamed that word at protests. I've burnt a flag, I've marched in DC with my babies, over Vietnam, over civil rights, over the horrors we have inflicted on the world. But then I came here, and my life for the past forty-six years has been a house, a valley, a small community full of people like the Kinneys and Jeff Zimet and Dolores and Rose and myself. Connection, not conflict.' She was watching Conor, so she saw the odd look that passed across his face as she spoke – a kind of shuttered panic. Then it was gone.

'Don't you pull that old lady stunt on me,' he said. 'You were at Woodstock. We're gonna fire up that spirit of sixty-nine. I've got the playlist, and we,' he squeezed Rose's arm closer to his ribs, 'must be in heaven, man.'

Liv laughed then. Conor was alluring, for sure, but she also saw that while he wanted to dictate the mood and she was happy to be led, he was loosening. She didn't know what she was going to say to Mary or Mishti and Sonny when they returned, but she had him to herself for the rest of the day and she was ready to listen, if he was willing.

Rose, leaning in towards Conor at the bottom of the steps, looked away and prodded Gunther with her shoe.

Conor gave her a nudge. 'Time to party.'

AREA OF DETAIL #6

C ONOR SLIPPED INTO the study. He knew from his previous investigations that Sonny kept a cheap Bluetooth speaker tucked next to the computer keyboard; now he quickly synched his phone and found the Woodstock Music and Art Fair playlist. The speaker wasn't great, but he raised the volume and scrolled down to the final song in the long opening set.

As the guitar strumming rang in his ears, insistent, almost feverish, Conor glanced up at the shelves of records and mix-tapes, files and photo albums. Sonny hadn't been as thorough as everyone made out. Dates were missing, sometimes names. Conor had been through them all over the course of several nights; he'd seen what he needed to see.

'What's this?' called Liv, from upstairs.

'Richie Havens.' Conor paused, listening. 'Yeah, at this point he'd performed for three hours already. The roads around Bethel were all blocked and no one else could get through. Then he sang this: "Freedom" spliced with "Motherless Child". You were there! Everyone stood up. Don't you remember?'

'No, I don't remember.' Liv and Rose's footsteps sounded on the stairs. 'It's so long ago. Just á blur, frankly – visitors often ask. You know more than I do.'

'*Communition!*' murmured Conor, taking a last look around the study. He pulled one of Sonny's cookery books from a pile next to the desk and used it to prop open the door.

PLEASE ENTER THROUGH
THE OTHER DOOR

MARY SAT AT the corner table in the coffee shop and took in the view beyond the window. If she leaned to her left, she could see a sliver of Lake Erie between the buildings, but she preferred to watch the electric street sweeper making its way along the broad sidewalk opposite. The vehicle looked like a giant bug's eye, and the woman inside seemed intent on her work, peering forward, using her mirrors. A small park lay on the far side behind a low wall, and she wondered if the sweeper would enter, but it didn't.

The day was breezy, with a weak sun that came and went between the clouds. Mary hadn't taken off her coat because the walk from the car had chilled her, and her order of decaf americano and tofu scramble was yet to arrive. When the sweeper had passed out of sight she checked her phone, scrolling through emails, most of which waved the red 'urgent' flag. A knuckle of anxiety pressed down on her chest. There would be a cost, she knew, if she took a leave of absence, as was her right, as per the bland message from HR. You had to set these things up carefully, reassure clients, weigh the risk of colleagues moving in. 'Eat what you kill,' they called it, yet she couldn't look away from what was taking place at Birdeye. She needed to be strategic on both sides of the Atlantic. Sonny and Mishti would be gone for at least an hour. First, she'd phone her mother.

It took several rings before she heard Liv's voice say, 'Hello, you.'

'Mom,' she said, briefly closing her eyes. 'How are you? How's Rose?'

'Good! Pretty good.' Liv sounded out of breath. 'Busy. We're moving the seedlings down to the porch.'

'Is Karin there with you?'

A pause. Enough to hear music playing in the background – some kind of growly woman's voice, which probably meant Liv was in the pickup listening to the radio.

'You're not driving, are you, Mom?'

'No! And yes, Karin was here last night. Please don't ask me whether I've remembered Rose's pills.' Something clattered – a saucepan, maybe. 'It's going to be a good summer, Mary. We'll adapt. I'm getting on top of the veggie garden, and I've been thinking – I might set up a website or a blog to celebrate what we do. Should have done it years ago. I want to get some young people back in, now that Sonny and Mishti's rooms are going to be vacant. How is it up there? Are they okay? Happy with everything?'

Mary waved at the teenage girl who was bringing over her coffee. Her mom sounded a little hyper, but she was probably working through the things that had been said in the kitchen before they'd left. Being told about Conor's pilfering must have been hurtful, so Liv didn't need to hear about how Mishti had had a wobble and started crying when Mary had driven off to her hotel for the night, or that Sonny seemed a little vulnerable, his face grey as he fussed about the whereabouts of the fuse box in their new accommodation. The place had seemed nice, to Mary – clean and well-furnished and bright – but she knew brother and sister well enough to see that this was exactly the problem. She'd been as surprised as anyone by their decision to leave Birdeye, and now she wondered if they were having second thoughts. In her opinion, they were being brave, because leaving was always hard. It also helped her make her case to her mother.

'Everything's fine, Mom. But listen. We're going to have to come home tomorrow morning, instead of tonight. Sonny and Mishti have been invited to eat with some of the people they'll be supporting – some kind of goodwill supper fundraiser thing . . .'

'Okay,' said Liv.

Mary frowned. 'You mean you're really okay with that? We should be down in time for a late lunch. I know it's our birthdays—'

'It's fine! I'm planning a celebration. I'll have more time to get things ready.'

'A celebration,' repeated Mary. It was almost as if Liv were glad that she wouldn't be home that night, which was good, she supposed, if she remained objective about it. Mary felt most secure about her feelings for her mother when they were separated, usually by an ocean.

'A little party – Eric and Dawn, Dolores and Jonathan – you know.' A pause. 'One, two, three, lots . . .'

'That sounds nice.' Mary's gaze wandered back to the street outside. A couple of thirty-ish men in roll-neck sweaters had stopped at the ATM next to the coffee shop. While one looked down at his phone, the other placed his hand on his partner's midriff and moved it in small circles as he turned to face the street. The casual intimacy, the way they didn't even look at each other in their physical connection made a space open up in Mary's belly. She caught her breath, filled with a sudden jealousy. This was something other people did – colleagues, friends, even Mishti and Sonny who touched each other all the time without thinking. She thought of GlennNevis66's image sitting in her phone, but intimacy wasn't something she could order. Boyfriends, over the years, had been few and far between. As she grew older, most men – well, the single ones – irritated her.

'Mary? Are you still there?' Liv sounded far away, and the music she was listening to seemed closer. 'I've got to go – but I hope you have a safe drive down tomorrow. Take it easy.'

Take it easy. Such a thoughtless phrase – one that didn't suit her mother. After she'd hung up, Mary called the server over.

'I ordered the tofu,' she said.

'Oh sure, I'll just go find it. Hey, your accent – are you British?'

Mary picked up her phone and flicked to her emails. She didn't feel like explaining.

Liv and Conor worked steadily all that morning: physical work that, along with the music, produced sufficient endorphins to keep Liv's aches at bay. They raked the backyard and rubbed the scum off the plastic chairs on the front porch and, when a warmish sun broke through, they opened windows, shook out rugs full of dog hair and swept the downstairs rooms. Rose seemed to enjoy the activity and hovered close to Conor, once or twice plucking at his shirt so that he and Liv exchanged looks of pretend surprise. Rose's liking for Conor was becoming obvious. She had fallen for a number of visitors over the years, and Liv, as always, was alert to her daughter's state of candid hyper-vigilance. She viewed Rose's longings, whatever they might be, as a matter for her attention, but not her action. Her daughter's feelings were her daughter's feelings, Liv's own heart notwithstanding.

By early afternoon Liv was ready for a break, and when she and Rose visited the downstairs bathroom, she sat there for a while and listened to Conor's music. A woman's voice, sad and insistent, seeped through the door.

Rose lifted her chin and looked out of the narrow window.

'Joan Baez!' called Conor, from the yard, but Liv had to admit that while she was familiar with the music, she had little recollection of the actual concert at Yasgur's Farm. She could barely remember the stage across the teeming hillside.

Anyway, she mused, by that first night she was already pregnant, or at least, there was nothing she could do to stop it. She had been so English, back then when she'd been bursting to escape. She'd sat her A-levels that June, then she'd flown to New York on a brand-new passport the month she turned eighteen to start her real life at Camp Pine Crest. She had known it would be wonderful, before she'd heard of Woodstock, or the counterculture, or conceived her twins with a stranger who called himself Otis one humid August afternoon. She was pretty sure Otis wasn't his real name – he seemed more like a Todd or a Jerry – but she liked the way it sounded, and she'd hitched a lift in his bus, and he'd looped his tanned arm around her shoulders and steered with one hand all the way to Sullivan County. Otis hadn't been much of a talker; instead, he'd watched her with his wide hazel eyes as they did it on the back seat of his bus parked up on a verge outside of Bethel. Liv had pushed her head back to peep beneath the curtain and saw helicopters criss-crossing the blue sky when he came. His tongue had tasted of peanut butter, and afterwards he gave her his sunglasses. Then she'd clambered down the steps and followed the crowds past the lines of cars to a gap in the fence and a life she couldn't yet imagine. She never saw Otis again, but she wore those sunglasses for the rest of the weekend, screaming at distant figures on the stage and hunkering in the rain, popping amyl nitrate and staring at all the cats and the dudes through those round green lenses.

❧

Conor was standing in the kitchen when Liv entered with Rose. His pale hands were covered in dirt and in the hair above his ear she saw the sticky remnants of a spider's web.

'Uh-oh,' she said, reaching forward to brush it out. 'You've got a look on your face. What's the matter?'

'You could leave Rose with me. You know, when you need some personal time.' Conor was blushing in the hollows beneath his cheekbones.

'I don't take her with me to the bathroom because I'm forced to,' she said. 'You follow me in, don't you, Birdie? Always have.'

'O-kay.'

'Cup of tea?' Liv took three mugs from the rack and removed the lid from the teapot, but Rose was already wandering out again. She lowered her voice. 'If you must know, I used to encourage it. Rose always had problems with her digestion. I believe the more she saw me – she saw it was normal, this stuff coming out of her body. I wanted to stop her being frightened of it. It was even more important when she started menstruating. She'd see me bleeding – Mary too – and using tampons and towels and all that – god, I don't miss it – but you know.'

'That's another thing you didn't put in your book,' said Conor, opening the fridge door and taking out the oat milk. Watching him do this made Liv feel oddly happy; it meant he felt at home.

'No,' she said, laughing. 'I guess I didn't. Are you hungry? Do we have any peanut butter?'

WHEN THE SKEWER
COMES OUT CLEAN

L IV'S BAKING SKILLS were rusty, but with Sonny away from Birdeye, she decided to tackle a cake for her girls. Sonny was better at it, though honestly, she was sick of his signature courgette and cardamom muffins or something clever with saffron, so she'd chosen a devil's food cake with three layers and plenty of chocolate frosting.

It was early evening, and the lights were on in the kitchen as she peered at the recipe she'd torn from a *Martha Stewart Living* magazine in an oncologist's waiting room a decade before. Rose was pacing her path around the parlour, and Gunther lay beneath the table, a heap of shaggy fur, his twitching nose the only sign that he was still alive. Conor, meanwhile, had offered to walk along to the liquor store with the last of the cash for a couple of bottles of Californian merlot that she thought Eric and Mary both liked. As he walked out, she had tossed him the keys to the pickup.

'I don't have insurance,' he told her.

'I won't tell if you won't,' she replied, hoping he saw this as a sign of trust, which he was owed. She knew she was strengthening the conspiracy between them, going against Mary, shutting Sonny and Mishti out. This was what it would be like from now on, she told herself. Conor – along with others too, she hoped – sharing the load.

Nevertheless, when Conor returned over an hour later, Liv masked her relief with a joke.

'Thought you'd done a runner!'

'Done a runner ...' Conor raised an eyebrow at her Englishness, though she knew he knew what she meant. He leaned in and ran his finger around the edge of the bowl with the frosting. 'I saw that girl – the one from the drugstore yesterday. Winter. She needed a lift. And some cash.'

'You didn't give her—'

'I didn't give her anything. She was high.' He hesitated. 'But I did invite her to the party tomorrow. She said she knew you. That's okay, isn't it?'

'Well—'

'Well, you tried to help her before, outside of Mishti's school.'

Liv nodded. She was letting things happen, today. It was what she wanted. There were some words in the Bible that Liv's grandfather had read out at her parents' memorial service and Karin had recited more than once at a Sharing. Liv had stopped believing in a god at boarding school, and Birdeye was built on the acceptance of no faith and all faiths, if practised humbly, and with love. Nevertheless, she'd always liked the yin and yang of the verse that came back to her now, as the light faded, and the kitchen filled with the smell of baking sponge, and Rose paced quietly through a pale filter of confectioners' sugar that made the air taste sweet on the tongue. '*A time to search and a time to give up, a time to keep and a time to throw away, a time to tear and a time to mend,*' and some other words about harvesting and dying.

'That day you arrived . . . why all that talk of burial places and memorials?' she asked. 'These things are always important, but you were making a point.'

Conor finished licking his finger, then hitched himself up onto the counter beside the fridge so that his stockinged feet dangled.

'My dad killed himself. Drowned. I don't really remember, I was too young, but I know they didn't recover his body. Just his sneakers that he'd left on the bridge. I mean, why would you take off your sneakers?' He paused. 'They hardly searched for him at all, which was super-hard on my mom.'

Liv thought about how her own parents had never been found, either. 'Oh Conor – I'm so sorry to hear that.'

'Yeah.' Conor's heel bumped against the cupboard door, soft and repetitive. 'No grave, right? I mean, say my mom dies. There'd be flowers, right? A memorial book, speeches. A fucking *mega* casket. You can get pre-payment. I don't want anyone to forget her.'

Liv looked down at the spoon and the well she had made in the bowl of dark frosting. She'd dug a grave herself, once, for Mishti and Sonny's baby. A long time ago now, but the image of that pitiful hole had never faded. It hadn't been deep enough. It could never be deep enough. She turned towards the sink, to hide her face.

'Well, I hope she's with you for a long time yet,' she said. 'But thinking about what matters to you – that's a kind of healing. Tell me about your dad.'

'He was a soldier – joined up straight out of high school. Tank operator. First Infantry. He fought in the Gulf War, bulldozed enemy lines – the whole nine yards. But he got that illness, Gulf War syndrome, and he was tired all the time, my mom says. He got the shakes, the shits, he couldn't sleep . . . He got a medical discharge.'

'Before he knew your mom?'

'Yeah. They met at some protest. She was super-radical, she showed him how war had fucked him – fucked the world.'

'And then they had you.'

'After my sister.' He held his breath in for a second. 'Shenandoah.'

Liv pulled out a chair and sat down. A wave of heat passed up her spine and spread across her shoulders, chest and neck, prickling like the hot flushes she remembered from twenty years before. There were aspects of his story that already seemed familiar, but the name – oh that name, Shenandoah – that was no coincidence.

'We had some trouble, once,' she murmured, feeling the words in her mouth, the deceptive simplicity of them. 'With a couple like your parents. Nearly destroyed us.'

'Oh yeah?' Conor's voice was bright, needling. 'I mean, was it like a takeover?' He leaned forward and Liv knew then that she had reached a place of shift. There were others in the room besides her daughter and this young man. Those shades of herself that had drifted off for a while were whispering at her shoulder, as if they'd known all along. He was the right age, and the way his forehead crinkled – she'd seen a frown like that before. She and Rose were exposed with him in the house, but she needed to stay calm; she needed to find out what he wanted.

'Is this my story, or yours?' she asked, looking up.

Conor said nothing, for a minute. His foot hung still, and when he did speak his tone had changed.

'You tell it.'

⁂

It had been a long, dry summer. Leaves had curled and browned too early and during the last week of August a faint pall from the wildfires on Long Island was visible from the top of Slide. Liv was still getting used to the departure of Mary, then Eric, but she and Sonny and Mishti were old hands at communal living. They could manage the shifting tide of visitors, or at least, they thought so. Evening meals and the twice-weekly Sharings were points of unity, and if someone didn't feel like working at the flea market in Woodstock or on the farm stand or in the kitchen, well, this was usually a prelude to them deciding to move on. Only the long-time Birdeyers slept in the house by that stage – Liv, Sonny, Mishti and Rose, along with a few others who'd been around for a while and whom Rose had come to know. Yet the community as a whole had grown big that year – over thirty people, by late July. There hadn't been enough work, or not the kind of work that young visitors wanted to do, so they hung out on the porch or in the donkey barn or in the huddle of tents they'd set up under the trees, keeping cool and getting high in the shade and watching the OJ trial live on someone's portable TV with a cable that snaked all the way down to the kitchen window. That was when Wren and Tyler showed up with their little girl, Shenandoah. Liv hardly noticed them at first. They blended in with their long hair and their sun-bleached clothes, but when Liv discovered that Wren and Tyler had another baby on the way, she waived the rules and gave them her bedroom at the back of the house.

Once they were more visible, Liv began to worry. Tyler suffered from stomach cramps. He had nightmares, and often shouted in the small hours, or prowled the woods, filming stuff on his hand-held camcorder. Shenandoah was a sweet thing, with a moon face and soft hair, but Wren seemed wary, hyper-alert, carrying her solemn daughter about on her hip, dressing in those cut-off vest tops and stretchy pants with her belly sticking out, tight and shiny. Her cheeks were gaunt and her arms too thin. She and Shenandoah didn't eat dairy, but she refused any food not grown at Birdeye, saying that Tyler was proof of the danger of chemicals, and farming was a government conspiracy with genetically modified crops entering the food chain undetected. That was all Liv could get out of her. She drifted away when Liv tried to talk, always finding somewhere else she needed to be.

'She's frightened for her baby,' Mishti told her, and Liv was glad to know that Wren was confiding in someone.

Labour Day came and went, but this year, for some reason, only a few people packed up and left. Liv never wanted to tell visitors to go, but the house was rapidly running out of food, so Sonny called a backyard meeting to ensure everyone understood the situation.

The whole community sat on the parched grass in the clear September light, picking at pine needles, waiting for the last few to join them. Looking at their faces, Liv, for the first time, sensed a shift in the collective mood – an unease, an indirectness of gaze. Then, as she and Sonny stepped forward to speak, Wren opened the bedroom window above them and leaned out.

'They are the self-appointed hierarchy,' she announced, pointing down. 'They're going to try to make us all leave, but we're not going anywhere, right? If you want to stay and overthrow the status quo, raise your hand now.'

Liv almost laughed with astonishment, then let her mouth hang open as everyone but Sonny put up their hand. Even Mishti, her bangles tinkling as she avoided Liv's perplexed gaze. In an instant, things had changed. Liv stared at her friend and wondered what she'd done to deserve such a betrayal.

That night, the Sharing was chaotic. Liv tried to re-establish the safe space within the circle – Sonny too – but again Wren hijacked proceedings and challenged everyone to confront anything they'd been too afraid to say before. People stood up in the evening gloom and spoke out of turn as they voiced their grievances about the organisation of work, about who camped and who didn't, and most of all, the way Liv controlled them through access to her inner circle. Their words rained like hammer blows inside Liv's head. Wren and Tyler, it seemed, had done the groundwork, moving among the campers, suggesting conflicts that hadn't existed, spreading discontent. Wren had been particularly skilled at discovering each person's weakness, so that now she could exploit it.

Liv should have been more decisive, of course, but clever Wren had found Liv's own source of anxiety and used it against her. She said that Liv had placed herself at the centre of things at Birdeye. Liv was the leader, and she fed on other people's insecurities. Their vulnerability was the source of her authority and her power. Shamed publicly for an ego that was – apparently – out of control, Liv tried to calm things down through accommodation, through a promise that she was listening. There were endless votes, angry factions as Wren accused individuals of revealing only what they could bear. Even Sonny was torn. Liv guessed Wren had something on Mishti, but Mishti just kept saying she wanted peace to be restored. Birdeye was being turned on its head, destroyed; so, after three days of madness, Liv told Wren that she was going to assert her rights as the legal owner.

'You can't,' said Wren. 'I know Mishti's little secret. If certain people heard, it would look pretty bad. You don't want to lose your guardianship of Rose.'

It was absurd, looking back. Wren had no proof of anything, but Liv's fear made her powerless.

All these events happened in the space of a few days, yet at the time it felt much longer. The dry spell ended when a low front moved up from the south-west, with a tugging wind in the treetops and rain that fell in sudden bursts, as if to catch them out. The campers darted across the yard, picking up sticks and rocks to secure the sides of their tents, or huddled on the dripping porch. Liv went about her tasks as though with every step she might tread on a tripwire. Increasingly she confined herself to the house where she watched Sonny and Mishti through a mist, realising they, too, had been trapped. Rose, meanwhile, was deeply disturbed by the changes around her. She was twenty-five years old, similar in age to the majority of visitors. Community living had worked for her when she could move freely, then retreat to a room where she could pace quietly as she needed to. Now though, as tensions rose, she didn't scream, or hit out. Instead, she stopped eating, stopped going to the toilet, and picked at a scab inside her nostril that became infected. Then, on that last morning, Wren, according to Mishti, caught Rose reaching out to touch Shenandoah's soft hair. Something must have switched in her, because she took Rose into the woods, past the tents with their flapping fly sheets, up towards a dense canopy of white oak and beech with the wind roaring through the high branches. No one saw whether Rose was cajoled or dragged, but perhaps her terror made her compliant. Fortunately, someone told Mishti, and Mishti ran to fetch Liv, who was hanging laundry in the donkey barn. Sonny helped them search, but still it was two frantic hours before they found Rose stumbling through a stream, covered in scratches, soaked through and blank-eyed. A length of nylon guy rope trailed from a loop around her wrist, and the skin beneath was red and bleeding. Rose couldn't speak about what had happened, but it made no difference. Liv knew that Wren had tied her daughter to a tree and left her.

The kitchen had fallen silent.

Liv kept her eyes squeezed shut, her head in her hands. She had never forgotten the sight of her own hurt child, but now other details seemed to rush at her: the dead leaves in the gutters, the overflowing septic tank, Tyler at the top of the stairs wearing fatigues Sharpied with anti-war slogans, and Wren's swollen belly, with its blue veins beneath near-translucent skin, as if she'd been the embryo.

'So, how'd you get rid of them?'

'What?' Liv looked up. Conor was still sitting on the countertop.

'I said, how did you get rid of them? You know – my parents?'

Liv traced one of the faded wood-block paisley patterns in the tablecloth with her finger. Rose, she realised, had wandered into the kitchen and was hovering behind her. She didn't want Rose to hear, but it was too late now. She had to finish it.

'I picked up the telephone and called Eric and then I called the police department. The cops came eventually, but by then Wren had driven off with Shenandoah and Tyler in the pickup. Eric went after them, and when he found them pulled up in Tanners Ridge, he hauled Tyler out and broke four of his ribs.'

'That's a bitch!' Conor slammed his heel against the cupboard so that Rose's chin jerked out and her hands opened wide like two starfish.

As Liv stood up and reached for her daughter, she realised she was trembling. Her shame about that time, about her own weakness, was a dark lake inside her. She had been led to this confession by a stranger whom she had welcomed but who turned out to be Wren and Tyler's child. He hadn't lied to her; it was her fault for not asking the right questions. She had no right to be afraid.

'What happened to Wren?' she asked, taking Rose's hand. 'To – your mom?'

'You know what happened.' Conor's voice had flattened now, all the anticipation spent. 'She had me, and straight after was put in a mental hospital for months. Pumped with all the drugs she hated. Dad couldn't cope – he had his own sickness. When I was four, he jumped off the Williamsburg Bridge. Shenandoah disappeared a few years later. She was only eleven years old. Mom – she was – she's not been sober since.'

'Conor.' Liv stepped towards him, helpless, needing to connect.

He shook his head. 'Don't say sorry. Don't you ever tell me you're sorry. I used to hate you for not helping them, for the empty words in your book, but then I came here, and I met you and now I think maybe it had to be this way.' His tone was level, yet his eyes seemed to plead, glittering, as he stared at Liv across the table. 'You kept Rose.'

⚜

Liv tried to focus on Rose as she helped her get ready for bed. She was cleaning her daughter's teeth in the bathroom, opening her own mouth wide to encourage Rose to do the same, when she caught sight of herself in the mirror and saw tears shining on her face.

There were no sounds from downstairs. Maybe Conor had gone. She wasn't sure how she'd feel if he had. She wasn't afraid, she told herself. Rather, it was as if a torch had been flashed in her eyes, and now all she could see was the afterimage. He was Wren's son. Wren the disruptor – yes – the manipulator – an alcoholic now, a widow, a woman who had lost her child.

'Shit,' she said. 'Shit and bugger.' She wiped her eyes on Rose's flannel, then leaned forward and rested her brow against Rose's collarbone. 'You like Conor, don't you?' she whispered, before listening some more. After a few moments she became aware of a light pressure on her back, and although Rose was probably just putting her hand somewhere, it could almost have been a hug.

After Rose was settled and Liv had blown her a kiss and turned out her bedroom light, she went downstairs. Conor hadn't gone; he was sitting on the floor of the study. He didn't say anything. He was pulling out the old photos: Sonny's Polaroids; snaps gifted by visitors; the annual birthday shots of cake and candles and bright, blurry smiles. When she knelt beside him, she noticed how he knew exactly which album to open. She watched his hunched shoulders, his pale hands brushing stray dog hairs off the pages and, when he twisted his head, the tendon at the side of his neck that stood out in sharp relief. The body was a marvellous thing, and terrifying, the way it stretched and flexed and held everything together. She skated over the faces in the images Conor showed her, and instead focused on the way an arm dangled or a spine curved. All that energy, all that vigour. She felt empty.

'Here,' said Conor, pointing to a man, Tyler, in combat trousers and an open, flapping shirt. He was holding up a hooked gaff pole, pretending to take aim, lining up his target in his sights. In another photo the same man carried a small child on his shoulders. The child was pushing her lips together, and Liv knew it was Shenandoah; she'd had a sad face, except when she was trying to whistle. In a third he was bunched up with several other people, including Mishti, and next to her stood a narrow-hipped, white-skinned woman who stared directly at the camera. Wren. The group were sheltering under a tarpaulin beneath some trees, and it looked like it was raining.

'That's me,' Conor said, tapping on the woman's protruding belly.

Liv leaned forward and pulled the photograph out of its little corner pockets. Wren had called a meeting outside, she remembered, in the middle of a downpour. She had declared the house a toxic environment and said that all decisions needed to be taken on neutral territory.

'Keep those. They're yours.' She flipped over the picture in her hand. *Sept '95*, Sonny had written. *Mishti and Wren*.

Conor read it too. 'I guess you don't want me to stay now.'

Liv laid the photograph down. She tried to imagine what he was thinking, as he sat with legs stretched out next to the woman who he believed had failed his family; the woman who had not been attentive, who let things implode. Where did he put his hurt? She thought about his tenderness with Rose, his way of waiting for her, as if he knew he had plenty of time. Perhaps they needed to strip things back – right back in order to move forward.

'You said you used to hate me. Is there anything else you've not told me?' she asked.

Conor closed the album. 'I could ask you the same question. I mean, what was Mishti's secret?'

'Oh!' He didn't know then. For a moment Liv felt the urge to laugh. She'd told Conor nothing, not really, about her life here with Mishti and Sonny and Rose, about how she still loved Eric, about how her daughter Mary frightened her, or about how she could never regret getting rid of Wren and Tyler, but she guessed he knew this.

'Well, I still want you to stay,' she said, finally. 'There are things to unravel, to work through, but not tonight. I need to celebrate my daughters' birthdays tomorrow, and I need your help with that. I'll tell the others they made a mistake about the fifty dollars.'

Gunther whined, softly, from the kitchen.

'Will you tell them I'm Wren's son?'

'No. Well, not yet. It would just upset them.'

'Right.' Conor regarded her. 'But that's not in the spirit of the Sharing.'

Sharing. The word seemed loaded when Conor spoke it. A profound tiredness descended then, as if someone had flapped that sodden tarpaulin and it had fallen across Liv's shoulders. She wanted to lie down, but the journey up to her bed in the attic seemed more than she could manage.

IF NOT YOU – WHO?

MARY WAS THINKING about butter pecan as she swung the car onto the bridge that led to Dutchman's Road. She hadn't meant to be so distracted; the long journey back from Buffalo should have given her ample time to mull over her mother's intransigence, not to mention a tricky client who wasn't happy that Mary was out of town. But today was her birthday – Rose's too – and childhood memories bubbled up and eddied while Sonny slept beside her and Mishti behind them moved her lips as though incanting her thoughts. Out of the window, by the first rusting truss, she saw the spot where, aged six, she had dropped her chocolate cone among the pine needles. To stem her wails, Eric had given her his own. Butter pecan – a taste she'd all but forgotten. She wedged her left elbow against the window rim and ran her hand through her hair, like a college kid.

'Almost home,' murmured Mishti once they'd crossed the river. She reached forward and tapped on Sonny's shoulder until he grunted and pushed his feet back into his sandals. A pretty gift bag sat in Mishti's lap, full of plant-based treats for them all that Mary had paid for at a mini-mall in Utica. While brother and sister had visited the rest room, Mary had checked her messages and viewed the virtual greetings card from her personal assistant. The animation revealed balloons, a box on a doorstep, a puppy of some kind jumping out and yapping. *So sweet!* she had tapped out, before it had finished playing. *Thank you!* Nothing from GlennNevis66, of course. When Mary signed up for the dating app, she had given her birth month as August, instead of April, for security.

'We've got company,' said Sonny, frowning. He tugged at his seat belt where it pulled across his chest.

Mary squinted as sunlight flashed through the bare trees. Several vehicles sat parked up at the bottom of the track, including Eric's Silverado. As her car climbed towards the house, she leaned over the steering wheel and saw the banner greeting nailed to the side of the donkey barn. Eric and Dawn's kids, Cori and Harrison, were dutifully carrying plates of food up the porch steps, but the bright bunting hanging between the posts could not disguise the fact that the old house was sinking on its bones. Rose was on the swing set on the south side, and other figures were milling. When a young man turned towards her, Mary saw that it was Conor.

A rush of bitterness obliterated the butter pecan. She switched off the engine and pressed her fingers to her temples. Half the neighbourhood was here.

'Well played, Mom,' she muttered, as Liv hurried down the steps to greet her.

'What the hell is he doing here?' said Sonny, getting out of the car.

'Don't start,' mouthed Liv, walking round to Mary's side. She opened the car door. 'Happy Birthday!'

Mary didn't move. 'Don't tell me. You've *forgiven* him. You don't care how the rest of us might feel.'

'Of course I care! He didn't take the money. He found it and pinned it to the notice board. None of us saw it. You were all too busy accusing him.'

'Right.' Mary knew sarcasm was pointless, but it reined in her need to sob. This was all so horrible. She should never have gone to Buffalo. All she wanted was to move Rose to London where she could keep her safe, but Liv stood there like some stubborn relic.

'Mary, please,' said Liv. 'We've worked so hard. Your dad's here. Come and say hello.'

Mary felt Mishti's hand touch her shoulder. 'Conor can't cause trouble with all these people around. We'll talk it out later. You can do this – for Rose's sake.'

179

Mishti, the peacemaker. Mary pursed her mouth and pulled herself together. She'd deal with Conor once the wretched party was over. Until then, she wouldn't let him out of her sight.

⁂

It could be any gathering, any birthday lunch, served buffet-style so that Rose could wander. Liv stood in the hallway while Karin's girlfriend, Alondra, chatted about whether dogs could get dementia and the lateness of the spring this year and how it made them all a little sluggish. The morning had been still, mild. Earlier, as the fog cleared, Liv had stepped down to the river and found that the red maple was finally flowering for her girls, and the trout lilies were poking up their pointy fingers. Already it seemed like ages ago.

'She's not wagging her tail,' remarked Alondra, meaning Gunther. She twisted her head to look for Karin. 'I guess she's not a party animal?'

'He's a he,' said Liv, vaguely. She stared down at the plate of chilli rice in her hand and realised she was out of practice when it came to small talk; she'd forgotten how, when the house opened itself to guests, their sounds and glances and gestures seemed to fill every corner, every room. From the kitchen came Eric's slow laugh, the clink of crockery and cutlery, voices drifting in from the backyard through the open window. 'Sorry. Since his pal Pinto died, he's not been himself.'

Karin came out of the downstairs bathroom and moved past Rose, who was heading for the parlour. Liv watched to make sure her daughter could push open the door. Rose liked a celebration; she enjoyed a bit of fuss, but she needed time out, too. There'd be cake later, a few gifts, though the ten or so invited guests knew not to overwhelm her.

'Hi,' said Karin, giving Liv a hug.

'You look nice,' Liv responded, pulling away to admire Karin's shining face and clean white t-shirt.

Alondra raised two carefully stencilled eyebrows. 'She's been

180

working too hard. She does all the chores at home, she comes up here and does yours, and she takes care of me. She needs to relax sometimes.'

'Hey!' Karin looked embarrassed. 'It's my choice.'

Liv frowned. Where was Mary? Where was Conor? Jonathan was in the doorway of Mishti's snug – she could see his tall frame leaning in, but she couldn't see who was with him. Was it Dolores? She couldn't deal with her right now.

'Well, we must catch up properly, Karin,' she said. 'Maybe sit down with a coffee on Friday. But first I need to do that thing – cir-cu-late.' She left her plate on the hall stand behind Jonathan and escaped through the front door to the porch.

Outside, the pale sunlight on the pickup's windscreen made her scrunch up her eyes for a moment. As the door closed behind her, she took a deep breath – in through the nose, out through the mouth – willing her heartbeat to slow down and her agitation to subside. Her fingers twitched, reaching for a dog's ears to fondle.

Small feet pattered around the corner of the porch, and for a moment, Liv thought it was Pinto.

'We got you a gift!'

It was Cherry, Jenna's little girl. She was wearing a dress with a net skirt that stuck out and she had circles of rouge on her pudgy cheeks. Jenna appeared behind her, hair loose, make-up done.

'It's not *Liv's* birthday, Cherry! The gift is for Mary and Rose . . . some fancy soaps. Two each.'

'I don't like Rose,' said Cherry.

Jenna rolled her eyes. 'Go say hi to Dolores. She's inside some-where. You can bet she'll be right next to the potato chips.' As she held open the door for her daughter, she looked at Liv, appraisingly. 'Need something?'

Liv smiled, despite everything. 'Mary found my baggie.'

'Oh shit.'

'Kind of how I feel, now you mention it. We're not speaking.'

'Because you smoked a little grass? She's so uptight—'

'No! No, it's because I won't go to England, and she wants to organise things with Rose. But I've got a new person staying – you may have met him already. He's going to help me move this place on.' Liv recalled her daughter's look of disbelief as she told her that Conor hadn't stolen her fifty dollars. If Mary heard the story of Conor's original connection to Birdeye, she would assume he'd try to murder them in their beds. 'It's complicated.'

'Yet here you are, having us over, pretending you and Mary don't drive each other nuts.'

Liv walked to the corner and peered out towards the veggie garden where half a dozen figures had gathered. Conor was talking to the young woman who had dropped her basket in the pharmacy – Winter, he'd called her. When he saw Liv, he raised a hand and grinned, as if to say she needn't worry.

'I'm not pretending,' she said. 'I just don't know what to do about it.'

'Oh well, I do.' Jenna was smiling when Liv glanced back, but her words carried an edge. 'No more free rides for college dropouts. Hey, don't pull that snooty face at me! Why not let Mary organise you a little? It's what she's good at. You gotta pay your goddam bills.'

⁂

Every birthday, ever since the girls had turned three, Eric took Mary and Rose by the hand and made a speech in their honour. It used to make Mary blush and squirm with pleasure, and nowadays he liked to point out that it was one of the few 'dad' things he was still allowed to do. So, once the rice and the bean salad and the vegan dips were eaten and the plates stacked up in the kitchen, he found his girls and led them both to the south-facing side porch. Here, guests could gather beside his sculpture of the twins being born. Mary tolerated it, Liv knew, because she loved Eric and because Birdeye was a great distance from her London life. But as Liv watched her from between the heads of Cori and Harrison, she saw the strain pulling at her daughter's eyes and mouth. She had been driving for six hours, and as soon as she arrived, they'd had words. My Mary, she thought. It was surely exhausting to be always so careful with oneself.

'Good chilli rice,' murmured Sonny, stepping in beside her. 'Lots of seeds, though. I've got one stuck in my back tooth.'

'Well hello to you, too,' said Liv. She'd barely spoken to him since he arrived back, and she smiled to show her appreciation that he was reaching out to her. She'd missed him, she realised. Not just while he'd been in Buffalo, but maybe all winter. She leaned her head a little closer. 'Where's Mishti?'

Sonny sighed. 'She's gone to meditate.'

Liv turned and looked at him more carefully. 'You mean, she's up in the woods, crying. Oh, I'll have to go to her.' She made to walk away, but he touched her arm.

'No. Stay here for Eric and the girls. Mishti's fine – she's wiped, that's all. The trip was – well, it was quite the deal.'

She resisted the urge to say something mean. 'I'd like to hear about it. Later.'

'And I'd like to hear what's been going on with Conor.' Sonny nudged her softly with his elbow. 'Later.'

Liv craned her neck, looking round. There was Conor – he was walking towards Dolores with a chair. He seemed at ease, solicitous. She should stop worrying, she told herself. Sonny, she was relieved to observe, noticed too.

'Halloo!' called out Eric, through his cupped hands, as if addressing a crowd instead of a few neighbours. He waved at Liv to move forward and join him with their daughters on the porch. 'Get up here, Liv!'

Liv smiled and walked around behind Dawn and Jenna. Earlier she had wrapped Mary's prom photograph in its new frame and placed it on the study windowsill, in easy reach when the time came. Mary's gift for her sister had joined it.

Eric started to read from a scrap of paper he'd pulled from his shirt pocket as she slipped her hand through Rose's arm.

'This is one of my favourite days of the year,' he began, clearing his throat. And here are two of my favourite people: Rose and Mary.'

'Hey, whaddabout me?' heckled Dolores, prompting Rose to twist her neck.

Eric scratched his ear and continued. 'Well, I guess you all know I like to make stuff,' he nodded at the birth sculpture, as Karin gave it an affectionate pat, 'and I was wondering what to make for my girls this year. So I got to thinking about how, when they were teenagers, they both ran rings around me. Round and round, I swear, until I got dizzy. They were in cahoots, you might say, and, somehow, spinning rings seemed appropriate this year . . .'

Liv sucked in her breath. She'd forgotten to return Mary's ring. When Conor had pulled it off her finger, he'd put it in a saucer and she hadn't seen it since. 'Eric,' she whispered, but he put his finger to his lips, and she saw then that he was reaching into his plaid jacket and pulling out a bulkier object made of silvery metal. It wasn't a piece of jewellery; this was more the size of his fist, with a flat central disc and two thin rings held by pins around it.

'What's she got?' piped up Cherry, pulling on her mother's hand.

Eric gripped the object's pin axis between his thumb and forefinger, then pulled at a tag of string, yanking it hard until it unwound, and the inner disc began to spin. He set it on the porch rail, where it wobbled, then righted itself.

'It's a gyroscope,' said Mary, as others murmured in recognition. 'I've not seen one in years.'

As several others made approving noises, Rose smiled her wide smile, swung out her hand and knocked it to the floor.

'Don't worry, Rose.' Eric stooped to retrieve it, then placed it back on the rail. 'I made it sturdy, and I've got one for each of you. When it's spinning, see, it will always correct itself. The two gimbals provide corresponding input and output forces. It won't be tipped off course.'

'Like Birdeye,' murmured Liv, as she admired the craftsmanship.

Mary frowned. 'I think Dad meant, like *him* . . .'

'Hey.' Eric winked at Mary, then leaned in close to Liv's ear. 'You've got a gift for Mary too, don't you?' But Liv hesitated. It didn't feel like the right moment. The frame she had chosen for Mary now seemed old-fashioned, and when she handed it to her, and Mary pulled off the gift wrapping, she saw the flare of dismay in her face.

'It's second hand,' said Liv, quickly. 'Or pre-loved, as Mishti puts it. You can change it if you want to – put the photo in something smarter.'

'There's nothing wrong with the frame,' muttered Mary, although Liv saw how she tucked the wrapping back around it.

'What you got?' called Jenna, hitching Cherry up to see.

A sudden screech of feedback made them all jump as Jonathan switched on his bullhorn in the front yard. Eric grinned, then waved them all into singing 'Happy Birthday' to the pre-recorded big-band accompaniment. It was too much for Rose, who pulled away from Liv and moved indoors.

'Chrissakes!' complained Dolores, from her chair. 'Where's the cake?'

⸙

The party was winding down. Liv could feel the energy draining from the house as people said their farewells and Jonathan's bullhorn blasted a final encore. Only Gunther remained in the backyard, sitting lopsidedly on his haunches, his jaw slack like a zoned-out security guard.

Rose had chocolate frosting on her chin, so Liv steered her to the kitchen sink to wash it off.

'Birthday Birdie,' she murmured, savouring the feel of her daughter's long fingers through the soap suds. 'So beautiful, from the moment you were born.' She turned over one of Rose's hands and massaged her palm gently with one thumb. In truth, she couldn't remember much beyond the panic of those first minutes after the twins' births. Rose had been whisked away, and the wrench had been physical; she had howled, and then she had been sedated. But she did recall the day after. The nurses had been whispering at their station as the sun rose over the London skyline and the ward was flooded with light. Liv had asked if she could help wash her babies, and after a doctor had glanced at the cheap ring on her finger and wandered off without answering, a kindly midwife had wheeled her down to the nursery to see Mary. Support her head like this, she'd been told. Keep the umbilical stump dry. Rose, whose blood flow had been restricted, whose brain had been starved of oxygen so that she almost died, lay out of reach in an incubator; yet to eighteen-year-old Liv, who had never held an infant until she herself gave birth, her tiny daughters were two peas in a pod.

'Thanks for a great party,' said Alondra, coming in from the passageway and interrupting her reverie. 'Karin won't want to go before the place is cleared up, but I'm ready.'

Liv wiped her hands and turned around. 'Great to see you,' she said, giving her a quick embrace.

'She's always talking about you, you know?' Alondra stood back and pushed her lips out, as if calculating how much to say. 'Worships you, in point of fact. Make time for her, won't you? Soon.'

When Alondra had gone, Liv cast her mind back. Had there been another scare, or some additional test? Karin, she knew, often worried about Alondra's health. Liv, of all people, should have asked, but she couldn't keep up; right now, her head was throbbing with the strain of playing hostess. Mishti had absented herself, and Mary was no doubt fuming somewhere. At least Conor had pulled his weight. She could see him down the passageway, near the front door, leaning against the wall as he chatted with Winter.

Liv switched her gaze to the old notice board and the faint writing that Conor had remarked on the day he'd arrived, scrawled by some long-forgotten visitor. She stared at it for a moment, then walked over, rummaged in the mess on the counter for a stub of chalk and wrote 'Karin' near the bottom edge, as a reminder. Then she slid the last slice of devil's food cake into a bowl and carried it outside.

※

Mishti had never been a hiker. Her meditation circle was only a hundred yards above the house. She had chosen the spot after Wren and Tyler left, and Sonny had shifted some rocks to form a run of steps for her small feet and short legs. Liv, climbing through the trees and around boulders, had to adjust her long stride so as not to stumble. She'd not been up there for a while, she realised. Thin, sappy branches brushed her shoulders, and she rejoiced, once she had retrieved her glasses from her breast pocket, at the hundreds of green shoots now poking up through the leaf litter. This same tiny feat, she knew, was repeating and repeating across the slopes and hollows of the Catskills. It made her want to carry on climbing, to reach the moment of hiatus between house and chores and people, and that upper realm of forest and mountain where the pressure changed in her ears and the temperature dropped, and a cleansing, watchful emptiness took over.

Instead, at a brief levelling of the slope, Liv made a left turn. She stepped over a fallen trunk, soft and pulpy with rot, then proceeded carefully until she saw a hunched figure through the twigs and branches. Mishti, facing away from Liv, sat on a plastic recycling box in front of the weathered stone shrine. For a moment Liv took in the scene: the spindly shadbush with its first white flowers bobbing; the moss near a tiny brook, glistening with moisture; the statue on its dais with its bird droppings, like offerings; and Mishti herself, wrapped in her Tibetan coat with its faded rainbow colours, as still as the implacable Buddha.

'Hey,' she murmured, circling around so that Mishti could see her. 'I've brought cake. For you, though, not The Blessed One.'

Mishti looked up. Liv noticed the dark puffiness around her

eyes with a pinch of irritation. She wanted to be kind, now; she needed to be kind.

'I missed you down there. So did Karin and Jenna.'

Mishti fumbled for a handkerchief and blew her nose.

Liv tried again. 'I want you and Sonny to live where you want to live, Mishti. Of course I do. But if your new place isn't working out—'

'Conor is Wren's son,' said Mishti, her voice quick and small. 'He told me.'

'He told you?' Liv frowned, taking in the new information, trying to work out what it meant. What had Conor said to her about not telling Mishti? *It wasn't in the spirit of the Sharing.* She had assumed that Mishti had absented herself from the party because she'd been upset by the trip to Buffalo, but this was something else. She squatted down and rested her free hand on her old friend's knee. 'It's okay – we've talked. It doesn't matter.'

Mishti, however, shook her head. 'Mary and Sonny were angry about Conor being here for the party. I hated all the bad feeling, so I waited until he was alone on the porch, and then I asked him why he'd come back. That's when he told me he is Wren's son – he was the child she'd been carrying.' She shuddered, crossed her arms and bent forward so that her thick plait of hair fell across Liv's hand. 'He said you knew, Liv. I wish you'd warned me. Why did you let him come back? What if he knows about me and – you know – Sonny?'

'Hush, stop that.' Liv wanted to stand up, not squat, but she set the bowl of cake down and stayed where she was. 'I mean, yes, he's Wren's. I found out yesterday. So what? He doesn't know about Sebastian, and nor did Wren – I'm pretty sure of that. She took a lucky guess about there being a secret, that was all. And no one could ever prove anything.'

'She knew I'd had a baby.'

Liv frowned, willing her brain to work faster. 'How? Are you saying I told Wren? Or Sonny, or Eric? Because if that's what you think, after everything we've been through—'

'No!' Mishti looked up and grabbed Liv's fingers. 'No. We promised each other.'

'So she couldn't have known.' Liv took a deep breath as she realised where this was going. 'Unless you told her. Oh Mishti, what did you tell her?'

Mishti's round brown eyes were pleading now. The kajal along her lids was smudged and sticky. 'When Wren and Tyler came, it was a difficult time for me. I was nearly forty – I didn't think I'd have another child, and Wren was pregnant, and seemed so fragile. I felt *close* to her. One time I told her that if she wanted, I'd take care of her baby. Maybe adopt it. I thought it might be the best thing for everyone. And you know what she did? She laughed. She said she knew I'd had a child – that it was written all over my body – and it must have died, and that I must have done something bad and that I'd have to live with that karma.'

Liv's mind was spooling back. 'You wanted to adopt Conor?' She felt the urge to cough, to clear her throat of something bubbling up. She had always needed to believe that they had shared everything, she and Sonny and Mishti, yet that week of Wren and Tyler's attempted takeover had frayed their bond. Now, at last, Liv saw why Mishti had sided with Wren; it wasn't because she was afraid of Wren knowing about her and Sonny, or even to prevent Liv losing Rose. It was because she wanted Wren's baby.

'Sonny didn't know I'd asked her,' whispered Mishti. 'I didn't tell him. He mustn't find out.'

That pin of steel again – Mishti's inner will, the one she usually kept hidden. She had decided for the two of them – the *three* of them.

'Conor knows more than he's letting on,' Mishti went on. 'The way he looks at me, and you – you must have noticed. What if he knows about Sebastian? Oh Liv, I can't bear it.'

'Wren guessed you'd had a baby, that's all. Nothing else.'

Now it was Mishti who looked at Liv. 'Why do you think Conor is always talking about graves? You know how he keeps asking where Pinto is buried. It brings it all back. All of it. That awful doctor my parents took me to, Sebastian, Baba's spit when he yelled.' Her voice was shaking, and her eyes had filled with tears. Liv felt like crying too. She struggled to her feet, and when Mishti also rose, she embraced her, pressing herself against her, not calmly, but in a kind of feverish anger: frightened, once again, that her oldest friends were abandoning her, wishing she could squeeze out the pin.

BUFFET CLOSED UNTIL OPEN

L IV DIDN'T GO back into the house straight away. Instead, she pulled out the wooden bench near the yard door so that she could sit and look up the valley while she ate the cake she had carried up to Mishti and brought down again. Too many memories had been disturbed, old pain turned over, cast up like flint in an English field. Rose, she was relieved to see, was in her bedroom; every ten or fifteen seconds she glimpsed the primrose yellow of her cardigan among the clouds reflected in the window. Liv waved a hand, to reassure her. What was Rose making of all this rupture?

Mary, meanwhile, was in the kitchen; the sash over the sink had been wedged open with an upturned saucepan, and a sudden clatter of cutlery from within sounded bad-tempered. All these people Liv needed to think about. She licked her finger and dabbed it at a piece of frosting. The cake was okay, she decided, but she couldn't taste the peanut butter. She tipped the bowl upside down and scattered the crumbs for the yard robins.

'Hi,' said a voice behind her. Conor.

Liv glanced up towards the trees, but it was all right, Mishti hadn't reappeared. She twisted around. 'I was just thinking about you. Come here, where I can see you.'

Conor moved so that he stood in front of her, a few feet away. He wore a grey beanie she hadn't seen before; it was pulled down low over his brow and his hands were pushed deep inside his jeans pockets. He looked wary; gone was the ease with which he'd chatted to a bunch of strangers, earlier.

'You told Mishti that Wren is your mother,' she said. 'I hoped you'd wait.'

'I told her because she asked me why I'd come back.'

'Yet you didn't say anything to me when I asked questions that first day you arrived.'

'I didn't know if I could trust you.'

Liv frowned, absorbing this.

'Anyhow,' Conor pushed at a snail shell with the toe of his hiking boot, 'I've been thinking. I'm gonna go. You need some space, here. I'm getting a ride over to Dolores' place.'

'Space?' A surprised laugh rose in Liv's throat. That was a word visitors often used when they came to Birdeye. *I found the space I needed.* He had to leave for a while, she saw that, but she was tired, and she didn't feel like being his interrogator. 'If that's what you want. Mary is going at the end of the week. Then maybe we can talk.'

'Jonathan's waiting, out front.' Conor motioned with his thumb, but he didn't move – he seemed to need her permission, somehow.

'Okay. I'll come and say goodbye.'

Liv pushed herself up from the bench and followed Conor as he skirted the house. Around the corner, Jonathan sat in his station wagon, fingers tapping on the steering wheel. Dolores slumped next to him, asleep. The porch light had popped on and Sonny was leaning against one of the uprights, arms folded, with the recycling crates stacked up beside him. He didn't look as if he'd heard anything to rile him. He just looked weary. Maybe Conor was right, maybe they all needed to re-set, in their own spheres. *Process* – another over-used word. *You've got to process it.*

'Bye,' said Conor, picking up the backpack he'd left on the bottom step. He opened the passenger door and pushed it along the seat.

Liv raised a hand as he slid in and reached for the seatbelt. 'See you soon.'

'You think?' murmured Sonny. They both watched as Jonathan laboriously turned the station wagon and pulled away down the track. In the old days, Liv thought, Sonny would put his arm around her at this point, maybe plant a kiss on her temple. She didn't doubt that Sonny still intuited how she felt, but it was what he did about it that counted.

A loud crash came from behind them, from the kitchen. A dropped plate or something similar.

'Liv . . .' Sonny turned to her, too late.

'I'm going in,' she said. 'On to the next drama.'

༄

It was so stupid, the traps they still fell into. Mary had worked herself into a rage and Liv ought to have left her to it, but instead she stood in the kitchen doorway and said what she knew, deep down, would provoke her.

'You don't need to clear up. It's your birthday. It's okay to leave it.'

Mary banged a drawer shut with her hip and rammed a dish of leftovers into the refrigerator. '*Leave* it.' She shoved a chair back under the table. 'You know what, Mom? Insisting on a messy house is just as controlling as making things tidy.'

Liv moved along the counter and stacked one plate on top of another to stop herself from saying she didn't mind tidy. She fished some Advil from her back pocket and pressed out a couple.

'You're right,' she said, instead. 'I just don't want to see you doing all the work.'

'My point exactly.'

'Oh please.' Liv was too tired to argue. She picked up someone's abandoned glass of water, then tried again. 'Can I sit down?'

'This is your house.'

Liv looked at the chair pushed neatly under the table and swallowed the pills.

Mary was watching her now. 'You're off the Oxy, right?'

'I'm off the Oxy.'

'You should see a physiotherapist for that shoulder. Build the muscle up, not rely on paracetamol and anti-inflammatories. Or get the joint replaced. In London – where I can take care of you.'

193

'Mary,' said Liv. 'Can we talk about what's wrong? You don't like Conor, but you got your wish – he's gone. This is your birthday. Let's go and find Rose. Let's celebrate.'

Mary wheeled about and flipped a dishcloth over one shoulder. She had a food stain on her blouse; her hair was messy. As she twisted her head to look out of the window, an old fear returned to Liv: *I repel her.*

'Susan Kinney came looking for you,' said Mary. 'While you were up in the woods with Mishti. She walked up to complain about the noise from Jonathan's sound system. She also mentioned safeguarding.'

'What?'

'Well, she's got a point, hasn't she? She needs some reassurance that her neighbours are reasonable people. You've got to see it from her side. You must know she's worried that you let Rose wander in the yard without someone watching her. I've said it before, Mom. It's an accident waiting to happen. Her episodes aren't diminishing – if anything, from what I've been hearing, I'd say they're becoming more frequent, and more distressing.'

Mary, siding with Susan Kinney. It was too much. Words wanted to come out and Liv no longer had the strength, today of all days, to keep them in.

'The Kinneys pay too much attention to other people's choices,' she said, moving around the table. 'And they're not the only ones.'

'Hush,' said Mary, warningly. She nodded towards the door, to where Rose was hovering in the passageway, but instead of keeping quiet, Liv held out her hand and beckoned Rose in.

'You know when Rose has "an episode", as you call it? You know when I say it's better for the whole house, afterwards, and you don't believe me? That's because you don't want to hear the truth, Mary. It *is* better, and I'll tell you why, and then you can go and reassure Susan Kinney.'

Sonny had stepped out of the study and stood in the passageway, listening. Rose was in the kitchen now, her bottom lip pushing over

194

her top lip, her head turned sideways, as if trying to hear some faraway sound.

'You're your own person, aren't you, Rose?' Liv went on. 'There is so much of you that's invisible to us – to Mary and to me – so when you scream or pull my hair I think, well, at least that's honest; at least that's feeling. Instead of suppressing it like your sister, you are telling me something true. Mary says I don't take care of you properly, and I'm sick of it. She hasn't actually *lived* with you for thirty years.'

The silence, as it settled, seemed to seep out of the walls, as if the house itself were passing judgement. Mary didn't react straight away, but after a few seconds her face closed in on itself, tight and pained. She pulled the dishcloth off her shoulder and walked out of the kitchen, past Rose, past Sonny. Liv started to follow her along the passageway, but Mary was bending over a refuse sack she had left by the front door. With one sharp tug she pulled something out. It was Liv's gift, the prom photograph, and Mary shook it at her.

'I may be as predictable as you imply, Mom, so here's the thing. I'm still surprised by you. I shouldn't be – it's absurd at my age – but I'm still surprised by how you manage to go that extra bit further to hurt me.'

Liv's legs felt unsteady. 'I thought you'd like it! We can change the frame . . .'

Mary, however, was already hurrying up the stairs.

How did it happen, this pain between them? Liv never meant to hurt her daughter, yet if she'd done wrong in her life, it was that.

꧁꧂

Some habits are harder to kill off than others. Later that evening, Liv and Sonny loaded the pickup with the bottles and cartons and cans from the donkey barn and drove them down to the recycling centre, as they had done every fortnight for the past five years.

'You should go back to curbside collection,' said Sonny, upending a crate of glass into the appropriate dumpster. 'See if Mary will set up a BetterWaste account, for when it's just you and Rose.'

The bottles glinted briefly in the pickup's headlights and smashed with bone-jangling discordance. It was nearly nine o'clock and the place was deserted, apart from the attendant watching TV in her booth at the floodlit entrance. Liv took the emptied crate and lifted it back over the tailgate before passing Sonny a box of cans. It was the last time they'd do this together, she thought, as she opened the passenger door and climbed in. When Sonny had disposed of the cans he opened his door and slid in too. He held the key in his hand, but he didn't insert it and when Liv looked at him, she saw his bald patch gleaming faintly. His little ponytail had loosened at the nape of his neck. He let out a sigh, and she remembered that he'd travelled down from Buffalo that morning. He'd had a long day.

'We used to talk a lot, didn't we?' she said. 'Now it's as though we've nothing more to say, but I don't know if that's true.'

Sonny grunted. 'It could be we're not sure how to say it. I keep thinking you'll stop being angry, but maybe you won't. That was ugly earlier, listening to you and Mary.'

Ugly. Liv considered the word. 'That photo I found of Mary – do you remember her prom at all? I mean, did anything happen?'

'Only that she couldn't go. Or maybe she did, but I'm pretty sure it was the day that woman Margie-something got lost up on Slide and broke her leg.'

'Oh.' Now Liv did remember a ruckus of some kind – the sort of thing she tried not to hang on to. Hadn't Mary taken Rose with her?

'You know she's changed her flight, right?' said Sonny. 'She says she's leaving in the morning. She's going to tell Rose while we're out.'

Liv absorbed this information for a few moments.

'I didn't mean to make this about Mary,' she said, finally. 'It's you and me here now. Who decided *you* had to leave? I thought it must be you to begin with, but now I think it's Mishti.'

Sonny sighed again. 'Please don't, Liv. I love you – we love you. We just need something else at this stage in our lives. I'm not even sure we know what we need, but I seem to have stopped searching, lately, and I guess that's the point.'

Liv twisted round and leaned the back of her head against the window. She shut her eyes and tried to gather her thoughts, but it didn't work. When she opened them again, she stared at Sonny straight on.

'You know when I was a child and my parents had gone and I lived with my grandparents?' Images of their rambling Hampshire rectory now came to mind with a clarity that surprised her: the herringbone path, the pillared porch, the thick, knotty coil of wisteria. There was an old-fashioned greenhouse that leaned against the southern wall where they grew tomatoes and tough-skinned purple grapes on a vine. Her grandfather would sit half-hidden among the leaves and play his birdsong recordings on a wind-up gramophone.

Sonny was waiting.

'Well, my grandpa had a game we used to play at teatime. I would climb onto my chair in the dining room and Grandpa would come in from the garden or the greenhouse with dirt under his fingernails or grass stains on his thumbs and when he had washed in the lavatory down the back hall he would say "No cake until you tell me one true thing." And I would say something like "Oh buttercups are yellow," and he would tell me that this was correct, but this wasn't the same as true. Then I would say something else, like 'Grammie has purple lips," and he would laugh and say that this was also correct, and maybe just a little bit true. So then I would think for a while and when I was good and ready, I'd come out with something daft like "Today I rode a ladybird all the way up to the top of the cathedral and we swung from the bells and spat gooseberries down at the ladies and the men," and he would wink and say, "Good girl – now you can have some cake."'

Sonny leaned forward across the steering wheel, stretching out his back. 'Why are you telling me this?'

'Oh, I don't know,' Liv said. 'It was a nonsense game. I can't say

I understood the rules, but when we played it, I knew something true had passed between us.'

'A nonsense game,' repeated Sonny, starting the engine. 'You think that's what's going on here.'

'Why not? Yes.'

⚘

Mary hadn't, in fact, changed her flight, but she had decided to leave Birdeye the next day. She went to bed early, then rose at dawn to blow a kiss through her sister's doorway before tiptoeing out, holding her breath as she started the engine, as if that might make it quieter, as if not breathing would help her slip away unseen. She checked her rear-view mirror as she pulled away, half-hoping that her mother might appear, but the house stood silent, and the front door remained closed.

She had regained some composure by the time she reached Manhattan. A couple of restful days were what she needed, so she had booked a hotel in Morningside Heights. She liked the sombre libraries of the neighbourhood, the anonymity, the way she felt at home there in her tailored clothes. The cherry blossom quivered prettily as she drove past Sakura Park, and at the Grant Memorial she saw tourists wearing shorts. It was always a few degrees warmer in the city.

When she had checked in, showered, wrapped herself in a robe and ordered tea, Mary sat down in an armchair by the window and thought about how remarkably quiet it was, how tiny and busy everyone seemed on the pavement far below. She had planned, after a rest, to stroll north to the bookstores around Columbia and maybe look up the Hungarian bakery that one of her London colleagues had raved about. Her room, however, was warm, and the week just gone had been extraordinarily draining. After a while, she found she didn't want to move at all.

When it was evening, and the sky had darkened and the uptown lights blinked their filmy auras, she dressed carefully, drank a glass of water and went out to a restaurant she had looked up earlier. The place was livelier than she expected; as the hostess showed her to a table near the restroom, Mary let out a sigh of displeasure. The woman turned inquiringly, and immediately a hot flush prickled between Mary's shoulders. Living by herself had made her mean. It wasn't pleasant to be reminded.

As she studied the menu her phone beeped. It was Eric, texting 'Hope you get home safe. Sorry not to say goodbye. Miss you. Dad x'. She replied immediately: 'I'm sorry too. Back soon, promise! Will call. Love you xx', but when she looked around at all the evening diners, she felt a knot tighten in her throat and she had a sudden thought that she should run out to find her car and drive straight back to the mountains. Then her glass of Sancerre arrived, and she took a sip and saw that nothing would be resolved by extending her stay. Rose, she was certain, ought to be in England. She would be safe in the house that Mary had worked so hard to pay for, with its long, airy hallway and the walled garden at the back with its pond and its blackbirds and flowers. Her mother was a different matter: intransigent, careless and – well, something else. Try as she might, Mary could no longer picture Liv curled up on the sofa in the sitting room or strolling along her street. The tricky prospect of a sabbatical was receding. There'd be no point if her mother wasn't moving.

It wasn't until later, while she was getting ready for bed, that she allowed her thoughts to shift backwards along the dark tunnel of the week. Things were said, hurtful things, but as she brushed her hair, she examined each one and concluded that nothing had been spoken that she could not bear. No, the worst thing was that photograph – the portrait from junior prom, the acquisition of which had done the worst damage, because she could never speak of it with anyone.

Now the photograph was in her suitcase. Mary walked over to the luggage stand, retrieved the hastily re-wrapped gift and removed the print from its frame, without looking at it. The print she put in the waste basket, face down, but the empty frame stared at her, the glass reflecting the electric light. She ran her fingers across the entwined leaves, the swollen, bulging heart. Had her mother chosen that particular frame, or was it merely what came to hand? Mary frowned and pushed it down between her sweaters. That awful young man, Conor; that last conversation in the kitchen . . . Oh, she was glad she hadn't driven back, or weakened. She wouldn't call for a few days, either. A sense of perspective required time. Let distance be the healer.

CARRY IN, CARRY OUT

L IV HAD WITNESSED Mary depart many times. She was used to the emptiness, the regret and the underlying relief that followed, along with a few days of distress from Rose and a need to regain lost rhythms. But this time Mary's leaving truly shook her. There had been no farewell hug, no mention of the next visit, no attempt to gloss over their differences for the sake of an easy goodbye. Rose wouldn't sit at breakfast, and instead lingered in the parlour, as if testing the renewed absence. By mid-morning the rain had set in, confining and claustrophobic, so when, that afternoon, Sonny reminded her about the Town Board meeting, Liv welcomed the distraction.

'I'll come with you,' said Sonny, checking the start time on Facebook.

'I'd rather go by myself.'

'I heard AJ and Susan are going. You might want back-up.'

'Oh please.' As far as she was concerned, the Kinneys had made a mountain out of a molehill, as if a few old mattresses down by the road were the Catskills' most pressing social issue. 'Watch the live stream on the computer. I'll wave if I need the cavalry.'

Apollonia Town Hall was a plain, two-storey building in a water-logged parking lot near the cemetery. The meeting was scheduled for six o'clock and Liv arrived a little late, having first settled Rose with Mishti. She missed the pledge of allegiance and the roll call and hurried in as Jeff Zimet was approving the minutes of the last meeting with a prim tap of his gavel.

The four board members sat at a long table, a drooping flag behind them, with everyone else scattered among the rows of wooden chairs in front. Liv shrugged off her dripping rain slicker, collected a photocopied agenda and chose a seat half-way down, on the side nearest the door. Jonathan, as usual, was filming for the town's YouTube channel in the corner. He swung his camera on its neat tripod in her direction, and she raised her hand in greeting. Dolores, who never missed a meeting, sat beside him in her Woody Guthrie cap and a see-through plastic poncho. She cocked her head and pointed conspiratorially across the aisle, and when Liv turned, she saw Susan Kinney, her hair flattened by the rain, and the round, heavy shoulders of her husband AJ; they were sitting on their own near the front. Further back, studying the paper agenda, sat Conor. He half-raised a hand, then moved across to join her, keeping his head and shoulders low as if he didn't want to draw attention or block the view of someone behind him.

'Hi,' said Liv. He was wearing his grey beanie again, and she wished he would take it off. It made him seem self-conscious in a way she didn't recognise.

'Dolores invited me. She said you wouldn't mind if I came.'

Liv wondered what he'd told Dolores, but she smiled and touched his arm. In truth, she was happy to see him. Things had become overcomplicated.

'Are you okay?' she murmured.

'Dolores sleep-walks. She talks all night. It's kind of funny.'

'Mary's gone,' she said. 'We could see about you coming back for a bit.'

Conor nibbled at the skin around his thumbnail. 'Maybe. Not tonight. I'm doing some things at Dolores' place, like fixing a hand-rail up her stairs.'

'That's great.'

'Yeah. She needs a lot of stuff like that.'

Liv noted the implied accusation. She glanced over to Dolores, who pulled her hand out from her cape and raised an arthritic thumb.

Up front, Jeff Zimet was making a meal of his financial report and kept saying things like 'Now ladies,' to the other officers, and 'I think we can all agree . . .' Then Molly Abers from the library was invited to read a statement about the town's poor cellular service and its effect on the senior members of the community, which was met with muffled handclaps from beneath Dolores' poncho and a call from the floor to petition Verizon. Next came a lengthy discussion, with photographs, about the next phase of the township's flood mitigation plan, at the end of which Jeff pointed out that current river levels were giving cause for concern and that, with more rainfall on the way, a message should go out to all householders of vulnerable properties to run through their emergency procedures. Liv tried to concentrate, to reacquaint herself with the concerns of the wider neighbourhood. Be attentive, she reminded herself, but after half an hour she gave up. Her tattoo itched, the room was fuggy, and Conor's proximity was an unexpected distraction. When the call came for Any Other Business, and the public microphone at the front was switched on with a screech of feedback, she wasn't ready.

Susan Kinney stepped up first. She kept her padded coat on, and wrapped it around herself as Jonathan repositioned his camera.

'I want to speak about the Beautification Committee,' she said, leaning in, as if she doubted the equipment. She pushed her hair back behind her ears. 'I'm here today to ask it to focus more on local. I mean, we shouldn't have to tolerate someone else's loud music blaring out along the valley road, or their dog wandering unleashed and snarling at our kids and coming to poop in our backyard. It's great to have volunteers to help out and hold fundraisers, but it's taking too long, and it means our neighbourhood is not beautified.' Susan turned her head to glance in Liv's direction. 'Not beautified at all.'

Jeff Zimet nodded and removed his glasses.

'Thank you, Susan. It's your right to speak on this, and we thank you for your contribution, but do you have anything specific you want Monica here to minute?'

Susan Kinney looked towards her husband who had his arm stretched across the back of an empty chair. 'I don't want to get too personal . . .'

'Yes, Jeff, we have specific incidents,' said AJ, so that everyone could hear.

'Here we go,' murmured Conor. His foot, Liv noticed, kept tapping the chair in front.

AJ spread his thighs wide and turned his head as if to address the room. He didn't stand up or ask for the microphone, but instead proceeded to list a catalogue of misdemeanours allegedly perpetrated by Liv and Gunther and 'the other come-and-goers at the Birdeye place'.

Liv sat still, listening, but she didn't move until he mentioned 'the mean-looking bitch, she's kind of bitey, a short-assed mutt that comes and frightens my boys'. This was too much, and she stood up.

'When did this happen, exactly?'

Faces turned to look at her. Jeff Zimet raised an eyebrow.

'Last week,' said AJ, with a dismissive shrug. 'Whenever.'

'Then it isn't true. Pinto died three weeks ago.'

'Well, it must of been your other dog, then.'

'No.' Liv felt a kind of dull anger rising inside her. She placed one hand protectively over her chest. 'Gunther is a German Shepherd. You said your boys were frightened by "a short-assed mutt". But mine died. Three weeks ago.'

'We are sorry for your loss,' murmured Monica, the town clerk, from the front. Susan looked as if she wanted to sit down, but AJ was twisting in his seat, taking up the space.

'I hope you didn't bury it on public land,' he said. 'Because that's another thing. Contamination. Not to mention vermin.'

'I'd certainly recommend a professional cremation,' said Jeff.

'No shit,' said someone else. 'Do you know what that costs? Those outfits are busting to rip you off.'

'Did you bury her?' asked Conor, quietly, but clear enough.

It was a simple question. One he'd asked before. Liv turned her head towards the row of windows and watched the slate-coloured rain clouds move along the valley. A sudden gust made the drops scatter against the glass; she wondered why somebody didn't drop the catch and let in a little air.

'No, I didn't bury her,' she said, remembering a different burial: a tiny baby, enclosed in Eric's old toolbox – the last dead thing she'd laid in the ground. It was Mishti and Sonny's secret, but Liv had dug the hole and threw the dirt back over afterwards. That part was her burden, alone.

She glanced towards Jonathan, towards the dark eye of his lens, because she couldn't look down at Conor. She knew he was staring intently at her now, as he did whenever he asked a question. The pressure was stifling her; she could hardly breathe. That afternoon when Pinto died, Gunther had been whining, or keening, and Sonny and Mishti were out, so she had wrapped her beautiful brave dog in a blanket, placed her in the back of the pickup and driven her down the road with Rose in the passenger seat.

'I didn't bury her,' she repeated, softly. 'The Kinneys get curbside collection, and we don't, so I put her in their trash.'

There was a moment of silence: time to draw a breath.

'Oh Christ. That is disgusting,' said AJ. 'That woman is bat-shit crazy. You got it on video now, Jeff.' He was pointing his finger all over the place rather than addressing Liv directly, but straight away Liv felt a rush of relief, almost euphoric, the way she used to feel after a Sharing. She closed her eyes as people started talking, and Jeff had to bang his gavel.

'Keep it clean, AJ. Now then, Liv.' He spoke in his father-of-the-town voice. 'The Kinneys' garbage is their property, and there are prohibitions about what can and cannot go to landfill. I don't think you've acted in the spirit of this community, although I am obliged to point out that it is more of a private dispute than a matter for the Beautification Committee.'

'You told me you buried her,' interrupted Conor. His voice was low, but clear. He sounded upset. A few heads turned.

'I suppose it was a kind of burial,' said Liv, looking down. Conor's gaze seemed fixed on the floor. 'Anyway, she's gone. I miss her. You never even met her. She was the best dog I ever had the privilege of owning, and I don't need a grave to remember her.'

AJ let out a snort. 'Don't you even *think* about putting that other dog of yours in my trash when it dies. Jesus, you got a sick mind.'

'That's enough, AJ,' warned Jeff.

'No, it fuckin' ain't. My wife and boys got to watch it dragging its back legs around – animal welfare should get involved.'

Again, Jeff banged his gavel. 'We'll have to bleep that on the recording. If you can't be civil . . .'

The room was full of voices. Liv didn't stay to listen. Conor had already risen to his feet and was shoving a path through the chairs, but by the time she had snatched her coat from the back of her seat and followed him outside, he was gone.

She stood in the parking lot, her breath quick and shallow. It was almost night, still raining; Conor had triggered the motion sensor light above the porch so that a pool of brightness pushed back the shadows and a blocked gutter spilled like a beaded curtain. She'd been a fool to ignore Conor's probing about graves. There had been no burial for his father. Those left behind needed markers.

For a moment she glimpsed two figures move along the verge by the road. She knew who they were, dim shades, projections of her own parents. *You left me,* she thought, aware of their pull as they slipped between the trees. When a truck rushed past, she felt the asphalt tremble. The puddles shivered and shimmered.

☙

Liv was still standing there when the Town Board concluded and people started to emerge, pulling on jackets and heading for their vehicles.

'He's gone and taken the station wagon,' grumbled Jonathan, peering across the dirt lot, his tripod tucked beneath one arm.

'Without your permission?' asked Liv, quickly.

'I said he could use it for a couple of days, if he ran us up here, but that didn't mean blasting off without making sure we had a ride home first.'

'Can you call him?'

Jonathan frowned. 'Do you have his number?'

He had a point. Liv had no way of contacting Conor. In the few days he'd spent at Birdeye, they had never spoken by phone or texted.

'He'll be running her over the state line,' said Dolores, with some satisfaction, as if she had seen this coming.

Liv dropped Dolores at her place first. Conor wasn't there, but as she looped back towards Apollonia via the river road, they encountered a huddle of people in glistening rain gear, flashing torches and holding clipboards. A woman stepped out and raised her hand, and when Liv slowed down to a stop, she felt a rush of fear, wondering if they might have found an abandoned vehicle, or worse.

She rolled down her window.

'Amphibian migration watch,' said the woman, glancing in over steamed-up glasses. 'We got three spotted salamander on the road.'

The woman sounded purposeful, confident she was doing the right thing. Liv remembered seeing the call-out for volunteers organised by the local conservation group. She had helped out herself a few times over the years. The cool wet night made for ideal conditions.

'We'll go carefully,' she promised, before inching the pickup forward around figures standing guard on the asphalt, pale hands waving her through, so that she could return Jonathan to his apartment behind the gas station.

'You'll let me know when Conor shows up, won't you?' she said.

Jonathan shook his head, his expression doleful. 'You mean "if".'

☙

Sonny was waiting for Liv back at Birdeye. She saw him in the dim passageway – he was leaning against the study door as she shook off her wet slicker and slipped her feet out of her shoes. The belt of his kimono was knotted across his jeans and his arms were tucked inside its sleeves, like some kind of ninja. Liv could tell he'd heard about the meeting.

'You watched the live stream, then,' she said.

'It cut out before the end. We heard you say you put Pinto in the Kinneys' trash.'

Liv closed her eyes for a moment. 'Right. And now you'll tell Mary, and she'll add it to her list of stupid things her mom's done.'

'No,' said Mishti, moving into view from the kitchen. She glanced pointedly at Sonny. 'No, we won't. We know you'd have been respectful, Liv. With Pinto.'

Liv pictured Pinto's slender forelegs, one brindled, one white, both stiffening in death. She had no wish to put into words her reasons for not being able to bury her. Anyway, from her tone, it seemed Mishti had guessed.

'Where's Rose?' she asked, changing the subject.

'Upstairs.'

'Liv—'

'We thought we could have a Sharing,' continued Mishti, speaking over her brother. 'We haven't shared for two weeks. And now that Mary and Conor have gone—'

'For old times' sake, you mean.' Liv rubbed her forehead, pressing her fingers into her skull. 'Okay. But I'm cold and I need tea. Let's do it in the kitchen.'

⁂

Mishti had orchestrated this. Liv gave credit where it was due. Here they were, Mishti, Sonny, Rose and herself, the old stalwarts, the ones who had stuck it out all those years. Gunther lay at Liv's feet, a warm, decaying presence. Rose sat quietly between Sonny and Liv, while the candle, a fallen-in-on-itself thing with a spitting wick, held them in its glow. As the rain tapped against the window and Mishti cradled her cup of tea, Liv resisted the impulse to reach for her daughter's hand, guessing she would probably flee at the sudden touch.

Fight or flight: be decisive. Liv hadn't sat down like this with brother and sister since the night they'd told her they were leaving. As individuals she could handle them, but together, she felt cornered.

'I'm raging,' she said, before they had agreed who would speak first. 'And I don't mean because of Mary, or Conor. They're not here. It's you two who make me sick. You say you're leaving, you've planned it out, you get Mary to chauffeur you off to wherever, but you keep going on with the chores and fussing around the house and over me as if nothing is about to change, as if you're not about to sever us.'

Sonny's gaze was fixed on a spot on the table. Mishti shifted and pressed her forehead into his shoulder; like a cat, thought Liv, against the silky fabric of his kimono.

'You've not explained anything to me,' she continued. 'I don't understand why you are doing this. Also, you've colluded with Mary against Conor. I welcomed him, Sonny - not to spite you - I invited him in because that's what we've always done.' She stopped, recalling two terrified faces: a teenage girl, belly swollen, already in labour, and her brother, his face sweating and strained. 'Ever since that first day, when—'

'Sebastian,' interrupted Mishti. She held Liv's gaze.

'Please don't,' murmured Sonny, his voice dry and small. He seemed stricken, and for the first time it occurred to Liv that he was oppressed by the force of his sister's conviction.

'You helped us,' Mishti went on. 'You did. You were strong, and you kept our secret and that's the trouble. I can't forget. This thing between us - it's sat there every day, for nearly fifty years! I want to be free of it. Not Sebastian - I don't mean my baby - I want to be free of the way you look at me. That knowing. It's there now, and I can't stand it.'

My baby. Oh, Liv felt a sudden pity for Sonny, even while she didn't think she could bear to sit facing either of them any longer. He didn't know about his sister's desire to adopt Wren's child, just as it wasn't his choice, now, to go.

'I never told anyone about your baby,' she said. 'I never judged. I only ever loved you both.'

'You're missing the point,' said Sonny, softly. 'It's not about love. It's about the burden.'

Whose burden, Liv wondered, in the silence that followed, until Rose raised her arm and pulled the fruit bowl towards her. An orange – one of several Conor had brought – fell to the floor and rolled in front of Gunther.

'It's always about love,' she muttered, reaching over to pinch out the candle. 'We're not finished here. But hey, fifty years, whatever.'

AREA OF DETAIL #7

CONOR HUNCHED OVER his phone in the donkey barn, his face tense in the screen's queasy glow. His thumbs moved rapidly over the keys, twitching, tapping.

The rain pattered on the roof above his head, sometimes barely audible, then with a needling insistence as the wind blew through the dripping cedars at the edge of Birdeye's front yard. The night was cold, and the barn's broken window exposed him to the damp, but he had found an old sleeping bag under a bench and with his legs inside it, drawn up towards his chest, he was relatively cocooned. Jonathan's car, backed into the undergrowth at the bottom of the track, was drier; he'd retreat there to rest when he was ready. First though he needed Birdeye's Wi-Fi for the stuff he was uploading.

He glanced up every so often towards the house. The downstairs lights had been switched off some time before, and he assumed everyone was asleep, but he was careful to keep his phone shielded with his knees. It would take him an hour, maybe two to put everything together.

It wasn't like he was planting a freaking tree or anything.

LISTEN TO THE RIVER

T HE RAIN CONTINUED all night. The thin mountain soil couldn't hold any more moisture, and by morning the runoff had made shallow lakes along the verges, while the Esopus had breached its banks of tumbled stones. When Liv shuffled downstairs in search of coffee, Sonny, already dressed, told her that a flood warning had been issued and he planned to drive the pickup to Tanners Ridge to see if they needed volunteers. Mishti would go with him. She was worried about a couple of families she knew with low-lying homes close to the river.

'I'll stay here then,' said Liv, stating the obvious. There was no sign of Karin, and someone needed to remain with Rose.

Before Sonny and Mishti left, Liv ventured down the track to see for herself. The downpour had stopped for the time being, and a damp grey mist was settling in, but Liv could hear the roar of the river as soon as she stepped off the porch. At the bend she sniffed the iron smell and glimpsed the deluge beyond the tree trunks, and when she drew near, the rust-brown surge seemed to twist and flail over submerged boulders like the heads of rearing horses. Dutchman's Road was high enough to escape the water that would continue to rise for the next couple of hours, and the mitigation measures put in place after Hurricane Irene meant Apollonia was protected, but Liv knew better than to underestimate the force below her. She decided not to walk with Rose to the diner for brunch. Maybe later she'd call Eric to come over and distract her from the deeper fears that plagued her.

'You won't miss this up in Buffalo,' she remarked to Sonny when she returned from her brief survey. He didn't answer, and as she climbed the stairs to help Rose get dressed, she could hear him filling bottles of water at the sink before fetching the emergency box from the cellar. Then he went out with Mishti.

The rest of the morning passed slowly. Liv did some physio with Rose, raising arms and circling wrists like creaking windmills. After that she stripped her bed and the bed that Conor had slept in and went down to the cellar to load the washer with dirty sheets. She found the roasted tomato soup that Sonny had left them for lunch, and while it warmed on the stove she stepped outside and scattered some bread and seeds on the bird table. In a couple more weeks the yard would be full of birdsong, but for now Liv had to make do with a nuthatch bleating from the fogged trees.

'We'll go to the diner tomorrow,' she said to Rose, as she tried to coax her to eat. But Rose didn't want lunch, wouldn't sit down, and instead raised her jaw and pulled her lips inwards so that the tendons in her neck stood out like ribs of fan vaulting.

'*Kic kic, kic kic!*' tried Liv. 'Do you remember the flickers? They'll be back soon. And the sparrows – *seee-saw, seee-saw!*'

It was no good. Rose was bumping her hip against each corner of the table as she moved around it, in a way that said something fierce was running along her nerves, raising her heartbeat, chaotic and unstoppable. She had heard too much lately: the words themselves, but mostly what lay behind them, absorbed like ink through blotting paper, like spilled milk on the parlour rug. Liv didn't move, didn't flinch as Rose passed behind her chair, but no fingers touched her head. Instead came the sudden sweep of an arm followed by the shock of warm soup on her neck and cheek. The bowl crashed to the floor in a bright orange burst. When Liv turned, Rose was tugging at clumps of her own beautiful hair.

'Oh, Birdie,' she breathed, rising up to put her arms around her, pressing her lips against her daughter's ear. 'Pull my hair, not yours.'

'Camptown Races' was ringing out on Liv's phone. It sounded far off – probably in the kitchen.

Liv had run a bath once Rose's outburst was over, but Rose wasn't interested, so she had climbed in herself. She lay now with her limbs adrift as the soup soaked away, though not the ache across her shoulders. Maybe it was Eric or Mary calling. Gripping the sides of the bath, she hauled herself up and out, streaming wet onto the mat.

'I'm on it,' she called to Rose who was walking up and down the landing. Rose paused in the doorway and looked at Liv's chest, at the tattoo there. Liv glanced down, too, at Pinto's head across her right side, good ear cocked, eyes solemn in their black inking. Rose hadn't seen it before, she realised. She should have shown her, not kept it to herself, but now she needed to answer her phone. She reached for Sonny's kimono which lay draped over the banister, tugging it on as she hurried downstairs.

The caller, however, wasn't Eric or Mary.

'Hey,' Jenna said. 'I take it you're at home?'

'Yep.' Liv's hair was dripping, making her shiver; she hoped Jenna didn't want to chat. 'What's up?'

'Okay, well, I'm at the diner with a bunch of customers and someone says there's a weird video posted on the Town Board's YouTube. Anyway, I pulled it up on my screen here and if you haven't seen it yet then I think you might want to.'

Liv stepped out into the passage to check Rose's whereabouts, but Rose was fine – she had followed her downstairs and was pacing around the parlour.

'You mean the meeting the other night? I was there. I don't need to watch the replay.'

'No, it's not a meeting. It's – something else.'

'Like what?'

A pause. Jenna cleared her throat. 'It's kind of personal. From that young man you had staying. What's his name—'

Liv closed her eyes. 'Conor.'

It took a minute for Liv to fire up the computer. The fan whirred loudly for a few seconds, and when the screen lit up she went to retrieve her glasses from the kitchen. Then she had to navigate her way to the list of videos uploaded under 'Apollonia Town Board, NY'. Once there, however, she soon spotted Conor's handiwork. The sample frame had frozen over a grainy image of a face illuminated in the darkness: herself, looking a little crazed, lighting a joint. She guessed it was that night when Sonny and Mishti announced they were leaving. It had fifty-three views already. No wonder Jenna was jumpy. Conor must have persuaded Jonathan to give him the password, or else he'd stolen it.

Liv pulled out the desk chair and sat down, wondering what she was about to see. She clicked on the video, and after a moment of blankness the harsh scrape of a match made her jump, but then a flickering candle filled the screen, accompanied by the Birdeye cowbell's familiar clanging. In fact, most of the first thirty seconds seemed blessedly tame: an outline of the house at night, split frames of people laughing at the birthday party, snippets of speech – fiddly to put together. Liv peered with a kind of morbid fascination at the jagged hole in Rose's window before Sonny fixed it; a glistening egg on the kitchen floor; the old mattresses with twiggy shadows playing across them at the bottom of the track while a deep voice intoned 'Fuck *orf*.' A bubble of surprised laughter rose in her throat as she realised the words were her own, slowed down and stretched on a loop. Was this all he'd got? She had nothing to be ashamed of; it could even, she told herself, be a kind of homage to the Birdeye lifestyle. It wasn't until the video switched to the kitchen table and zoomed in on an oddly familiar Polaroid that something clenched inside her. The Polaroid showed Conor's father Tyler pointing the gaff hook like a shotgun towards the lens.

'I've been hearing things about you,' said a man's voice. Absurdly, it sounded like Super Jeff. Then the camera panned across the front of Conor's copy of *The Attentive Heart* before settling on the blackboard with a new word chalked in thick, emphatic capitals:

Liv pressed pause, nerves fluttering in her belly. She pushed up her glasses to rub her eyes. Hadn't she wanted to understand Conor better? Hadn't she known he was keeping something back? Sonny liked to rant about how people said anything they wanted on the internet, regardless of the truth. A glance at the progress bar showed the video was halfway through.

'Spit it out, then,' she murmured grimly, jabbing at the keyboard.

This time, when the screen lit up again, the quality of the recording was different: flatter, less contrived, the colours brownish and muted. Shards of sunlight dazzled between leaves. Birds chittered, and someone was breathing heavily, as if their mouth was too close to the microphone. There seemed to be some problem with the focus, and the picture jerked sharply as Liv heard footfalls across soft ground. Then a man said 'over here' as the camera panned past a drooping canopy slung between the trees, a couple of fold-down chairs, and the back of someone's head. The location was familiar, but Liv knew this wasn't Conor's work. This was filmed in the days before camera phones, with a hand-held video recorder and a cassette of Hi8.

'Listen up, people.'

Liv pulled back, startled. The new voice was high and soft and peculiarly childlike. You couldn't forget a voice like that. The camera pointed down to the ground for a moment, showing pinecones and a man's boot before refocusing on a circle of mostly young folk sitting cross-legged in the dirt, like kids waiting for show-and-tell. Now she pushed her face close to the screen, searching, until she found who she was looking for. Wren was walking around the circle, in and out of the sunlight, her pregnant frame simultaneously tiny and enormous. The sight of her was shocking, after all this time.

'Birdeye ain't what's advertised,' she was saying, her hands cupping her swollen belly. 'I'm telling you this in case something happens – something big. Liv Ferrars is a control freak, and Birdeye is a cult – yeah, the cult of Liv Ferrars. She's trying to kick us out, man! I mean, this baby's coming soon, and Tyler's gut is sick, and we have a child! How is that healing? How is that loving? No, she wants to own you, or you're gone.'

Faces turned as Wren wandered. Every few steps she stooped and whispered something, or her fingers fluttered and touched a shoulder as if weaving everyone into her way of thinking.

'That's how dictators do it, right?' A few murmurs of agreement. 'And we don't need to look hard to see the way she picks favourites – her little slaves. We all know how that works. I mean, Mishti and Sonny?' Her hands made exaggerated air quotes. '*Weird* shit, the way they are together. I pity Rose.'

The video spat a line of static. It seemed to finish, the picture disappearing, but then, like a magic trick, Wren was up close, swinging her blanched face to camera and staring straight into the future.

'Hey, Liv! I know you want *this* –' she indicated her bump – 'but I'd never trust you with my baby, not now, not ever.' And in the final moments before the screen froze, Wren leaned forward and picked up moon-faced Shenandoah, who took her thumb out of her mouth, made a fist and flipped up her soft pink middle finger.

Liv felt sick. She put her hand over her mouth and stood up hurriedly. The video was old, but the hurt was raw, brand-new. Conor knew how his parents had infected Birdeye, and his timing, coming here, giving her hope then pulling it away, was cruel. She needed Jonathan or Super Jeff to take it down and fumbled for her phone, but when she tried their numbers, they were out of service. The thought of sitting around at home, waiting, was unbearable to her.

'Birdie,' she called, stepping into the passageway. 'I have to—'

Cold air moved against her legs. Gunther stood by the open front door, his tail drooping. Liv had always believed she could sense when the house was empty, when she was the only person in it, but her instincts had been disrupted, and now Rose was outside. She hurried out to the porch; another moment and she would have been too late to see the yellow smudge of Rose's cardigan disappear round the bend in the track. Such an exodus had been triggered by something, and in Liv's agitated state she could only think that it must have been hearing Wren's voice. She grabbed her rain slicker from its hook, pushed her bare feet into her gumboots and set off after her daughter.

It was tricky, running in gumboots. Her ankles chafed against the rubber, and the kimono flapped around her legs. The rain was softer now, materialising from the mist that concealed the treetops and the mountains, settling like a damp net across her face. As she rounded the bend, the noise of the river filled her head as if she had somehow plunged beneath the water. The surge hadn't risen as far as the road, though, and when she reached the bottom of the track, she spotted Rose a short way ahead. Rose was moving steadily along the verge with her distinctive, swinging gait. She might have been heading for pancakes at Caspar's, even though there were puddles to negotiate, and she was still wearing her slippers.

'Birdie,' Liv puffed when she drew level. 'Where are you going?'

Rose kept walking. Liv fell into step beside her, draping her coat across her daughter's shoulders and taking her cold hand. Liv herself was shivering, but she didn't want to force a turnaround, not after what Rose must have heard back at the house. Besides, something else had caught her eye. As they moved forward, a low-slung shape began to emerge from the mist in front of them, parked up above the river. A distinctive protuberance sprouted from its roof. It was Jonathan's station wagon – the car Conor had taken.

That boy.

As Liv walked on beside her daughter, a cold, quiet rage seized hold. She didn't care what others thought, but each frame of Conor's video had been designed to hurt her. If the key was in the ignition, well, she and Rose would drive straight into town and make Jonathan delete it.

She steered her daughter across the asphalt. 'Let's take a look.'

The nearside windows were clouded with condensation. Liv tried the driver's door; when it opened, she leaned in. Old clothes lay scattered across the seats along with a sleeping bag, its grubby pink interior opened out. It smelled of mould, and sour milk. Jonathan would never have left his vehicle in such a state. She checked for a key – nothing. Discouraged, she straightened up and removed her glasses to wipe the fogged lenses. As she pushed them back into place, she glanced over the roof to where the deluge hurtled downriver. Now she could see the faint geometry of the bridge and the way the muddied water pushed and surged around its piers. The struts and trusses formed grey triangles in the mist, and there, half-way across, something blue. She blinked and looked again. Yes, Conor's blue nylon jacket – almost, but not quite as she'd observed it nearly two weeks before.

'Conor!' Her throat felt tight, her voice useless against the roar below her. '*Hey!*' She needed to reach him. She needed to look him in the eye and shout in his face and shake him, but as she turned around, Rose began to zig-zag away from her across the asphalt, stumbling in her soaked slippers, her hair glistening wet. Liv went after her and manoeuvred her back towards the station wagon.

'Stay here, where it's dry.' She opened the passenger door, but Rose wouldn't get in. 'It's just for a minute, Birdie,' she pleaded, pressing her hand on her daughter's shoulder until she sat down, then taking hold of her calves and swivelling her until her legs were folded inside. Once the door was shut, Liv gave her a quick wave through the glass. 'I'll be right back, okay?'

The rain was falling steadily as Liv hurried along the verge. She gave no thought to what she would say, too intent on running, out of breath, the kimono sticking to her knees. At the junction she swerved left and continued onto the bridge, looking for Conor's blue jacket. Then she saw his backpack on the ground. She glimpsed his booted feet up on the guide rail almost half-way along, and the denim fabric of his jeans. The rest of him wavered between two diagonals.

He was leaning out over the water, like a kingfisher ready to swoop.

Not here, she thought. Not now. She slowed down, resisting the urge to shout. As she drew level, she saw that his right arm was slung around one of the rusty uprights. He was clutching something in his free hand. A book. Hers, she guessed, grimly. Its pages were crimped and darkened with moisture.

'Conor.' She leaned forward slowly, to let him know she stood beside him, but when he turned his head, his eyes were red and streaming as if he was high on something. A strange look passed across his face, so she tried again, groping for words that might shake him out of whatever course of action he was contemplating.

'I need the key. For the station wagon. Where is it?'

Conor didn't answer. Instead he faced the oncoming river, seeming to ready himself, shifting his weight. Instinctively Liv reached out and took hold of one leg, but in the same moment he pulled his left arm back and swung it sharply forward, letting go of the book so that it spun away from him, out over the water. It fell open, pages flapping. A wave tossed it briefly before it disappeared beneath the swell. Liv swore under her breath. Was that all he meant to do? In that one second, one fraction of a second, she imagined herself giving him a push. A swift nudge. Then he'd be gone.

Aghast, she let go. Immediately his arms flailed as he lost his footing. His hand clawed the air as he tipped sideways with clownish slowness, until, as if it took a tremendous, grotesque effort, he crashed against the guide rail and slid off towards the asphalt, towards her.

He landed heavily, bringing her down beneath him, pinning her to the gritty road. The two of them lay unmoving; Liv, dazed, could hear his breath close to her ear. Thought and action scrambled over one another – had she really come close to pushing? Had he been about to jump? Her relief that he was safe brought back the fury at all the stupid things that had brought them here.

She tried to shift him off. 'You shouldn't have come. I said you could stay, and you lied to me the whole time. You filmed us!'

Conor untangled himself, but he didn't get up. Instead he rolled onto his side, his back to her, a few inches of puddle between them.

'You think you know how people feel. It's all bullshit.' His words came in short breaths. '"At Birdeye we acknowledge this pain, we listen to it, sing it, walk with it. We cast it into the river and let it flow down to the ocean." Remember?' He was taunting her, quoting her own words back to her.

Liv reached for the guide rail and hauled herself to a sitting position. 'I let you into my house. I took your side against my own daughter.' Conor was still lying on the ground, like a dog. She wished he would move. She poked him with her foot. 'Hey.' His body was shaking. He was saying something, but she couldn't hear him. 'Are you okay? Conor?'

'She's dead.' He made a harsh sound like a sob. 'Mom's dead.'

Liv took in the words, although she didn't understand them. Did he mean Wren? He'd said she was in Idaho or somewhere. She shunted closer, but Conor was wiping his eyes with his sleeve. She remembered how he'd been evasive about Wren's current circumstances, and yet he'd always spoken about her in the present, as if she were alive.

'When?' she managed.

'Two weeks before I got here. She told me to come, and I did.'

Liv pushed her face into her knees. Wren's blanched forehead in the video, those disturbing blue veins across her skin . . . She recalled the white shirt Conor had been wearing on the day he arrived, the dark necktie by his bed. An awful thought came to her – that he'd pitched up straight from his mother's funeral. He'd talked about memorials, although he never explained why. She should have realised.

'What happened?' She raised her head. 'Were you with her?'

'She was in this hostel place. It was her liver. She turned yellow.' Conor shifted, manoeuvring into a crouch. 'She asked me to show you the tape. When she died, I knew I had to.'

Liv tried to think back, to what he'd said to her, to what she knew. 'Except you didn't show it to me until today.'

'So how the hell was I supposed to figure out what to do?' His right hand was bleeding from the fall, and he looked at it, then rubbed it on his knee. 'I was going to show you at the Sharing that first day, but then you seemed okay – nice, even – and Sonny and Mishti were leaving, and I thought I could be different, or make things different, if you let me stay. I thought I could handle it.' He shook his head, as if what had happened was unbelievable. 'But then I heard what you did – you put your dog in the trash. Mom always said that's what you did to people. She swore you'd have thrown me out if she'd let you adopt me.'

'*Adopt* you?'

Liv didn't trust what she was hearing. Conor's words revealed a horrible symmetry, and for some reason she thought of Axel and the tattoo so nearly reversed out. It was Mishti who wanted him, but she couldn't tell him that. Wren had played people to the end – even her own son. He'd come to Birdeye to find Liv, and she'd loved him for a few days, but Wren was right, Liv had had enough. She was done.

Conor was up on his feet. She watched him fetch his backpack and stumble away from her. She wondered whether to go after him, but her legs felt too weak.

'What about Shenandoah?' she called, picturing again that pale, shy toddler flipping her middle finger. Conor seemed not to hear her; he kept moving towards the mist-draped pines on the opposite bank. Shenandoah, he'd told her, had gone missing before she was even a teenager. If this was true, then he had no one now, and all at once she felt his loss descend around her, the entirety of it, with its dreadful simplicity. She closed her eyes, wanting not so much to erase everything that had happened as to spool back and excise the moment when her heart had begun to fail in its duty of care.

'*Bring out your dead! Bring out your dead!*' A new sound was beginning to push through the tumult of the river below. Then a screech of playback from Jonathan's bullhorn.

Liv's eyes shot open. Rose.

PEOPLE WHO CREATE THEIR OWN DRAMA DESERVE THEIR OWN KARMA

A COLD STONE sank in Liv's belly. She was sixty-seven years old. She thought she had lived a whole life of loving and listening, of heartache and sickness and all kinds of grief. Now, after everything, she had lost her daughter. How long had she left her for? Ten minutes? Fifteen? The station wagon's tailgate swung open, and the sleeping bag lay spilled in the mud.

She wrenched open the other doors to check the footwells, because maybe Rose was crouched there, but the tang of urine stung her nostrils instead. Refuse sacks lay torn open, clothes scattered about. Liv veered round, looking first along the bank and downstream. No Rose, but fallen branches swirled in the current. A stark white trunk of paper birch hit a rock and disappeared so that only the dark tracery of its roots above the surface showed its agitated passage. There was other debris, too: pieces of metal sheeting, more branches, a Sunoco-yellow plastic container bobbing dementedly in the shallows.

'Conor!' she yelled, hoarsely, but Conor was gone. Her terror was incapacitating her; all around, the shrouded trees, the river, the bridge seemed to urge the threat upon her. Jonathan's recording was still playing on its loop; she reached in and yanked out the wire that connected to the bullhorn, then pushed herself clear. Her old brown rain slicker, she saw, lay in a hollow on the opposite side of the road, in the direction from which she had just come. Rose hadn't gone back to Birdeye, then; she could be anywhere, and Liv had no phone, or anyone nearby who could help her.

Unless, perhaps, the Kinneys were at home.

The entrance to the Kinneys' place lay a few yards beyond the bridge. The house itself was single storey, at the end of a broad, waterlogged yard. To Liv's dismay, she couldn't see their truck, but there was no one else she could try. Up she ran in her gumboots and bedraggled kimono, past their trash bin, past the kids' detritus – the bikes and the saucer sleds and a bright plastic slide.

'Hey!' she shouted, panting as she neared the porch. 'Hey – Susan, anyone!'

After several moments the front door opened part way, and a boy inched out. Susan's youngest, Kason. His fair hair was pushed up from his forehead and he stared at her, wide-eyed, brows quirked exaggeratedly in his soft child's face.

'You look weird,' he said.

'I need help. I've lost Rose – my daughter, Rose.'

He turned his head. 'Mommy!'

Liv heard the insistence in his voice, the uncertainty. 'Have you seen her? Has she been in your yard?'

'Yup,' said Kason, still looking back into the house, still holding on to the door handle.

Where'd she go?' Liv's chest was heaving, her lungs raw. She bent forward and placed both palms on the porch step; her legs wouldn't hold her much longer.

'She's here,' said Susan Kinney, appearing above her son, one hand resting on his shoulder. The door opened fully, revealing a pale blue carpet, scattered with bits of mud. 'Sweet Jesus, the state of you! She's here. Come inside.'

꧁

Liv sat down heavily on the closed lid of the toilet in the Kinneys' bathroom. Susan had told her to towel herself dry, but she didn't have the strength. Instead, she watched Rose through the half-open door. She was pacing up and down the narrow hallway, her expression distant, her hands clasped behind her back. Susan, it seemed, had removed her soiled jeans and replaced them with some grey sweatpants that looked as if they belonged to one of Kason's older brothers. Rose's settled demeanour was almost stately, although Susan had told Liv that she'd found her rocking beside their trash bin, and that she'd needed to take her arm and tug her quite firmly towards the house. These last details were almost more than Liv could bear. She saw now that Rose's earlier flight from the house had little or nothing to do with Wren. She'd gone looking for Pinto in the place where Liv had laid him.

'I hope you're decent.' Susan pushed the door wide and stepped into the bathroom with a cup of coffee for Liv to drink. She set it down on the floor and stood there with her arms crossed, hands tucked beneath her armpits. 'You'd better get that thing off,' she said, nodding at the wet kimono. Liv pawed at the tie ineffectually. Her fingers were numb; it would take some time for the warmth in the bathroom to penetrate her frozen bones. Susan shook her head and went to fetch a pair of scissors.

Liv shifted sideways and rested her shoulder against the towel warmer. It seemed easiest to focus on something that wasn't moving, so she stared at the three plastic battleships ranged around the edge of the tub, not quite hiding spots of mildew along the grouting. They didn't look very sea-worthy, she thought, distractedly; one of them had a hole in the gun turret. Mary, as a child, had loved to fill her bath with toys. There had been a whale that squirted water, and sometimes sloughs of mould came out. Liv turned her gaze to the toiletries on the shelf next to the mirror – the de-lousing shampoo, the lime-green shower gel, the jar of pastel-coloured bath bombs, the row of electric toothbrushes. The more she looked, the more these objects seemed necessary, and vital in this house – profoundly connected to the acts they witnessed, and intimately linked to a world that wasn't her own. They'd be missed if they weren't there. To her surprise, she found herself blinking away tears.

Susan returned and deftly snipped the belt in two while Liv remained seated. Then she peeled off each sleeve, exposing Liv's chest, as if undressing a child. If she was surprised by what she found, she didn't show it.

'That's your dog,' she said, quietly. 'The one you put in our trash.' She stared for a moment, then reached for a towel and flapped it across Liv's shoulders. 'You should take a hot shower. AJ's not here, in case you're wondering. He's out.'

Liv regarded her neighbour. She saw the complicated thoughts behind her eyes, but right now there were more important things to attend to.

'Birdie!' she called, softly.

Rose paused outside the door and tilted her face towards the light fixture.

Liv sat up and shrugged back the towel. 'Look at me, Birdie. See this? It's a tattoo of Pinto, like a photograph. But Pinto's gone. She's not coming back. The tattoo is to help us remember her.' Trembling, she pictured her beloved dog all stiff and lifeless in the blanket. Then in her mind's eye she saw Wren, and also Mary, accusing, and felt herself falling into the empty space inside her. 'Except you *do* remember, of course you do. It's me who needs the reminder.'

Rose had clamped her front teeth over her bottom lip. Liv reached out for her daughter's hand, but young Kason was sliding around her, so she set off again along the hallway. He was wearing his pyjamas, which Liv hadn't noticed before. They were decorated with turtles in karate poses.

'That's your dog,' he said, echoing his mother as he peeked at her chest. 'It's got funny ears.'

Liv managed a smile. 'You're lucky. No one else has seen this, apart from Rose and the tattoo guy.'

'And Mommy.'

'Get!' Susan was back, shooing her son away, but as soon as

he'd disappeared her voice took on a sudden harshness. 'So what the hell were you doing leaving your daughter running loose like that? Maybe if you took better care of her, instead of leaving your crap around and smoking pot in the woods and letting your homo friends broadcast offensive language around the valley . . . She could have injured herself, or fallen in the river.'

Liv rocked herself forward and stood up, sucking in her breath with the effort. 'Is the internet down?'

Susan's face puckered, then righted itself. 'No, I don't think so – I was online before.'

'Well then, I'll head home. Thank you for your help.'

'But your things aren't dry.'

Susan voiced ugly opinions, yet Liv knew she had goodness within her. She loved her boy. She had taken care of Rose.

'It's okay,' she said. 'I need to send a message.'

※

It was after 5 p.m. by the time Liv walked with Rose back to Birdeye. The skies had finished emptying themselves, and the twigs and pinecones washed down from the woods sat forlorn in puddles along the road. Liv dragged her legs up the steps; her body ached, every part of it, and her knees couldn't seem to bend, just like her daughter's. She then had to climb the stairs to her bedroom, though Rose, impatient, tugged her hand, which helped her. Up on the landing, Liv slipped off the coat that Susan had lent her, then pulled on some trousers and a sweater. The memory of Conor's wet hair across his forehead came to her as she retrieved some thick socks from the laundry basket, but she blinked him away and dragged the comforter from her bed to wrap around her shoulders. Rose seemed warm enough in the sweatpants Susan had given her. Nevertheless, Liv found an extra cardigan and helped her put it on.

'We are going to live with Mary,' she said, as she fastened the buttons. The words, once she had uttered them, seemed quite easy

– plain and ordinary. She watched as Rose's dark eyes rolled up and took in the ceiling. For a moment, Liv pictured the aeroplane in which they would travel, and felt the shudder of its take-off. Then she recalled the open door of the station wagon, and the gaping sleeping bag, and with the same sense of inexorability she had experienced in the Kinneys' bathroom, she made her way downstairs. She sat down at the computer in the study, and within five minutes had composed her short email to Mary. She pressed 'send' without hesitating and imagined the little envelope icon being sucked through a hole and whooshed into the ether. Finally, she checked the outbox, to make sure it had gone.

Twenty minutes later, as she and Rose ate toast and drank sweet liquorice tea in the wheezy quiet of the kitchen, Sonny and Mishti arrived home. Liv felt the push of cold air and heard 'Hello hello!' along the passageway.

'What a day!' said Mishti, appearing first, her hair tucked under her pink ear warmers. She was still wearing her boots, and she trudged around the table to kick them off into the pile of footwear behind the yard door. 'Not flooding so much, but the bridge up past Lazlo's place was knocked out and some homes north of Big Chogan had no power. I stopped by the community centre while Sonny went over to the Schreibers. Their sewage was up again, would you believe it. He was crawling around most of the day and he's whacked.'

'I'll make more tea,' said Liv, standing, relieved that they hadn't seen Conor's video. As she turned to fill the kettle, she heard the downstairs bathroom door open, followed by the double click as Sonny tugged the light cord. They would all be leaving soon, she thought, and then who would sit in the kitchen or leave stinks in the toilet or pad along the passageway in search of a stub of candle?

'How are you two?' asked Mishti, settling herself into a chair. 'Did Karin come by? I saw that note for someone to call her.'

Liv glanced at the reminder she had scribbled on the noticeboard at the end of Rose and Mary's birthday party. Karin – she'd needed

228

something, hadn't she? Alondra had said so, but Liv couldn't remember what. Karin, with her strong legs and her broad back and her green hair. Liv could picture her clearly now, as if she had stepped beneath a lamp, or rather, as if Liv had raised the lamp towards her and looked closely, maybe for the first time. Karin had the energy to make a go of things, she thought. Of course.

It wasn't until she heard a rasping sound behind her, like a dog with something caught in its throat, that she realised she'd not considered Gunther in her plan. Turning, looking for him, she instead saw Sonny in the doorway. He was staring straight at her, and his gaze was so direct, so stripped of complication that Liv knew something irreversible was happening. Instinctively she began to check off the whereabouts of her daughters: Rose – *beside her* – then Mary – *across an ocean*.

A coil of panic tightened beneath her breastbone. Sonny's face was grey. His clenched mouth slackened.

'No,' Mishti said, rising to her feet. Then Sonny grasped his chest and leaned forward until it seemed to Liv that he was folding himself in two. By the time he pitched sideways and fell in an oddly modest heap, Mishti was already reaching for her phone to call 911.

࿇

Sonny was declared deceased forty-five minutes after admission to the Margaretville Emergency Room, sixteen miles away. Liv, when Mishti called to tell her, stood in the darkness of the kitchen and pressed the phone tight against her ear, as if this might bring her closer to brother and sister, one gone now, one left behind.

'This is what will happen to his body,' Mishti was saying. 'There won't be an autopsy because he passed under a physician's care. An ambulance will come. They have to be quick. He – it – needs to be kept at the right temperature. They are on their way now. I'm going to wait here. I need to see him go.'

Mishti's voice, though very small, seemed unexpectedly calm.

She was following Sonny's instructions, she told Liv. He had signed the documents, and so had she. There would be no marker, and it would cost them nothing. His body would be transported up to the new forensic research facility overlooking Lake Erie, and it would be laid out in a field, or folded into a refuse sack, or lowered into a pond or buried beneath a woodpile and left to decompose, gradually, so that people could study how the robins and the worms and the bacteria took what they needed; how its tissues decayed, how its bones became exposed. They would observe how long it took, in outdoor conditions, for Sonny's physical remains to return to the earth, and through this symbiotic act of giving and receiving, assist his being towards Nirvana.

Did you know he was going to die? Liv might have asked, if she hadn't already guessed the answer.

༄

'Liv,' whispered Mishti, her voice a rasp in the darkness. 'I want to go up to Sebastian's grave in the morning. Will you take me?'

Liv couldn't talk. She couldn't even turn her head. Sonny's smell was all around her: on the pillow, within the sheets. She and Mishti had crawled into his bed a couple of hours earlier and had clung to each other until the ache in Liv's shoulder had forced her to stretch out on her back. She thought about how she and Sonny had sometimes slept together right there, on his old saggy mattress. She couldn't remember the details, it was several years before, but there'd been no one else since her cancer. It was a strange thing to think about, now that he was dead. The two of them had made a pact that whenever they were intimate together they had to look each other in the eyes. Liv needed to be honest about what it meant, and what it didn't.

Now Mishti lay curled beside her, and Liv knew that Mishti's pain took precedence, and that Liv would do what she asked, because Sonny had been Mishti's brother.

'Yes,' she said, finally. She could feel the dampness from Mishti's tears on the pillowcase by her cheek. She pushed her hand across to Mishti's hip and let it rest there.

After a minute, Mishti rolled away onto her side. 'I'd like to be alone now,' she mumbled.

Liv got up and went to her own bed.

IN MEMORIAM

'WE'RE CLOSE, AREN'T we?'

Mishti was a slow walker. She trod uncertainly across the loose rocks in her worn leather boots, and when her foot slipped, Liv took her arm to steady her. Every couple of minutes they stopped and peered into the trees: the red maples with their miniature floral fireworks, and the beeches, still bare, although the leaf buds were finally swelling.

'I can't see the rock cliff, but here's the bend. If we try through there . . .'

Liv nodded. The sky was a dull grey sheet above, and she could hear the sound of water, a small stream, trickling its way under logs and ferns and spilling over moss-drenched boulders. A junco issued its staccato warning note in the branches to their left. There was no one else on the path, and they had seen no other vehicles at the trailhead at Mink Hollow. Eric had driven over at breakfast to pay his respects and seemed keen to stay and look after Rose and Gunther. Sonny had been his friend, too.

They stepped left, away from the trail and climbed north-west for a couple of hundred feet, across dry leaves and wet rock, holding hands now, although if one of them fell she would take down the other. It had been a couple of years since Liv had hiked the slopes of Olderbark. The place formed part of the Indian Head Wilderness, north of Woodstock, from where she'd made the journey decades before, speeding along Rock City Road in the Wagonaire, onto the Glasco turnpike, past the artists' colony and the moonlit waters of Cooper Lake to find a burial place for the bloodied bundle folded away in Eric's toolbox on the seat beside her.

She'd been in shock, back then, of course. She had carried the toolbox up the trail and then veered off just as they were doing now, bushwhacking away from any witnesses, stumbling wide-eyed with her burden. But the truth was that Liv had never been able to remember the exact spot. Sonny had asked her not to draw attention to it in any way, and in the darkness one rock was very much like another. Mishti knew this, or guessed it, but from time to time she still asked Liv to bring her up here. Sebastian's bones lay on Olderbark somewhere. That was what mattered.

Once they had found a dryish spot in the lee of a boulder, Liv took out a flask of coffee, and they sat there together.

'Are you cold?' asked Liv.

Mishti shook her head. 'You know what? You and Eric are the only people left who know I was a mom.'

'Correction. You're still Sebastian's mom.'

'I'm not sure that's true.' Mishti began to cry, silently, tears coursing down her cheeks. 'He'd be forty-six now. He'd have his own family. He'd look like Sonny – I tell myself that, but it's stupid, because he wasn't ever going to grow up, or have his own children – he was never meant to survive.'

'But you still love him,' said Liv. 'I mean, here you are, after all these years, feeling his loss, thinking about every day, every minute he might have lived. You'll always be his mom. And Sonny—'

'Oh . . .' Mishti bowed her head, shrinking into herself. 'It's my fault. I wanted to get away for the last bit of our life together. I wanted to try living someplace where no one knew what we did a long time ago. I couldn't bear you still remembering. Sonny agreed to come because of me. Maybe the wrench was too much for him. Maybe that's why he died. Sonny didn't want to leave you, or Birdeye.'

'Hush.' Liv raised a hand to Mishti's face and brushed away her tears. What had happened when Mishti was seventeen was still there; she still carried it inside. That was what Sonny had meant on their last evening together, when he talked about the burden. Liv thought of Sonny, and how Mishti had made him be the one to break the news at the Sharing the day that Conor first arrived. She leaned her head back and stared up at the sky beyond the gaps in the branches. There were patterns, she knew, like the seasons, like the wheels of cause and effect. You could look back along the events of a life and thus try to anticipate what might happen next, and maybe she could have foreseen the jolt from Sonny and Mishti.

But if she had seen it coming, maybe it would have happened anyway.

Directly above them, a hawk was rising on a thermal, intent and unhurried. No wonder the songbirds had stopped their warbling.

'Will you still go?' she asked.

'I think so. Yes. I want to go to Michigan. I want to find my family. I know Mommy and Baba are gone, but Baba's brother – cousins, maybe – they need to know about Sonny.' Mishti's voice juddered and Liv nodded, thinking what a lonely trip that would be. A few years back she had walked into the study and found Sonny moaning into his hands. He'd been stalking on Facebook and discovered that their parents had died. She hadn't been present when he broke the news to Mishti.

'I meant to tell you yesterday. I'm leaving too. With Rose. I've told Mary. We're going to London at the end of the summer.'

'No!'

Mishti's obvious dismay made Liv twist round and stare at her.

'That's what you wanted, isn't it? I mean, you and Sonny – you were both on Mary's side.'

Mishti frowned. 'It was me who wanted to leave.'

'Yes.'

'And Sonny said that meant you'd go, too. But I thought you'd stay.'

'Sonny was right,' said Liv. 'I can't stay on without you two.' In her mind she saw again the spilled sleeping bag, the toys in the Kinneys' bathroom – dreamlike things from a different life. Clever Sonny. He'd known her better than anyone.

'I'm sorry,' said Mishti.

Liv nodded. She wasn't entirely sure what Mishti was sorry about. Not specifically. Not that it mattered.

'So am I.'

They sat quietly for a few minutes watching the wheeling bird rise out of sight. Then Mishti said she was ready to walk back to the pickup.

'You carry on aways without me, Liv,' she urged. 'I know you want to hike.'

'You'll get cold.'

'I'll run the engine a little. Go on.'

Once Liv was alone, she reached forward to tighten her boot laces, then fished inside her daypack and pulled out the drawstring bag that contained Sonny's trail crampons. She had picked them up from the desk in the study before they'd left, and now, as she opened the bag and pulled them out, she thought about the way Sonny had always stored things tidily. They were clean, freshly waxed and they slipped easily over the toe and heel of her walking boots. With the spikes on her soles, she began her ascent of Olderbark, following the gaps between the rocks, shielding her head from snagging branches. It was a demanding climb – gruelling, even – the terrain pocked and unpredictable. She reached the snow and ice after twenty minutes, by which time her lungs were burning and her ankles ached. Still she pressed on, until she had cleared the deciduous forest, emerging into the boreal realm of red spruce and balsam with the sky unmoving above her, a raven's distant cawing, the shapes of the neighbouring mountains like absent friends and Cooper Lake far below her, a rinsed eye, unblinking.

Grief, Liv already knew, came from behind, from in front, from above and below; it wasn't possible to predict how you'd be doing on any particular day, or at any particular hour or moment. The future was hypothetical, with no bearing on whether you lay your head down on the bathroom tile, or pressed it against the steering wheel and never raised it, or whether you held on, kept going.

One warmish morning towards the end of May, she stood in the Hannaford desserts aisle with Rose beside her, trying to decide between dairy-free mint choc chip and salted caramel.

'Which do you want, Birdie?' she asked. 'Help me out.'

Rose twisted her head to one side and made a sound that caused a boy by the frozen yogurt to shuffle away from them. Liv looked up and there was Karin, with her shock of hair and baggy dungarees, hovering next to the cookie counter. Liv had last seen her when she walked up with a bunch of flowers the day after Sonny had died. Karin hadn't been back for a while though, and in a house that felt blown open by loss, Liv hadn't considered her absence. Now, she realised, she had missed her.

'I'm so sorry,' began Karin, as Liv opened her arms to embrace her. When she stood back, she saw that Karin looked different. She had a flush on her cheeks and her eyes had a new brightness.

'How's Alondra?' asked Liv, quickly.

'She's okay.' Karin touched Rose's arm in greeting. 'We're not together anymore. I've moved out - back to my mother's.'

'Ah.'

'It's fine,' said Karin, looking down. 'It was something we agreed on. She kept saying I should go back to college. She didn't want us to start a family.'

Liv thought about how she hadn't called Karin when Alondra asked her to. The reminder was still on the blackboard. She thought about the Sharings where Karin had talked about Alondra and she had kind of switched off, or at least not been fully attentive. All of that was over, now. She'd had an idea for Karin, she remembered - just before Sonny died.

As they walked together towards the checkouts, Karin asked about Mishti and Liv told her that she and Rose were shopping for food for Mishti's last supper at Birdeye; that in the morning she'd be leaving.

'Up to that place near Buffalo?'

'Not straight away. She's going to Michigan, where she was – where her folks are.'

'What will you do then?' asked Karin.

'Oh,' said Liv, as she put the ice cream on the conveyor belt. 'Rose and I are leaving too. In a couple of months. We're going to London to live with Mary.'

Karin's face crumpled.

'It's okay,' said Liv.

'I'm sorry,' said Karin. 'I mean, I'm happy for you, if that's what you want. Mary's so lucky. But I'll miss you guys like crazy. I did a test two days ago. Looks like I'm pregnant.' She took a breath, her eyes welling, as if her own words had shocked her. 'I wanted a child with Alondra, but it isn't what she wants, so I'm doing this on my own. All those times at Birdeye when I didn't know what to do . . . Now I'm certain. I realised I needed to decide, Liv, that night we shared – you, me and Conor. It feels right. I've wanted you to know.'

'That's eight dollars and sixty cents,' said the grey-haired cashier, pushing up his cap. 'You got coupons?'

Liv opened her purse, her mind whirling, glad her hands had something to do. 'I've got a house going spare,' she said.

Karin laughed and scooped up the tub of ice cream for Liv.

As the doors opened, and Liv took Rose's arm and the three of them walked outside into the sunshine, Karin threw a sideways glance at Liv.

'How is Conor?'

'I think he's gone back to the city. I've not heard anything.'

'Me neither.' As Karin spoke, her fingers brushed against her abdomen.

'What?' Liv stopped moving as the penny dropped. '*What?*'

'Oh.' Karin was blushing. 'He helped me. It's not complicated. He wanted to help, and – well . . . trust me, I've not got into guys.' She shrugged, and Liv, recalling Conor's insistence on looking for signs and leaving traces, started to laugh, which in turn made her suck in air and shudder.

'I honestly did not see that coming,' she said after a moment, wiping her eyes. 'Jeepers, now I'm weeping again. I can't seem to stop. But Karin, here's the thing. Come over tonight. About the house – I wasn't joking. It's yours.'

AN ARMY OF LOVERS
CANNOT LOSE

HAMPSTEAD HEATH, LONDON.

Mary pushed open the squeaky metal gate to Kenwood Ladies' Pond and looked around for somewhere to pay. The path ahead of her wound down through some trees, and off to her right she could hear a ripple of female laughter.

'It's that way, if you're swimming,' said a woman's voice behind her. Mary turned and peeped over the top of her sunglasses. The woman was young – mid-twenties, with bleached hair tied up with some kind of bandana. The coconut scent of cheap sunscreen rose up from her and she had a bulky canvas bag from Daunt Books slung over one shoulder; the strap was digging into her soft skin, just above a small tattoo – an armadillo.

'Oh, I'm not . . . I'm just looking,' said Mary.

The young woman raised an eyebrow and moved past her. 'Okaaay.'

Mary put her hand up to shield her eyes and waited until there was enough distance between the two of them for her to follow without it feeling creepy. She tried to remember what her assistant had told her. *It's very relaxed. No one cares who you are. Just don't take photos.*

After a short descent she came out into the sunlight where she stood and squinted at the shower hut, the lifeguard on the decking and the wide brown oval of pond with the heads of women, young and old, bobbing about in it. There was a plastic heron, she noticed, stuck on a lifebuoy in the middle. Ugly, in a kitsch way; something to strike out for.

Mary found an empty patch of bank and sat down to watch the

bathers. Someone wearing goggles swam a sleek, efficient crawl, but most of the women glided slowly, like toads, or floated on their backs. Mary hadn't come prepared to take a dip herself. Now, though, lolling on the grass with her bare legs stretched out before her, she weighed up the pond's attractions. It was outdoors. The place was fenced, which was good for Rose, and young children who might stare at her mother's scarred chest were few and far between. Indeed, the pond seemed both libertarian and decorous – a place of watery communion beneath non-judgemental murmurs. It was a relief, frankly, after her mother's message, followed so swiftly by the shock of Sonny's death and all the sorrow, as well as wrangling with a builder to ensure that everything at her new house met the necessary safety requirements. *You are right*, her mother had written. *We need you.* Mary had longed for this acknowledgement her whole life, yet she couldn't help but worry about how Liv would fit in once she came to North London; what on earth she would do with herself all day, especially if they got a carer. The Ladies' Pond could turn out to be a godsend. Bohemian, but in a nice way. Mary knew how much her mother loved the water.

As the afternoon grew hotter, Mary found herself less and less inclined to leave. She had trudged across Parliament Hill to reach the secluded enclosure, and two of her toes had blisters. A short distance in front of her, a middle-aged woman – Mary's age – drifted by, casting her arm above her head with a languid splash. You didn't have to wade through any mud to swim, Mary noted; you just lowered yourself in from a ladder. She pulled out her shirt and glanced down, peeking at her bra. Navy blue, hardly any lace, matching knickers. More coverage than some of the bikinis around her.

The water, when it slipped over her thighs and stomach, was as cold as she imagined, but no worse. She gripped the ladder for a moment, then took a deep breath and stepped off the last rung. One quick gasp, then another, kicking out and splashing, before she calmed herself and found her rhythm, a steady breaststroke, her chin held high above the surface. She wished her mother could see her now, swimming in her underwear in a reedy pond in the middle of London. Really, the perspective at eye-level was quite peculiar. Other women's faces loomed at her, some in shiny swim caps, and some with a slick of lipstick, mouths simultaneously smiling and straining. *One, two, three, lots,* she counted, remembering, with a kind of joy, the feeling of her mother's hands beneath her ribs when as a child she had screamed and floundered.

She glided on towards the middle, then over to the far side where the willows dipped down low, and the long shadows made her shiver. Afraid of touching the bottom, she circled back, faster now. There was the buoy, slick with mildew, with its hunched-shouldered heron on top. As she passed, the heron opened an eye: not an ornament, but alive. She held her breath, treading water as it levelled its charcoal-streaked head and held her in its stare. Then it rose up on its stick legs, unfolded its great ashy wings and, with a few ungainly flaps, took off across the pond.

Liv was down at the swim hole with Rose when Conor showed up one afternoon near the end of August.

The air was warm, heavy with the thrum of crickets, golden with the sun. The river was glassy and sluggish, disturbed only by the occasional flick of a fish or a dragonfly skimming its surface. The first leaves were already falling – silky yellow precursors, though you wouldn't guess that Labour Day was just around the corner from the whoops of the bathers upstream, or the ice-cream money that Jenna would, most likely, be making.

Rose sat on a warm rock with her knees pulled up to her chest. She wasn't a swimmer, despite Liv's efforts over the years to entice her in, but she seemed happy to stay close while her mother dived for slippery pebbles or trod water. The swim hole wasn't wide enough for more than half a dozen strokes, but it was deep enough for Liv to point her toes and not quite touch the bottom as the mountain cold sank into her ankles. She hung there for a while, feeling the water press against her, until Rose raised her chin and sucked in breath through her gappy teeth; someone else had stepped into the clearing.

'Hello, Rose,' he said. 'Hello, Liv.'

Liv squinted up, her arms and hands circling in the water. Conor stood in the sunshine with his hands his pockets. A backpack was slung over one shoulder – the same pack he'd once filled with fruit. For a split second she remembered how she had imagined herself pushing him off the bridge not five months earlier.

'You've come back.'

'Yeah.' He swung his pack down and set it on the ground. 'I joined the Adopt-a-Highway Program. They gave me a two-mile stretch east of Woodstock in memory of my mom and dad. They're putting their names on a sign. I thought I'd have to pay, but it turns out you just pick up roadside litter four times a year. Done my first one. You'd be amazed at what people chuck out of their vehicles. Food and diapers, mainly, but I found a beautiful fountain pen – still runs.'

He stopped talking.

'I didn't think I'd see you again,' Liv said.

'Eric came to my work. Found me stacking shelves. We talked.'

Eric. He'd been going to the city on a visit and Liv had asked if he would try to track down Conor. She had told him what she knew: that Conor worked in a Home Depot and that he lived in Rego Park. It was just like Eric to do everything Liv could ever ask, except come back to her.

'Pass me that towel, would you?' She swam across and her feet felt for the tree root that would help her clamber out without too much hauling. Conor, she could see now, was fully clothed in his usual jeans and t-shirt. She, on the other hand, wore her old denim-blue bikini bottoms, and her top half was naked.

Conor stared at her chest as she rose out of the water.

'Sorry.' He looked away. 'Isn't that your old dog?'

'Pinto. Yes.' Liv didn't care who saw her tattoo anymore.

'When did you get it done?'

Liv reached for her towel and bent down to dry her legs. 'About when you arrived, I think. Maybe after.'

Conor said nothing for minute.

'So you *did* mark her passing, then . . .'

'Have you come back to talk about that?'

'I guess not.' Conor had the grace to sound uncomfortable. 'Hey, I'm sorry about Sonny. He didn't want me here, but I wish I'd had the chance to say goodbye.'

Liv put her head on one side, regarding him. Same flat hair; same blueish-white complexion, even at the end of the summer. She didn't mind seeing him, she realised. He'd lied to her about Wren and filming stuff, but his mother had lied to him, too. She knew as well as anyone that grief made you a little crazy. Whatever his troubles had been, he had made her feel more alive.

'How's Gunther?' he asked.

'Asleep on the porch, I expect. He won't come down here now. He's an old boy. Want to swim?'

'I can't.' He peered over the bank into the water. 'Don't know how. Maybe I'll learn. You could teach me.'

'Are you thinking of staying?'

Conor raised his eyebrows, as if seeking permission.

'Well, that would be up to Karin,' she went on. 'You should know I'm giving the house to her.'

'That's what Eric said, so I called Karin, and she said to ask you.'

Liv shook her head, then rubbed it with the towel before she sat on the bank and wrapped it around her. 'I've told Karin repeatedly to use her own judgement.'

Conor laughed softly. 'Maybe she has!'

'Maybe,' echoed Liv, wondering what it was he wanted. 'Birdeye is her place now – her rules.'

'But will you really let go? I mean, Karin says you two are moving to England, but you'll come back, right? She says I can move in – maybe bring Winter – so if there are conditions, you'd better say now . . .'

His voice trailed off, and Liv thought about what he had asked and what she had made at Birdeye with Mary and Rose and Eric and Sonny and Mishti. She saw no need for answers – for Conor or herself. Only acceptance. *Be attentive*, she thought. He'd learn that.

'The house is Karin's,' she repeated. 'No conditions. Not from me, anyway.' She turned away, reaching for her shirt. There had been a brief period when she had considered gifting Birdeye to him, but Karin was better suited. She was tolerant; she listened, and soon there would be her baby. Perhaps her friends would join them. Such thoughts still felt a little unfamiliar, and Liv wanted to be alone, to pay her respects to the hollows deep inside, but Conor was waiting. He needed to say something else.

'I promise I'll help look after it – I mean, you know that, right?'

It? Was he talking about the house, or the baby? Liv was glad her face was hidden. Conor wanted her approval, same as Karin. Well, they would have to make their own minds up about that.

After Rose had taken Conor's hand and led him back into the house, Liv sat down on the porch steps and looked up at the sky. A small white cloud was passing from north to south above the crease of the valley, alone and purposeful in the blueness. From within the house she could hear voices: Karin's greeting, a reconnection, or the beginning of something new. Liv was the guest, now. She closed her eyes. Conor seemed to think she could come back if it didn't work out, or if Rose wasn't happy. She pushed her shoulders forward, letting the old pain greet her, then settle. Her toes squeezed the fine dirt; she listened again, but the hum of insects cloaked her ears, and as her mind drifted, she heard the shush of the river – nearer now – between the sun-warmed rocks and boulders. Children's shrieks carried down the valley – tubers or kayakers, tumbling and turning through the shallows. All that life, she thought, passing through, and then she heard other children, far away but closer, their bare feet thumping across the yard, and she heard the strum of a guitar and adults murmuring and the clinking of bottles in the cool box. She knew, without looking, that the shadows had lengthened, and she could smell the yellowing grass along with Eric's musky skin as he pulled the mattresses into a circle and lit citronella candles to keep the black flies at bay. Evening was almost here. While the older children hung out in the woods, the little ones dawdled back from the sprinkler for glasses of Kool-Aid and a cuddle on a lap. Adults brought out bottles of rosé and salty pretzels. Soon the sun would set, and the lightning bugs would jig in the darkness beneath the trees, and someone would start spitting watermelon seeds and there'd be a competition. Mary, aged nine, would sidle close along the porch, wriggle out of her wet bikini, then run upstairs for a pair of shorts. Sonny would hunker on the steps, shucking peas, and Liv would laze with Mishti on the swing set - Rose tucked between them, their feet up on the rail - and they'd lean their heads together and smile as the warm air kissed their skin, and all was right in this dream of the world.

EGGPLANT

L IV HAD A couple of final tasks to complete before she and
Rose made the journey to England. She had been putting them
off, but departure was fast approaching, so, one dampish morning
towards the end of September, she left Rose in Karin's care and
took Gunther for a ride in the pickup. Lately he had refused to
climb into the cab unaided; Liv was forced to lift him, an awkward
manoeuvre that made them both yelp. Now the old dog slumped
in the passenger footwell as she drove, his body swaying with the
turns in the road, his sad eyes never faltering in their steady, upwards
gaze.

They waited for a trio of logging trucks at the junction that
led on to the highway, then got caught behind the school bus. A
light wind nudged grey clouds over the mountain tops and shook
spots of rain across the windscreen. Liv tried not to think about
the splashes of burgundy and pumpkin in the woods that blanketed
Tremper; she had always loved the fall, and when she pulled into the
parking lot, she was glad, almost, that it was busy – some meeting
at the realtors, maybe, or a hiking party up from the city. Nothing
to miss; nothing to make her feel sentimental.

Once she had found a spot and switched off the engine, Liv leaned
forward and rubbed Gunther's jaw the way he liked. Beneath the soft-
ness of his jowls, she could feel the bumps and fissures of his gums.
His head drooped. He had loved Pinto, and he had mourned her
with remarkable tenacity, but grief, like age, had become exhausting.

'I'll get you a pancake,' she murmured, opening her door. 'With
bacon.'

As Liv pushed open the glass door to the diner, the bell above her head clanked dully. She looked up. Someone had stuffed a paper towel inside the cavity.

'Needs some TLC!' called Dolores, sitting at her usual table with a magazine in front of her and a cup of coffee. 'How's Rose doing? Hey, I bet you're going soon, are ya? You oughta send me something nice from London. English tea. No, switch that – mail me a Beefeater.'

'Will do, Dolores,' murmured Liv. She looked around; the place was quiet after the breakfast rush, and the lights had been switched off at the far end of the bar. She walked along and sat up on a stool, away from Dolores yet facing her, so as not to seem unfriendly.

As soon as she smoothed out the paper menu on the counter, the young server, Thomas, came with a pad to take her order.

'Is Jenna here? Can I speak with her?' Liv asked.

'Sure thing.'

'Okay, in that case I'll have buckwheat pancakes with a side of bacon, to go.'

'You not stopping?' Dolores called. 'They got eggplant on the specials. Parmigiana.' She raised her hands in the air and spoke out of the side of her mouth. 'Or so they *say*.'

When Jenna appeared, she poured Liv a coffee from the jug and leaned forward over the counter. Cherry stomped around behind her, her little jeans tucked into a pair of glittery cowboy boots clearly meant for an older child or a teenager.

'Her daddy sent them,' said Jenna, rolling her eyes. 'Need a refill?'

Liv nodded. 'Oxy.' She raised a hand with her thumb tucked across her palm.

Jenna looked surprised. 'Only four?'

Without answering, Liv hooked a folded envelope out of her shirt pocket and placed it on the menu. 'It's all there,' she said. 'All I owe you.'

Jenna picked up the envelope and tucked it into her apron. 'If you need more . . .'

'No.'

247

Jenna narrowed her eyes briefly at Liv before shooing Cherry in Dolores' direction and disappearing back into the kitchen to fix her order.

While Liv waited, she thought about the other thing she needed to do. She would call the tattoo guy, Axel – ask him to finish what he'd started. She hoped he would fit her in at short notice. But instead of pulling out her phone, she stared out of the window, past the little decking area with its plastic table and chairs, along the street and above the pitched roofs of KeyBank and Hope Springs Eternal to the wooded mountain. The Esopus lay there somewhere, flowing down from its source, then along the fold of valley past Birdeye and the Kinneys to where it joined with another creek at the eastern edge of the town. On it went, in her mind's eye, over the drowned buildings of Olive, across the Ashokan reservoir and on to the city, to its cisterns and tanks. Beyond the city lay the ocean, and beyond the ocean lay another city.

'Here you go,' said Jenna, placing a take-out box in front of her. 'Thomas!' she called, turning. 'The pancakes are on the house.'

Liv kept one hand on the box as she drank her coffee. She didn't need to check the contents – what she had asked for would be there. If she took her hand away, she felt, if she didn't leave soon, she might not do it, but she didn't move, not yet, because one cup of coffee wouldn't change anything; she couldn't take Gunther to London, and she wouldn't leave him behind.

When the bell clanked again, she jumped.

Two new arrivals stood in the waiting area. One was a man in a khaki jacket with lots of pockets, mid-forties, while the other was a lanky, awkward-looking teen. Both wore the green caps of the Philadelphia Eagles: father and son, if their matching dark eyebrows were anything to go by. They were strangers, and Liv might have looked away, but the boy rubbed his cheek several times with his knuckles, and while there was nothing obvious about his appearance to draw attention to the profound nature of his difference, she could tell, by the way the father led him by the hand, then sat him down in a quiet booth before Thomas could reach them, that these two were mapping the same universe she had navigated ever since she had first glimpsed her baby girls.

Oh Rose, oh Mary. Liv passed her hand over her eyes, ambushed, suddenly, by love. Mary had seemed happier, when they last messaged; she had talked of swimming in a pond somewhere, and she had sounded hopeful, in the way that Liv, too, was hopeful when they were apart. Liv had prioritised Rose all those years before because she had been the one with the cord around her neck. Nothing could change that fact, so she had made her own truth. She had ridden a ladybird all the way up to the top of the cathedral and swung from the bells and spat gooseberries down on the ladies and the men, and now she was taking Rose to London to pay for it.

'Excuse me,' said a low voice beside her. Liv raised her head. It was the man in the khaki jacket. He held up his phone. 'No signal. I'm trying to find somewhere called Birdeye. Do you know it?'

'O-Livia!' called Dolores from across the diner. 'I got a word in my wordsearch. "Eggplant" – like the special! I'm telling you, it's telepathic.'

Liv looked at the man. He had worried eyes. Worried and tired. He and his son were seeking something, the same as everyone. She thought about Gunther, waiting trustingly in the pickup, and when she slipped down from the stool and dropped the box of pancakes in the trash, she felt the old, familiar unclenching of her heart, like a leaf unfurling, like a hand opening, as it still knew how to do.

'I'm heading that way myself,' she said. 'Let me show you.'

THE END

ACKNOWLEDGEMENTS

M<small>ANY</small> <small>PEOPLE</small> <small>HAVE</small> been generous with their expertise and support during the writing of this novel.

My thanks to those Catskills residents who patiently answered my questions during recent visits. I have written a work of fiction, but I still needed to know about waste collection and signal blackspots and where to get a tattoo. Any errors are mine alone.

Special thanks to Daphne Vaughan, who graciously shared her experience of being a camp counsellor in New York in 1969, and to the University of Winchester for providing me with travel bursaries on two occasions.

I remember with great fondness my friends from the L'Arche Kent community where I lived in the late 1980s.

To writer friends who have discussed countless intricacies with me, huge thanks, especially Sarah Butler, Claire Fuller, Susmita Bhattacharya, Carole Burns, Louise Taylor, Amanda Oosthuizen, Claire Gradidge, Richard Stillman, Rebecca Fletcher and Tim Fywell. Janet Macdonald, Bob Smith, Robyn Dylan, Adrian Goldszmidt and Paul Ayling have also made valuable suggestions.

My agent Jane Finigan's belief in this story has been immensely sustaining; I'm so grateful to her, and of course to Chris and Jen Hamilton-Emery at Salt for understanding what I've tried to do.

My parents Michael and Gill Heneghan took my siblings and I to New York State in 1970 and again in 1973, and my fascination with the Catskills began with those trips. It has been a joy to share memories with Patrick, Sarah and Jonathan Heneghan, and also with family who weren't there but who listen anyway, especially Rory and Francesca, Nellie, Jeremy and Meriel Anderson. Thank you.

This book has been typeset by
SALT PUBLISHING LIMITED
using Neacademia, a font designed by Sergei Egorov
for the Rosetta Type Foundry in the Czech Republic. It
is manufactured using Holmen Book Cream 70gsm, a
Forest Stewardship Council™ certified paper from the
Hallsta Paper Mill in Sweden. It was printed and bound
by Clays Limited in Bungay, Suffolk, Great Britain.

CROMER
GREAT BRITAIN
MMXXIV